D1487152

# SEEDS *of*
# INTENTION

# SEEDS *of*
# INTENTION

ANDREA THOME

*hesse*
*creek*

*media*

*Seeds of Intention* is the second book in the Hesse Creek series, following *Walland*, which was first published in 2016.

This is a work of fiction. Names, characters, organizations, places, events, and incidents are either products of the author's imagination or are used fictitiously.

Published by Hesse Creek Media, Chicago
www.andreathome.com

Edited and Designed by Girl Friday Productions
www.girlfridayproductions.com
Editorial: Stefanie Hargreaves, Michelle Hope Anderson
Interior Design: Rachel Christenson
Cover Design: Sherwin Soy
Image Credits: Cover photographs © Andrea Thome

ISBN-13: 9780997850420
e-ISBN: 9780997850437

First Edition

Printed in the United States of America

*For my incredible children. You're the most important seeds your daddy and I ever planted, and it's been the joy of our lives watching you grow. May you live each and every day with the purest of intentions. And above all, be kind.*

*Though I do not believe that a plant will spring up where no seed has been, I have great faith in a seed. Convince me that you have a seed there, and I am prepared to expect wonders.*

—Henry David Thoreau

# CHAPTER
# ONE

Garrett Oliver had a knack for being in the right place at the right time. Or the wrong time, if you asked his new boss and mentor, Finn Janssen. One heart attack was one too many, according to Finn's wife, Susan, who had owned and operated the rural resort in Walland, Tennessee, for over forty years. Finn's new wife had firmly suggested it was time for the renowned heirloom farmer to take a step back and enjoy life, which was how Garrett had found himself being groomed to take the lead in the resort's gardens.

It was quite a success story, really. Garrett had moved to Tennessee from Washington State to work at the resort a few years earlier. His grandparents had owned a farm that had employed heirloom techniques for decades, so Garrett had always dreamt of studying under a true master gardener. His entry-level job, despite his impressive academic and agricultural credentials, hadn't been as a gardener, though, rather as a member of the bell staff. That's how badly Garrett had wanted the chance to soak up everything he could from one of the pioneers in the field. He'd decided that he would stay as long as he had to in order to work his way into a farming position. He spent his days off milling around the fields, willingly taking any opportunity to learn. Once Finn realized Garrett had an unusual passion for farming, the kind he hadn't seen in a long time, they'd become fast friends. It was unexpected but not unbelievable that Finn had chosen to groom Garrett as his eventual successor.

Garrett was flying solo this week, though, since Susan and Finn were on a well-deserved vacation. Finn had left Garrett with a spectacular garden staff at his disposal. And there was Garrett's close friend, Wyatt Hinch, who had been working alongside him outside the potting shed all morning long. As one of the proprietors of the resort, Wyatt had his own ideas about which of the late-summer harvest crops could be used for the upcoming dinner events being held in the garden.

Wyatt was about to make a suggestion when something caught his attention. Garrett followed his friend's gaze, lifting his hand to shield his eyes from the late-morning sun. India Hinch, Wyatt's wife and coproprietor, had parked a golf cart near the shed, smiling at them both as she approached.

India was one of the loveliest women Garrett had ever seen, and she was just as kind. He remembered the day she'd arrived at the resort as a guest, shortly after he'd been hired himself. He'd been working at the time as a bellman, so he'd had the pleasure of checking her in and showing her around. He'd sensed even then that she and Wyatt had a special connection, but he never could have imagined they'd be married the following spring, and now just a little over a year after their wedding, she was pregnant with their first child, due just before Christmas.

Garrett had a great life, and he knew it. But it didn't stop him from wanting what they had.

"Hey, guys. Thought you might like some lunch. I was up in the main house and saw they had trout sandwich boxed lunches for guests, so I snagged two of them," India said.

She smiled at Garrett and handed him a lunch before reaching up to give Wyatt a kiss. Wyatt lay his open hand across India's blossoming belly, the look of awe in his eyes making Garrett instinctively look away to give them a private moment.

It was hard not to feel like a third wheel around the two of them, but it was no fault of their own. These were two people who'd taken the long way around to love, so they intended on making every moment together count. Garrett often felt himself experiencing pangs of envy when he watched them together, but he'd come to care for both of them so much over the past year that the feeling was always quickly replaced with happiness.

"Thanks, India. I didn't realize how late it had gotten. Wyatt gets to talking about the menus, and before we know it, both of us forget about all the hard labor that has to be done to provide for them."

Garrett took his ball cap off and rested it on his knee. In the sun, his thick dark curls took on a slight russet tone as he perched on the edge of the old wooden table to unwrap his lunch. The smoked trout sandwiches at the resort were legendary, and he was grateful India had thought to bring one for him.

Wyatt sat down in one of the blue rockers that were scattered around the garden, pulling India down into his lap, his hand still resting on her belly. "I think we've got these dinners nailed, Garrett. After lunch, my wife and I will clear out of here so you can get back to the real work. I'd hate to get any new calluses on my hands."

Garrett knew Wyatt was all talk. He'd made himself too comfortable in that rocker to be going anywhere soon—not that Garrett minded. Wyatt and India were his bosses and his best friends. They'd all taken their new positions around the same time and were unofficially considered the new guard at the resort.

Returning to Walland and making a life there with India was the best decision Wyatt had ever made. With Susan and Finn retiring, Garrett knew it was a daunting task to try to fill their shoes, but with India's background in television, they'd managed to take the marketing of the resort to the next level, really building upon the established brand. Most of the calendar year was filled with special events, encouraging guests to return for their favorites year after year. The upcoming Smoky Mountain Table event, set to kick off on Friday evening, was arguably one of their biggest and most popular.

Garrett finished his sandwich and reached into the box for the homemade oatmeal cream pie he knew he'd find. Making short work of it, he sighed and replaced his ball cap, pushing himself up out of the chair, signaling his return to work.

"These tomatoes aren't going to pick themselves. I've never seen such a beautiful crop. In Washington State, my grandparents had a pretty good variety of heirloom seeds, but nobody comes close to having the stash that Finn's been squirreling away."

The three of them laughed, but they knew that Garrett was right. Finn was a true pioneer of heirloom farming in an industry that was finally making a comeback, despite it being the age of the dreaded GMOs.

"I heard your girl's coming in for the weekend, Garrett," Wyatt said. "It's been a while since we've seen her. How long is she staying?"

Garrett covered his mouth as he coughed, stalling for time. It had been almost five months since Lindsay's last trip from Seattle, and he knew people were wondering how serious things could be when they never really saw each other. He was planning to ask her if she'd consider staying in Tennessee with him after her college graduation, but he wasn't ready to share that bit of information with his friends just yet.

"She's coming on Thursday and staying until Monday. Her sister is getting married next weekend, so she has to get back to Seattle for that. But, hey, I'll take what I can get, and I'm pretty busy this month anyway. I'm sure she'll come out again during her fall break."

Wyatt raised his eyebrows in surprise. "Do you need the time off to go to the wedding with her, man? You know we'd cover for you."

Garrett shook his head quickly, busying himself with the piles of recently picked greens on the table. "She knows this is a busy time for us. She's fine with going alone. Besides, she's in the wedding, so we'd hardly see each other anyway."

He didn't want to admit to them that Lindsay hadn't technically invited him. He knew she was just being considerate, but it occurred to him that it might not look that way to his friends.

India stood up, and Wyatt followed suit. The two of them held hands, turning to walk back toward the golf cart.

"If you're sure. But if you change your mind, I've got your back. How hard can this gig be?" Wyatt smirked sarcastically as he gestured toward the vast fields before them. "After all the time you've spent on this girl, you should be thinking about a different kind of karats, my man."

"I'm one step ahead of you."

The words tumbled out before Garrett could stop them.

*Damn.*

He had a hard time being careful around Wyatt. No one needed to know that he'd spent almost every night of the last two weeks staring at the ring he'd bought, wondering if a proposal would convince Lindsay to move to Walland. He wasn't even sure he would go through with it. He wanted Lindsay here; he was so tired of being alone. But marriage was a big leap. They hadn't spent any measurable time in the same city since Garrett's move to Tennessee, and Lindsay was just now starting her final year of school.

India flashed him a grin, rushing back to give him a big hug. "I knew it, Wyatt," she said over her shoulder. "I told you something was up with him." India turned back to face Garrett. "You haven't been yourself these past couple of weeks. We were starting to wonder if you were having second thoughts about living in Tennessee." She took his hand in hers. "Garrett, she'd be lucky to have you. We promise, your secret is safe with us. If I didn't have to interview candidates for our new GM back at the main house, I'd stick around and ply you for more details. Consider yourself lucky."

Garrett couldn't help but smile. India was the best kind of person, and the way Wyatt was looking at her as they walked away together, it was clear he knew it too.

All Garrett really wanted was what they had.

He hoped Lindsay wanted that too. But somewhere deep inside, he wasn't so sure she did.

The cozy decor of the reception area was supposed to put people at ease, but standing among the others who'd gathered in the Hickory Cottage to await their interviews, Willow Armstrong was a nervous wreck. Looking around, it wasn't lost on her that she was the only female candidate in a sea of capable-looking men. She knew she had the credentials and experience, but she recognized now that she was considerably younger than most of the other applicants. Sighing, she looked out the window and studied the dense woods behind the building, watching the squirrels running back and forth on the forest floor collecting nuts to prepare for the cooler autumn days ahead. Their frenetic energy matched hers, and the coffee in her hands wasn't helping. As she turned around to set her cup down on a nearby table, the door opened and a stunning blonde woman walked in. She'd done her research before the interview, so Willow immediately recognized India Hinch.

"Thank you for your patience, everyone. I know I asked those of you who've already met with me to hang around for a while, but I'm finding it harder to choose than I thought. So if you've already interviewed, you're free to leave, and we'll be in touch very soon, I promise."

Willow watched as the majority of the men in the room gathered their things and prepared to depart. Willow hadn't yet met with India, so she sat back down with two or three others who were still waiting as well. She was just about to pick up a nearby magazine when she realized India was standing next to her, a warm smile on her face.

"I'm going to make an educated guess here and say that you must be Willow?" India's eyes were twinkling as she spoke.

Even though the woman's beauty was more impressive close up, it wasn't intimidating. Willow instantly felt at ease and sensed she was going to nail this interview. "I am. Willow Armstrong. Thank you for having me, Mrs. Hinch."

Willow gathered her handbag and résumé and followed India outside as they strolled in the direction of the main house. It was an unusually warm fall afternoon, but the breeze made the heat more tolerable, coupled with the shade of the large oak trees that had already begun to change color along the walkway.

India smiled again at Willow. "I know this humidity takes some getting used to, especially coming from someplace as dry as Utah. But I see you went to the University of Tennessee, so you know that late September can still feel like summer around here."

They were inside the main house now, walking down a short hallway before coming to a stop in a small office just off the gift shop. India gestured for Willow to be seated.

"I'm actually from Knoxville originally," Willow answered. "I studied retail and hospitality and tourism management at UT before working my way up to the assistant general manager position at Stein Eriksen Lodge in Deer Valley."

Willow was proud of the fact that she'd worked in almost all areas of the esteemed Park City hotel. She'd been in housekeeping management and sales, worked as a concierge for a while, and even managed the restaurant for a time. She felt experience gave her a unique holistic perspective of what it took to make a hotel great.

India nodded her head, setting the résumé she was holding to the side of her desk. "There's no doubt you're qualified. I've reviewed your résumé and spoken to the folks in Deer Valley. They couldn't have been more effusive about you. They told me I'd be lucky to have you." India leaned forward, propping her elbows on her desk. "They also told me they'd offered you the general manager position there but that you turned them down. I'd love to know why."

Willow worked hard to hold India's gaze, her cheeks warm from the woman's direct question. "Honestly? I've loved living and working out West and always thought I'd make my life there. But circumstances have changed, and I need to be closer to my family."

She hoped that would be enough to satisfy the woman's curiosity, and after a moment of locking eyes with India, she knew it would be.

"Fair enough. I know it must not have been an easy decision for you to leave, but I certainly understand the importance of being near loved ones."

They chatted a few more minutes about the duties of the job, then India suddenly stood and excused herself for a moment.

Willow allowed herself a few deep breaths, hopeful that she'd made a good impression. She glanced around the small office, her eyes landing on a photo in a silver frame on the desk of India with an exceptionally handsome man. He stood in front of an Airstream trailer, a teasing look in his eyes, with India next to him, her head thrown back in laughter.

Willow was smiling to herself at the image when she startled at the sound of someone entering the office.

"Hey, India, you and Wyatt want to hang out tonight—"

A tall, handsome man wearing jeans and a mud-covered gray T-shirt stopped midsentence when he saw Willow sitting there, her big brown eyes staring back at him in surprise.

He smiled at her, his suntanned face half covered by close-trimmed whiskers that matched the hair on his head. Or at least what she could see of it, since most of it was tucked up under a ball cap with a *W* on the front. There were enough short dark curls peeking out at his neck, though, to confirm the reddish-brown hue.

"Oh, I'm sorry. I didn't mean to come in here guns blazing. I forgot that India was doing interviews today."

His eyes were remarkable—blue-gray and feathered at the corners with soft lines, indicating that this was a man who liked to laugh. He studied her quietly, his large frame filling almost the entire doorway.

Willow was just about to introduce herself when India came around the corner and stopped short at the sight of him.

"Garrett, what can I do for you?"

India spoke in her professional tone of voice, so Garrett knew he'd better make himself scarce. He smiled at the two of them as he backed out of the small space with a nod. "Nothing that can't wait. Give me a call when you're finished for the day." He glanced back at Willow. "Sorry again for barging in. And good luck."

Willow murmured her thanks.

India sat back down, this time in the chair that was on the same side of the desk next to Willow. "I hope you were serious when you said you wanted to be closer to your family, because we're about to host our biggest event of the season starting on Friday, and I've just dismissed the remaining few candidates." She extended her hand, smiling. "It's likely to be a baptism by fire, but, Willow, how would you like to become the new general manager here at the resort, effective immediately?"

# CHAPTER

# TWO

The week leading up to the Smoky Mountain Table event was a busy one, made more so that year by Finn's absence. Garrett loved the quiet hour of the morning when the sun crested over the mountains and he could brew a pot of coffee in the shed and shore up his to-do list for the day. That Thursday morning, the mountains were living up to their name, the cool air meeting the still-warm ground under a shroud of smoky-looking mist. The effect was mesmerizing, and Garrett took a moment to enjoy the view as he finished his first cup.

He needed to be on top of things, especially today, so he could get his work done with enough time left over for a quick lunch with Lindsay, who was set to arrive on property around the noon hour. Once she landed in Knoxville, one of the resort's courtesy cars would meet her.

Because of the tight schedule Garrett would be keeping that weekend, Wyatt and India were letting him stay in one of the suites in the guest house, which was temporarily closed for renovations. It would save time not to have to make his usual thirty-five-minute drive from his loft in the city. He imagined what he and Lindsay might do with that extra half hour every morning while they were all alone in the guest house, and the thought put a little extra spring in his step. It would be a rare treat to have the entire building to themselves.

He uncapped a marker, walking over to the dry-erase board where he and Finn always jotted down their notes for the day. After the usual walk around the fields, his first order of business was to head up to the Dogwood in the main house for a quick all-staff meeting. Wyatt had e-mailed that morning to tell him they'd hired a new general manager earlier in the week whom they wanted to introduce to everyone before the weekend's festivities kicked off. Garrett was interested to see who they'd settled on to run the day-to-day operations at the resort. He hoped it would be someone who was as easy to work with as the outgoing GM, who was retiring after working there for over two decades.

Garrett was just about to step outside to walk the garden rows when his phone lit up and buzzed across the wooden table. It was a text from Lindsay, letting him know that she was in the air and due to land on time. He picked up the phone to text her back, trying to ignore the feeling in the pit of his stomach. It was probably just the second cup of coffee that was making him jittery. He was excited to see her, even if he was still a little anxious about proposing. He figured it was like anything else; he just had to close his eyes and jump before he had the chance to chicken out.

They'd met back at the University of Washington during Garrett's second year of his master's program. He'd taken the extra time to get dual degrees in both horticultural and plant sciences, with a minor in natural resources, so he was one of the older students on campus. He'd never forget that spring day when he was proctoring a class for incoming freshmen as a favor to a professor friend and he'd seen Lindsay walk into the lecture hall. She was tiny, only five feet tall, with the features of a doll. Her blonde hair and slightly upturned nose gave her an aristocratic look, but when she happened to catch his eye and then smiled sweetly at him, he decided maybe she wasn't the snob that her features had given her license to be. The hour dragged on, and when he was getting ready to leave at the end, he was surprised to find her standing on the other side of his desk, waiting for him to look up.

"You're new. Where is Dr. Crawford?"

She was adorable, and he was instantly smitten.

"Uh, he had a dental thing, so he asked me to proctor for him today. I'm Garrett." He tried to act nonchalant, but her piercing eyes were unsettling. He decided to keep it professional. "Did you have questions about the exam?"

He unscrewed his water bottle and took a sip. She smiled slyly, as if she could sense she had him rattled.

"Oh no, I'm sure it went fine. I'm taking this class pass-fail, so I'm not too worried about it." She stuck out her hand. "I'm Lindsay, by the way."

Garrett shook her hand quickly, and she proceeded to prop herself on the edge of the desk, closing the gap between them ever so slightly.

"So what's your story? Are you communications? I am. Advertising, actually." She smiled again, confident now that she was making him nervous and enjoying it very much.

He shook his head and told her he was studying to be a farmer, steeling himself for the usual reaction he got from girls. A quick exit stage left. But Lindsay surprised him. It turned out she was from a farming family outside of Portland, so she understood that the trade was about more than just wearing Carhartt pants and riding around on a tractor. There was a lot of skill in land management, and Garrett had plans to follow in his grandparents' footsteps and become a master gardener. It was a lost art, but one he was excited to carry on.

Lindsay was intrigued, and after a few minutes of small talk, they agreed to meet the next day for coffee. And that was that. They dated for the next year until the job at the resort in Walland had opened up. Lindsay was beginning her sophomore year by then, and while neither of them was crazy about being apart, they were in love and willing to at least attempt a long-distance relationship.

Garrett promised her that if it got too hard, he would return to Washington, even if it meant giving up the opportunity to work and study under an industry superstar. At the time, neither of them could have imagined a scenario in which Garrett would eventually replace Finn, but still they agreed to push ahead with their relationship, despite it becoming harder to find time to spend together.

Lindsay was just about to begin her final semester, needing to pick up a few additional credits after she'd spent the past spring and summer interning at a large advertising agency in Seattle. With Garrett unable to travel during the busy spring-summer season, it had been almost five months since they'd seen each other in person. Garrett knew if they toughed it out during her last semester at UW, they'd be OK. That morning, when he'd fished the little black box out of his sock drawer and buried it inside his duffle bag, he'd convinced himself that an engagement ring would make the remaining time apart easier for her. He hoped he had the guts to put it to good use once she was standing in front of him.

Garrett walked into the Dogwood just after eleven. He grabbed a bottle of water and something from the pastry platter, then slid into one of the few remaining seats at an outlying table. He'd chosen to wear jeans with a plaid button-down over a white T-shirt rather than his usual basic gray T-shirt, so he wasn't surprised by the good-natured ribbing he received from his coworkers and friends. Making an effort for the new GM didn't hurt, but he'd mostly wanted to look nice for Lindsay's arrival—not like he'd been rolling around with the hogs.

Garrett felt a hand on his shoulder as he finished up the last of his muffin, and he turned around to find Wyatt greeting everyone at the table.

Wyatt looked down at Garrett, letting out a low whistle. "Someone's all gussied up. When's the photo shoot?"

Garrett wiped his mouth with his napkin and rolled his eyes, letting Wyatt have his fun. He stood, pushing back his chair, so he could stand facing his friend. "Sorry I bailed on you guys Monday night. I was trying to finish up a few things early in the week so I'd have a lighter load today. Lindsay should be getting here pretty soon, and I wanted us to be able to grab a quick lunch together."

Wyatt smiled. "This shouldn't take too long. India ran to the ladies' room, but when she gets back, she'll say a few words, introduce the new GM, and you'll be free." He lowered his voice a little and gestured for Garrett to listen close. "Just so you know, I made a small change and put you over in Woodshed. I also stocked it with a bottle of Basil Hayden's and some champagne. It's been a while since you've seen your girl. Besides, my wife knows you have something special planned, so it was the least I could do. I know you said you'd be fine in the guest house, but there is nothing better than those screened-in porches."

Garrett just shook his head in amazement. Woodshed was one of the most private and luxurious accommodations on the property. He'd been thrilled with their initial offer to be one of the last people to stay in the guest house before the upcoming renovation, but this was a special treat. He could hardly wait to celebrate by the fire with Lindsay later that evening.

"Thanks, Wyatt. That's so cool of you guys."

He felt his phone buzz, so he slipped it out of his pocket to take a look. Lindsay was walking out of the airport to meet the courtesy car. *Perfect.* She was right on schedule. Now he just hoped the new GM didn't prove to be too long-winded.

India had taken her place at the front of the room, so Wyatt headed up to join her, and Garrett sat back down at his table, shifting his chair so he could see better.

"Hello, everyone. Thanks for joining us. Hope you're all well rested and ready to welcome our incoming guests for Smoky Mountain Table. As usual, we are sold out, so it's important we're all in top form heading into the big weekend."

India had only been a part of the management team at the resort for a little over two years, but in that time, she'd worked tirelessly to gain the respect and admiration of the staff, and she'd done so in spades.

She laid her hand on Wyatt's forearm and glanced out over the crowd, finding Garrett seated in the back. "I spoke with Garrett and Wyatt on Monday, and I know that the menus they've put together with Chef Mend and the kitchen staff for our garden dinners are some of our strongest yet. The rain we all cursed early this past spring and summer really turned out to be a blessing for our gardens and ultimately our menus. Let's make sure that we complement the positive dining experience our guests will most assuredly have with the very highest level of customer service, from check-in to turndown each night, and every hour in between."

India took a quick sip of water before continuing. "To that end, we've conducted an exhaustive search to replace our nearly irreplaceable Michael Cummins as he sails off into the sunset of his retirement. While we had hundreds of solid candidates to choose from, I believe we've settled on the perfect person to carry on and build upon Michael's successes while blazing a few trails of her own in the process. She comes to us from the renowned Stein Eriksen Lodge in Deer Valley, where she was the youngest assistant general manager to ever be offered the top position, which she turned down to join us here. Their loss is certainly our gain. Please join me in giving a warm Walland welcome to our new general manager, Willow Armstrong."

It took Garrett a moment to realize his jaw was hanging open, but he needn't have worried; he wasn't the only one. She was even more stunning than he'd remembered from their encounter in India's office. He shifted uncomfortably in his seat as he suddenly recalled a forgotten dream he'd had a couple of nights ago. He shook his head, trying to clear the image from his mind, especially since his girlfriend was getting closer by the moment.

He watched Willow look around the room with those fawn eyes of hers. She appeared to have the confidence necessary for such a position, but he couldn't help remembering that he'd thought she'd seemed so vulnerable when he'd encountered her up close.

She wore a fitted camel-colored dress that enhanced her long brunette hair, which was loose and wavy. Willow thanked India before turning her attention to the room full of faces staring back at her. Taking a deep breath, she was about to speak when she caught sight of Garrett in the rear of the room. Recognizing him, she gave him a shy smile and an almost imperceptible nod.

He didn't hear a word she said after that, but just as she finished, his phone buzzed again in his pocket.

Lindsay had just pulled into the reception area.

Garrett stood quickly and left the meeting as quickly as he could, ignoring the nagging sensation that he was running from something.

# CHAPTER
# THREE

It wasn't unusual to see Lindsay surrounded by admirers, so Garrett wasn't surprised to find the bell staff hovering around her outside the reception building. Lindsay had only one small bag, which wasn't like her, but three of the most strapping men the resort employed were currently trying to take charge of it. Garrett chuckled, knowing he'd better step in before they got their hopes up.

"Fellas, thanks, but I can take it from here."

At the sound of Garrett's voice, Lindsay turned and smiled at him, the kind gesture failing to reach her eyes. She looked a little nervous, but Garrett supposed that was normal, since it had been so long since they'd last seen each other. Garrett reached down and wrapped her in his arms.

It never got old how small and delicate she felt. The two of them really were a study in opposites. Garrett was almost a foot and a half taller than Lindsay, and he wore the evidence of hard labor across his muscled back and shoulders. She was the definition of petite. Being with her made him feel needed, like he was protecting her from the world.

Lindsay hugged him back briefly, but she turned her face ever so slightly when he bent down to give her a kiss so that it landed just to the side of her mouth.

"Not here, Garrett. Let's get checked in and go somewhere more private," she whispered.

She tried to ignore the hurt look in his eyes as she discreetly pushed away from him, reaching down to dislodge the handle on her wheeled suitcase. He brushed her hand aside gently, lowering the handle and picking up the bag himself. He accepted two boxed lunches from one of the staff with his free hand as he led her away from the portico.

"I parked my cart over here by the Dogwood. We can jump in and head over to Woodshed after a quick lunch. Wait until you see the place where Wyatt and India are letting us stay. It's right next to the garden; it's a small red cottage with a tin roof. Anyway, it's really cool. I think you'll love it."

It occurred to Garrett that he was rambling as they climbed into his cart and started it up. He was just pulling away when he noticed India walking out the door of the main house with Wyatt. His pulse quickened a little when he saw that Willow was with them, and he was able to get an even better look at her. She was as tall as India, and if the bell staff had seemed enamored with Lindsay, they were downright captivated as they were introduced to their new boss. He was irritated with himself for feeling a little jealous, and he blew out a frustrated breath as he steered the cart away from the reception area and down the hill toward the boathouse.

"Who was that?" Lindsay was looking at him with a curious expression on her face. She didn't appear jealous. Just interested.

Garrett parked the cart at the entrance of the boathouse and got out to grab their lunches from the back. Lindsay watched him, then stood up to follow him to the picnic table in the shaded pavilion overlooking the pond.

"That's the new general manager. They just hired her. I haven't even officially met her yet myself."

He busied himself with setting up their lunches side by side. He didn't know why, but it suddenly felt very awkward between them.

"She's pretty. Beautiful, actually. But she looks awfully young to be running this place." Lindsay slid her lunch box to the other side of the table and sat across from Garrett, popping open the top of the iced tea he'd set out for her. Taking a drink, she puckered up her face.

"I still can't get used to sweet tea. It amazes me that everyone in the South likes things so sugary. All those unnecessary calories. Ugh." She replaced the cap, reaching down into her purse for a bottle of water.

Garrett just shook his head and smiled at her. She had no reason to be thinking about calories. He'd noticed she looked even smaller than usual when he'd first spotted her. He supposed that working all summer at her internship hadn't left much time for indulgences.

They ate their chicken sandwiches together in silence, enjoying the serenity of the boathouse. It was a warm day, but the breeze helped, and the humidity wasn't as bad as previous days.

"I'm glad you're here, Linds. It feels like it's been forever. I wish you had longer than a weekend to spend. This event is going to be pretty hectic, otherwise I'd have a lot more time to hang out. I was hoping we could at least get in a hike before you leave Sunday. The trails are beautiful this time of year. Not muddy like they were last April when you visited."

He stopped talking when he saw her face. She was staring at him with those blue eyes of hers, something unsaid. She stood up and walked to the edge of the dock, looking out over the water. He watched her, wondering what was on her mind. He was about to ask when she started to speak.

"I'm glad you're happy here, Garrett. It's so obvious when I talk to you on the phone, and seeing you now, it's even more clear. This is totally where you belong." She sighed, turning to face him again. "It's a beautiful place, and I love coming to visit you here. But it's really hard. It's not enough. I don't know if I can do this for another semester." She held up her hand to stop him when he started to protest. "I know you offered, but I would never ask you to come back to Washington for me. That's crazy. Your life is here now." She paused before continuing. "I just don't know how I fit into it."

It was quiet except for the gentle sound of the water lapping against the canoes moored to the dock. While he'd known the subject would come up, Garrett hadn't expected it to be so soon after Lindsay's arrival. He'd hoped to have time first for them to remember how good they were together. He wanted to convince her that they could make this work. They just needed a reason to get through the next few months.

He walked over to where she stood and took her face into his hands. "I know it's tough, babe. But there are plenty of great ad agencies in Knoxville, and I know you'll have no problem getting a job. By the time Christmas rolls around, we'll be together for real. For good."

He looked down at her and smiled before dropping his head to brush his lips against hers. It was like no time had passed, but there was also a desperation in the kiss. It felt less like hello and more like good-bye. He chose to ignore the sadness in her eyes and took her by the hand. "Come on. Let's ride over to Woodshed. I'm sure you want to rest up, and I have a few things to do in my office before dinner tonight."

He started to lead her away, but she pulled on his hand to stop him.

"Garrett?"

He looked back at her.

"I love you. I always will."

Garrett smiled, relief washing over him. He squeezed her hand then as they walked to the parked cart and set off together.

Willow had changed into more informal clothes and was headed down the hill on foot when she saw him again. He was holding hands with a petite blonde as they emerged from the boathouse and got into a golf cart. She noticed the way he tenderly helped the woman in before taking his own seat, and it surprised her when she felt a pang of sadness.

She knew who he was now; she'd asked India about him after spotting him again at the staff meeting. Willow was surprised to learn that he'd been a bellman before becoming Finn's heir apparent. It was rare to find someone like herself who was willing to work different positions within a resort, especially two posts that were so diverse. She was looking forward to meeting Garrett one-on-one, but watching him drive off with the petite blonde in tow, she sensed that it might be better to seek him out later that day. She'd stop by the garden in the late afternoon after she'd finished exploring the property on her own.

Willow was glad to be staying in the guest house for a couple of days. It was the ideal home base from which to explore the property, and she'd have the chance to experience one of the resort's original accommodations before a planned winter renovation.

There was a cozy common living room with a fireplace, where she could picture herself unwinding with a glass of wine and a new book at the end of long days. And the coffee-maker and breakfast bar would make her very early mornings more tolerable too. Best of all, she'd have the entire multi-room building to herself.

Willow spent the next couple of hours stopping by the various venues scattered around the resort. First, she introduced herself to the young men who ran the Orvis fly-fishing shack, watching as they skillfully outfitted guests who were already on property with waders and fly rods. She couldn't wait to try her hand at the sport. The guides told her that women usually picked it up quickly because they had a gentler rhythm, whereas most men tried to muscle the line in an attempt to get it to land where they wanted it to. Fly-fishing was all about finesse.

She took a drive by the stables next and met the staff, who made sure the horses were well cared for and ready for riding. She was pleased to see that they offered both Western and English saddles, and she made a mental note to come out and ride as soon as she had some free time. She'd grown up with horses and missed the sense of freedom riding provided.

By the time she'd wrapped up her stable visit, Willow noticed it was getting close to dinnertime, so she figured she'd better get over to the garden before she missed her chance to introduce herself to Garrett.

She borrowed one of the carts parked near the horse barn and took the short ride over to the other side of the property. As she pulled up, she feared that she must be too late. The potting shed appeared closed for the day, and the fields were empty, except for the picnic tables that had been lined up in anticipation of the following evening's welcome dinner. The sun was setting over the trees, but the last few angled rays were lighting up the charming red cottage known as Woodshed. When she put her hand up over her eyes to shield the sun and take in the stunning view, she saw them. Garrett and the small woman from the boathouse were standing in the screened-in porch together. She watched, mesmerized, as Garrett suddenly bent down on one knee. Willow heard herself gasp, and she whirled around, feeling ashamed that she'd unintentionally intruded on such a personal moment.

She hopped into her cart and headed back down the lane in the direction of the guest house, deciding to skip dinner in the barn and order room service instead. She wasn't feeling much like company after all.

# CHAPTER
# FOUR

That afternoon, Garrett had gone back to work for a few hours, but he was still feeling a little uncomfortable about how things had unfolded during lunch. He'd left Lindsay alone in Woodshed, after giving her a brief tour, so that she could take a short nap and he could finish up his work in the garden. But after replaying their conversation in his mind, he couldn't get back to her fast enough. He needed to get that ring on her finger as soon as possible.

Garrett knocked softly on the door before entering so he didn't startle her. She was finishing up a phone call and hung up just as he walked in the door.

"You're back early. I thought you'd be working until sundown tonight? I was just thinking about hopping in the shower." Lindsay stood up from the sofa, tossing her phone onto the table and moving toward her suitcase to select some fresh clothes.

Garrett had stopped by his Jeep on the way to dig through his duffle bag and grab the small black box, which was now burning a hole in his jeans pocket. He walked up behind her and took her hand. "Come out onto the porch with me for a minute, Linds. I want you to see how beautiful the light is. It's my favorite time of day in the garden."

She hesitated for a moment before setting down the stack of clothes she was holding and letting him lead her out onto the screened porch. The sun was shining in at a low angle, lighting them both up in a warm glow.

Garrett knew it was now or never. He took a deep breath, ignored the panic, and went for it. "I know it's weird between us right now, babe. I feel it too. I know we haven't seen each other for so long, but you have to realize by now what you mean to me, Linds. I'd do anything for you. Just because I'm far away doesn't mean we've lost our connection. It's just one more year."

He reached into his pocket just then, pulled out the small velvet box, and dropped to his knee.

Lindsay took it all in, and when she realized what was happening, her eyes registered complete shock.

Garrett wasn't prepared for what came next.

Willow was grateful that India and Wyatt had left the bottle of Far Niente on the living room counter in the guest house with a note welcoming her to the resort family. She'd showered and thrown on her gray cashmere sweats and a white tank top. The only thing missing was a long straw to stick directly into the wine bottle. She made do with a glass instead and was sitting in the dark, on her second or third drink, when she heard the main door click open.

He was drunk.

It was obvious by the way he stood at the threshold, swaying a bit before deciding whether or not to come in. She was pretty sure he hadn't seen her sitting in the dim light next to the dying fire, so she held still, trying to figure out how to handle the situation.

Garrett paused, his duffle in one hand, the doorknob in his other. After a moment, he walked in, pushing the door shut behind him with a thud. He reached down and opened the small refrigerator, grabbing two bottles of water with his free hand. He closed the door with his knee, almost falling over in the process. She watched as he turned around and walked up the stairs, presumably headed to one of the second-floor guest rooms. She heard his heavy boots fall to the floor and then a loud creak as he fell (hopefully) into bed.

Willow blew out a breath she didn't know she'd been holding. She felt sick for him, knowing that his presence here must have meant things hadn't gone well back on the porch. She stood and walked quickly to her room on the main floor, just off the sitting area, trying to shake her own head loose from the wine fog she was in. She locked her door, set her alarm for the morning, and used the water on her nightstand to swallow an Advil. As she fell asleep, she was vaguely aware of feeling a tiny bit relieved by the whole scene, which made her head ache that much more.

Garrett woke to the sounds of birds chirping in the morning darkness, and his first thought was of coffee.

That wasn't true.

His first thought was to wonder whether or not Lindsay had left for the airport yet.

He hoped she had. He couldn't tolerate the thought of having to see her again after the way things had gone.

He rolled over, vaguely aware that he'd slept in his clothes. Dragging himself up out of the bed, Garrett stumbled into the bathroom, peeling things off as he walked, needing to feel the hot water on his skin as soon as possible. He stood there for a time, trying to feel human again. When he realized that wasn't going to happen without copious amounts of caffeine, he shut the water off and draped a towel around his hips, opening the door to the hallway.

As he walked down the stairs barefoot, running his fingers through his hair with his free hand to shake out the excess water, he considered the possibility that the coffee bar wouldn't be stocked since no one was expected to be staying in the guest house. He stopped short at the bottom of the landing, trying to figure out if his eyes were playing tricks on him.

Willow was standing at the counter, the spoon in her hand hovering, forgotten, above her steaming mug, staring back at him with those chocolate-colored eyes of hers.

He grabbed ahold of the towel around his waist to make sure it was secure and tried to act nonchalant, clearing his throat first. "Morning. I'm guessing there's coffee after all? I wasn't sure. Thought I was the only one staying here."

He waited for her to speak, although it didn't seem like she was able.

Finally, after a moment, she answered him. "Uh, sorry. I thought I was the only one staying here too. There must have been a miscommunication."

She smiled weakly and offered him the mug in her hands while trying to avert her eyes. "Here, take this one. It has cream and sugar, though. Hope that's OK."

He could see now that she was blushing, and it occurred to him that it was because of his current state of undress. *Damn.*

Holding on to the towel for dear life, he couldn't help thinking she looked remarkably beautiful standing there in her simple sweats. Garrett thought she looked even younger with her hair piled on top of her head like that. He could hear a trace of a Southern accent in her voice, and he wondered where she was from. "Thanks for the coffee. I guess I'd better go find some clothes and get myself to the garden. This is a late start for me. I usually beat the sun by at least an hour."

He paused for a moment, realizing he hadn't introduced himself yet but questioning the wisdom of the timing. He decided it would be weirder if he didn't say anything at all. "I'm Garrett Oliver, by the way. I'm one of the gardeners here. And you're our new GM. Willow . . ."

She smiled, remembering his hands were full and shyly withdrawing her hand. "Willow Armstrong. Nice to meet you, Garrett. I missed you last night when I stopped by the garden." She realized her mistake in mentioning last night when she saw the shadow cross his face. "Anyway, I'm sure we'll be seeing each other around. Hopefully dressed a little more appropriately."

She gestured weakly at her own clothing and blushed before turning to head back toward her room.

"Have a good morning," she said over her shoulder as she stepped over the threshold of her room and closed the door.

Garrett took a sip of coffee and headed upstairs to pull himself together. Suddenly, the day didn't seem as bleak as it had just a few moments before.

*Oh my God.* Willow leaned back against her closed door, trying to collect her thoughts, but they kept defying her and racing straight back to his insanely muscled torso. She could get her laundry squeaky clean on that washboard. She'd had a little wine headache up to that point, but now she felt only an adrenaline rush from their encounter. Clothing sure had a way of hiding things. Granted, he'd looked pretty great in the jeans and plaid shirt from the day before too, but it was nothing compared to what a white towel had done for him.

And for her.

She hurriedly got ready and packed her day bag before heading out to work. Garrett must have beat her to it, because his empty coffee mug was turned upside down next to the coffeepot, a note beside it thanking her and welcoming her to the resort family. She smiled at the gesture and thought to herself that she was glad she'd chosen to come back to Tennessee. She felt at home.

As she walked over to the main reception building to say good morning to the staff before heading to her office, Willow noticed Garrett's girlfriend standing off to the side of the door, her back turned and her hand over her mouth as she talked on the phone. Her suitcase was beside her, and it appeared she was waiting for the courtesy car. Willow couldn't help but overhear her talking as she walked by.

"I couldn't tell him, Will. It would have crushed him. But believe me, baby. It's over. I'm coming home now. I'll see you in a few hours. Love you too."

Willow didn't want to hear any more. She brushed past the woman and into the lobby, forcing herself to smile at the employees manning the front desk. After saying hello to them and to the concierge, she stepped into the small hall powder room and locked the door behind her.

She was surprised by how angry she felt. Obviously, the girl had broken up with Garrett, but it sounded like she hadn't been completely faithful to him. It was none of Willow's business, but she couldn't help despising the woman anyway. She took a moment, then headed out of the reception building toward the building that housed her own office. She was relieved to see the Lexus pulling away, presumably with Garrett's ex-girlfriend inside.

Willow sighed, pulling out her chair and sitting down to a hefty to-do list. It was time to put all of the morning's events behind her and get down to the business of being a general manager.

Garrett's shirt was soaked through, and it wasn't even noon. The day was going to be a warm one. He was busy clearing and plowing where plants had already been harvested so the garden would look as tidy as possible for the dinners that weekend. If he had time, he'd start planting a few potatoes and root vegetables as well. But the combination of heat, humidity, and a wicked hangover had him feeling like he was moving through molasses, so he wasn't too optimistic. He'd just stopped for a quick drink of water when he saw Wyatt approaching, a big smile spread across his face. Garrett took his time chugging from the water bottle, trying to figure out what he would say to his friend.

"Well, what's the good word, my man?" Wyatt slapped him on the shoulder, his face lit up in anticipation. "Do I need to get fitted for my tux?"

Garrett had spent the better part of the morning feeling humiliated about the way Lindsay had flatly turned him down. He wasn't sure he was ready to talk about it just yet, but he didn't want to lie to his friend either.

"She isn't ready, as it turns out. She dumped me, actually. But, hey, thanks for that bottle of bourbon. I tucked into that as fast as I could and then proceeded to walk my sorry ass over to the guest house to sleep it off. Hope you don't mind." Garrett returned his attention to the water bottle.

Wyatt looked stunned, running his hand though his hair as he searched for the right words.

"It's OK, Wyatt. There's nothing to say. This thing between us ran its course. I don't know what I expected. My life is here, and hers is in Seattle. She was offered a job at the agency where she interned this summer, so I guess that's what sealed our fate."

Wyatt shook his head in disbelief. "Damn, I'm sorry, Garrett. I never saw that coming. I thought I'd find you whistling Dixie this morning. I sure would have kept my big mouth shut if I had any sense."

Garrett smiled at his friend. "You couldn't have known. Hell, it definitely caught me off guard. And if that weren't embarrassing enough, I met our new GM this morning, wearing nothing but a towel and a giant hangover. So, that was awesome."

Wyatt stared at Garrett for a moment before exploding in laughter. It was contagious, and both men allowed themselves the moment.

"Oh man, I totally forgot to mention that she's staying in the guest house. For the weekend at least. We figured it would help her get a sense of the place if she hung around for a few days. It never occurred to me to tell you once I'd switched you over to Woodshed."

Garrett grimaced. "Yeah, she thinks I'm an idiot. I stood there half naked and carried on a full conversation with her—even took her cup of coffee. Nothing I can do about it now."

Wyatt couldn't stop laughing. "I can't wait to tell India. On the bright side, though, Willow isn't exactly hard on the eyes, man. I'll bet seeing her first thing took the sting out of your morning?"

Garrett smirked, the resulting ache in his temples reminding him not to get too excited.

"I hadn't noticed. I was about to get engaged, remember? What would that say about my character if I was checking out other women, with a ring in my pocket?"

In his own mind, Garrett was trying to ignore the answer.

Wyatt started to walk away, then changed his mind. "Remember, we're getting together in the barn at twelve thirty to go over tonight's menu. Hey, I guess you'll get a second chance to make a first impression. Did I mention that your new boss is going to be running all of our meetings from now on?"

Wyatt pumped his fist in the air as he walked away, clearly pleased with himself.

Garrett, on the other hand, suddenly felt even worse than he had that morning. He rushed into the shed and splashed some cold water on his face, trying to make himself as presentable as possible. At this rate, his second impression wasn't going to be any better than the first.

# CHAPTER
# FIVE

Willow arrived at the barn early for the menu round table, so she used her extra time to wander around the kitchen, watching in awe as the talented staff prepared the bounty of ingredients for that evening's garden feast. There were greens she didn't recognize on cutting boards next to the most luscious heirloom tomatoes she'd ever seen, in shades of green, orange, red, and even brown. The warm weather they'd been experiencing for most of September had extended the life of the harvest. Willow understood now how this food had inspired an entire movement.

Finn Janssen was passionate about maintaining the integrity of everything grown on their land, so much so that it had inspired a book. Violet and Rex, the staff photographers at the resort, had produced it. Willow had been pleased when India mentioned that they'd be attending the dinner that night to autograph copies of their critically acclaimed book for guests. She was looking forward to meeting them.

The large glass entrance door to the barn opened soundlessly, and India and Wyatt walked through it, smiling when they saw Willow emerging from the kitchen. India wandered over to greet her, and Wyatt nodded hello as he passed them to set down the stacks of menus he'd carried in for the meeting.

"I still love to come and poke around the kitchen myself when they're prepping for a big event. Isn't it a sight to see?"

India waved to the chefs as they called out greetings to her. It was obvious that India had completely won over the staff in her short time there. Willow hoped she could do the same.

India turned her attention back to her new GM. "So I heard you had an interesting morning? I'm so sorry Garrett barged in on you like that. He had different plans. . . . He thought the guest house was empty, which is our fault. I hope you weren't too mortified?"

India watched Willow's face for any signs of irritation, but what she saw was something altogether different. A slight pink crept into her cheeks, and Willow cast her eyes downward, but not quickly enough. India thought she saw interest there. No, Willow definitely wasn't too upset about the intrusion.

"Oh, it's fine. He was very nice, and it was certainly a first encounter neither of us will forget, I'm sure." Willow was looking at India now, a smile on her face. "Besides, the guest house has more than enough rooms to spare. I'm happy to share with anyone you want to put there for the weekend. Is that where your photographer friends will be staying too?"

India shook her head. "Violet and Rex will be with us. You wouldn't get a moment of sleep with their little girl running around. And they have a new baby boy, who has his days and nights mixed up. So it's just you and Garrett staying in the guest house. And I think he's only planning to be there through the weekend, then he'll go back to his loft in Knoxville."

Willow was surprised. He didn't look like someone who would live in the city. "Is that where his girlfriend's from?"

At India's surprised look, Willow rushed to explain. "I saw them having lunch yesterday in the boathouse. I just assumed . . ."

The door opened once again, and they watched Garrett walk in and say hello to Wyatt.

India lowered her voice so only Willow could hear. "Ex-girlfriend. And no, she lives on the West Coast. I doubt we'll be seeing her again. Garrett lives in the city, near Market Square."

India was momentarily distracted by activity in the kitchen, and didn't seem to make the connection that Garrett and Willow would eventually be neighbors in nearby Knoxville, once Willow settled in at her father's house the following week, as she planned to do. After a brief chat with the sous chef, the women started walking together over to where the men were talking, India gesturing toward Willow as they joined the guys. "Garrett, you've met Willow Armstrong, yes? Now that we're all here, why don't we grab some seats over on the couches in the demo area, and we can finalize the details for tonight."

Garrett nodded toward Willow. "Sure, we've met. Just this morning, actually. Welcome again, Willow."

India could tell Garrett was horrified by his actions as he went above and beyond in order to be polite. She sighed, hoping this wouldn't make things weird for everyone.

She needn't have worried. The meeting proceeded as planned, with everyone acting professionally. India could tell they'd made a good choice. Willow had distinct ideas of her own, but she was also a good listener, and she went out of her way to compliment others when they suggested a better option. The four of them worked seamlessly together and knocked out the final touches for the evening in under an hour.

When they stood to go their separate ways, India excused herself to use the restroom while Wyatt stepped away to talk briefly with Chef Mend.

Willow fiddled with her earring as she found herself alone with Garrett once more. "I can't wait for tonight. It sounds like an incredible experience to have such a special meal served in the garden. You must be really proud of what you've produced this year."

Garrett was excited about the evening too, but he rubbed the back of his neck absentmindedly as he tried to think of a way to answer her with humility. "I'm really proud, but I can't take too much credit. The entire garden staff is so talented, and we've got a true pioneer as our leader in Finn Janssen. Only an idiot could screw this up. Luckily, I didn't."

He grinned at her, his eyes twinkling, and they laughed together, easing any leftover tension.

"Hey, listen. I'm really sorry about this morning. I couldn't have made a bigger ass out of myself if I'd tried. I had a rough night, but that's no excuse to be anything less than a gentleman, which I certainly was not. I hope we can forget about that and let today be the start of a great working relationship."

Willow wasn't so sure she wanted to *totally* forget all the details of that morning, but she nodded, her smile reaching her eyes. "Of course. You didn't exactly see me at my best either." She extended her hand to shake his. "Forgotten?"

He reached for her and almost completely engulfed her small but strong hand in his. "Forgotten. Now, back to work before my new boss hears that I've been loafing around. Rumor is she's pretty tough."

Willow smiled as she watched him walk away from her and head back to the garden.

India had just caught the tail end of their conversation as she emerged from the hallway, and seeing Willow's face, she smiled to herself. Maybe this would be the start of something great after all. For everyone.

Wyatt heard them before he saw them. The baby was fast asleep in his infant car seat, but Sadie couldn't wait to bound up the porch steps and throw open the screen door in search of her aunt and uncle. India got to her first, drying her hands on a kitchen towel that she quickly threw aside so she could scoop the little girl up in her arms.

"Aunt Indy, you got so round!" Sadie was rubbing her hands on India's belly, which was growing bigger by the day. It had been almost a month since they'd last seen Violet and Rex, and in that time, she'd really popped.

Wyatt walked up behind her, laughing the whole way. "She's not round, sweet girl. She's got a baby in her tummy, remember? Now get over here and give your uncle Wyatt some love!"

Sadie wriggled down from India and went running into Wyatt's arms. "I'm gonna be six, Uncle Wyatt. My mom and dad said so. I'm in kindy garden, but next year, I get to go to first grade!"

She covered Wyatt's face in kisses, which never got old. He couldn't wait to experience these moments with his own child, but Sadie would always hold a special place in his heart.

"Hey, guys, are you ready for this traveling circus?" Violet looked tired as she let the screen door close softly behind her. But she was still sporting a huge smile on her face, which was just as beautiful without a stitch of makeup on and sur-rounded by her mane of red hair. India was pea green with envy.

"Let me take the little man off your hands, Mama." Wyatt reached for the carrier that held their six-week-old son, Evan, and then lifted him up for a closer look. "Wow, he's so small."

Wyatt looked at his wife. "I can't believe we're getting one of these, Indy."

Wyatt was still in awe over his good fortune. He truly had everything he'd ever wanted. And more. Violet kissed him on the cheek, touched by his expression.

"Evan is small, but his lungs are big and powerful. He does some of his best work in the middle of the night, so we apol-ogize in advance."

Rex came through the door, a diaper bag and Sadie's pink duffle hanging off him at all angles. "That's not the only thing my son has that's huge." Rex had a wicked grin on his face, and he broke out into laughter at the same time as Wyatt.

India and Violet just shook their heads. The band was back together. They were in for all kinds of tomfoolery that weekend, if their history together was any indication.

"Yep, he's got a big mouth too, just like his daddy," Violet said without missing a beat, leaning over to smack Rex on the butt as he passed by.

India went back into the kitchen to finish preparing a few snacks for everyone while Wyatt took the family upstairs to get settled. Once they'd gotten Evan down for a nap and Sadie was happily playing with her dolls, the four adults reconvened around the kitchen table, like they'd done so many times before.

"So, how are you feeling, India? You look incredible. I look like that when I've had too many tacos. I can't believe you're almost seven months pregnant!"

India laughed at Violet's description of her. Violet practically had a newborn, and she still looked like she could book a modeling job at any moment. Her figure was flawless as usual but sported a couple of new assets that India was sure Rex didn't mind. "I feel great, honestly. The new wardrobe is a bit of an adjustment, and I don't look so great in a bikini, but I couldn't ask for a better pregnancy so far."

India glanced over at Wyatt. "Should we tell them?"

Wyatt mulled the idea over for a moment. "Nah. Let's keep it just between us for now."

He reached over for the cheese knife, but before he could grab it, Violet's hand came down over his with a thump.

"If you don't start talking, Hinch, I'll make sure Evan has his uncle Wyatt change all his poopie diapers."

She switched her gaze to India. "Tell us what?"

Violet looked back and forth between the two of them, waiting for an answer.

"To resist is futile, brother. Trust me, in this case, her bite is definitely much worse than her bark." Rex crunched a tortilla chip, watching with growing interest.

"OK, OK. I'm kidding," Wyatt said, rubbing his hand in mock pain.

Violet released her grip, and Wyatt sat back to join hands with his wife.

"We caved at our last appointment and found out the sex of the baby. Do you want to know or should we keep it a surprise?" Wyatt grinned, because he already knew what their answer would be.

"Tell us!" they said together and without a moment's hesitation. Violet was leaning forward in anticipation, and Rex had a huge smile on his face.

Wyatt took a deep breath and stared back at their friends. "It's a boy," he announced proudly.

"Yes!" Rex jumped up to bump fists with Wyatt, who just beamed and looked at his wife.

India was smiling mischievously as she leaned forward toward them. "And a girl. We're having twins!"

It was quiet for a moment while the news sunk in, but after a few seconds, Violet leapt out of her chair too, and offered hugs all around as well as words of congratulations.

India and Wyatt were still reeling from the news themselves. They'd just found out the week before, which was why India had accelerated the search for the new general manager. She'd planned to try and pick up the extra workload herself and then conduct a more leisurely search when things slowed down in November. But her doctor recommended she allow herself the final eight weeks just in case she needed to be on bed rest for any reason.

She'd been relieved to find such a qualified candidate, and India knew that being a woman would likely make Willow more empathetic toward her situation as she prepared to become a working first-time mother. Not to mention India sensed that she and Willow could be friends, which would be important with the two of them working together so closely.

When it was time to go up and change for dinner, Violet helped India carry the dishes from the table to the sink. She hadn't stopped smiling at the news, so happy for her friends. Violet still couldn't believe the twist of fate that had brought India and Wyatt together. It had truly been a miracle.

"I can't wait to introduce you to our new general manager, Willow Armstrong," India told her. "You're going to love her. She just started, but I already know she's the perfect fit to lead our team. And maybe the perfect fit for a certain young farmer friend of ours, if you ask me."

India rinsed the last of the plates, setting them on the sideboard to dry.

Violet looked surprised. "Wait, are you talking about Garrett? Isn't he serious with that college girl from the Northwest?"

Rex had become pretty good friends with Garrett through Wyatt, so he kept Violet up to date on all the gossip during their pillow talks.

"He proposed to her, and she turned him down. Broke up with him on the spot, if you can believe it. He's better off without her, if you ask me. He can do better."

"And by better, you mean Willow?" Violet asked, raising her eyebrows in surprise. "I've taught you well, grasshopper! Aren't you the little matchmaker?"

India giggled as they walked up the stairs together, pausing before heading into their separate rooms to get ready for dinner. "Who knows? Men are tricky. You can lead a horse to water, but it's a little harder when you're working with mules."

Violet laughed out loud and hugged her friend, promising to meet downstairs to leave for dinner within the hour.

# CHAPTER
# SIX

The weather that Friday evening couldn't have been better. Dinner was scheduled for seven with a cocktail hour beforehand, timed so that the sun would still be peeking over the trees when guests arrived. As warm as the day had been, the waning humidity and slight breeze that had picked up again would keep everyone comfortable as they mingled. Staff members were dressed casually in jeans and plaid. All they had to do now was wait for Willow's signal to start passing appetizers once the guests arrived.

There were local musicians setting up a short distance away at the edge of the field, and Willow knew the happy sounds of the fiddle and steel guitar would be the perfect complement to the rustic dinner.

Willow had arrived early, taking her time to make sure the table settings were perfect. She'd double-checked the spelling of the guests' names on the place cards to make sure even the smallest details were polished. This was not only her first big event as general manager but also one of the most popular weekends of the year. The Smoky Mountain Table event usually sold out as soon as the schedule was released, oftentimes with repeat guests. Late September was a perfect time to experience the resort. There would be expectations, and Willow wanted to exceed them.

Garrett found her standing just outside his potting shed in a patch of shade when he arrived fresh from showering and changing his clothes. He could see she'd done the same, and the thought occurred to him that he'd never seen denim look that good before. She wore a sleeveless light-blue denim dress that stopped just above her knee, with buttons running up the front. She looked even taller, with legs a mile long in her tan wedge sandals. Her hair was still loose around her shoulders, but she had it pinned up on the sides now, framing her face in a very flattering way. She was striking, and he had to remind himself after a moment that she was, for all intents and purposes, his boss.

He cleared his throat to let her know he was there, and she startled even though he'd meant for the gesture to have the opposite effect.

"Sorry, I didn't mean to spook you while you were deep in thought." He looked around the garden. "Everything look OK to you? I walked around before I left to get cleaned up and thought we were in great shape. Did I miss anything?"

She sat down in one of the blue rockers, slipping her feet out of her shoes ever so slightly and wriggling her toes. "The only thing I missed was the memo not to wear wedge sandals in a garden. I didn't think that one through." She gave him a rueful smile. "It's gonna be a miracle if I keep my ankles intact."

Garrett rubbed the short whiskers on the side of his face with his hand and shook his head. "I'm sure glad I'm a guy. It was between the hiking shoes or the boots for me. I chose the ones that were less muddy."

She laughed, thinking to herself that he'd done a fine job of cleaning up. He had on gray jeans and a white shirt, with a black-and-gray plaid shirt layered over it. He'd tried to tame his hair back with some kind of product, but he needn't have bothered. She remembered how hot he looked with his hair damp and loose after his shower.

*Cancel that.*

She was not going to think about that right now. She had to focus on the event, which, from the looks of things, was just about to get under way. In the distance, she could see a trail of golf carts winding up the path, carrying guests to dinner. She stood and smoothed her hands down the front of her dress and smiled at Garrett. "Ready or not, here they come."

The start of the evening was flawless, save for a bleating sheep that kept interrupting Wyatt's welcome toast, causing murmurs of laughter across the tables and a joking suggestion of mutton on the menu the following evening. Wyatt promised that the meal would be sublime and assured guests that the sommelier had chosen some incredible wines to pair with each course.

Willow was seated next to Violet, and she found the woman to be even more interesting than she'd anticipated. Willow had paged briefly through the book Violet and Rex had produced, and she was impressed by the wealth of information it contained about heirloom farming practices around the world.

"It must have been something to travel to all of those amazing places and record the stories of the way people live and farm. Was it hard to settle back in to your normal routine after that much excitement?"

Willow couldn't imagine traveling the world with a young child in tow. They'd included several pictures of their daughter, Sadie, in the book, one a close-up shot of her small hands holding a big juicy tomato in Bologna, another a photograph of her from the back, standing among a group of village children in Guatemala.

Violet chuckled, shaking her head. "Honestly, I thought it might be, but once we got home and I found out about the pregnancy, I was never so happy to have our simple lives back. Besides, with Wyatt and India running the place now, they didn't have time to pick up our slack too. Shooting the farmstead catalog is a full-time gig." She looked at India, who was sitting across the table from them, listening in. "And now I guess we're both busy breeding."

The three women laughed.

"All kidding aside, I'm so glad our babies will be close in age, India. I can't wait to see what kind of trouble they'll get into together."

The food started coming in waves and never let up. Plates of gorgeous crimson tomatoes and handcrafted mozzarella were soon replaced by slow-cooked farm eggs over grits in a delicious smoked-chicken broth. Wines were poured in a perfected synchronization, and it was safe to say that no one saw the bottom of their wineglass if the waitstaff could help it. The meal ended simply but spectacularly with a warm cookie served with a side of homemade vanilla bean ice cream, ensuring that the workout facility would be a popular destination the next morning for those who were hoping to at least play for the tie in terms of calorie consumption.

Rex had been seated at the other end of the table, but Willow was able to meet him briefly when he'd come to fetch

Violet near the end of the evening so that they could mingle with guests and sign copies of their book. A short time later, they circled back to say their good-byes. The baby was fussy, and the sitter they'd hired for the evening thought he might want to be fed again.

The first night of Smoky Mountain Table had been a success, and it was close to ten when the last of the guests left for the evening, some of them still clutching their half-full wineglasses.

Willow finally felt herself relax. She'd made it over her first big hurdle and had done so in fine form. She'd already had a fair amount of wine, but she decided to live a little when one of the waiters offered her the rest of a delicious bottle of the zinfandel they'd enjoyed with the main course. She noticed that Garrett and Wyatt had also said yes to another glass of wine as they approached her with India leading the way.

"It's so strange. I love wine, but for some reason, despite seeing the three of you with that delicious red, I'm not craving it at all," India said. She shrugged her shoulders. "I wish I could say the same for chocolate gelato."

Turning to Wyatt, she gestured toward his drink and raised her eyebrow. "Why don't you throw that in a to-go cup, and I'll drive us back to the house? I'm beat, and there's a half-pint in the freezer with my name on it."

The look Wyatt gave his wife made Willow blush. The love between them was palpable. He reached over to give India a quick kiss before grasping her hand and saying good night to the others.

Garrett was alone now with Willow, with the exception of a few servers who were clearing the remaining tables. Maybe it was the beautiful autumn night, or maybe it was the magic of the fireflies canvassing the space above the darkened fields.

It might have simply been all the wine. Regardless, he found himself not wanting the night to end.

"Do you feel like grabbing one more bottle and getting out of here?" He held up his hand in explanation when he saw her shocked face. "I only mean, we're both headed back to the guest house, and it would be nice to have a nightcap out on the rear terrace if you're up for it? I'm sure we'll get treated to more of these firebugs."

Willow thought that didn't sound half bad, actually. She was still riding a high from the success of the night, so what harm could a drink with a coworker do? She smiled at him. "I'll grab the wine; you grab a golf cart. My feet aren't going to make it up that hill in these shoes."

Garrett was right; the view from the veranda was spectacular that evening. It was situated high above a hill that sloped down toward Walland Pond and the boathouse. Thousands of lightning bugs were flickering in the darkness, and it was an incredible vantage point from which to see the waning moon. They were each in a rocking chair, their feet up on the stone wall in front of them. Willow was barefoot now, her shoes in a pile on the bluestone patio next to her. She'd grabbed a light sweater from inside and slipped it around her shoulders, glad to have a barrier from the oncoming chill of the late-night air. Garrett could tell the wine had her feeling relaxed, because her accent had thickened up quite noticeably since they'd sat down. He could listen to her all night, so he kept finding ways to keep her talking.

"So word on the street is you were offered this same gig out in Deer Valley. I've been to Stein Eriksen Lodge," Garrett told her. "I know what we've got here is special, but what possessed you to uproot your life and turn that job down?"

He glanced over to see if he'd offended her by asking, but her face was open and eager to share.

"Oh, I loved Park City. And Stein is an amazing place to work. The people are great. It was tough to leave, because I felt like I belonged in the mountains. But I'm from Knoxville originally, and it was the right time and opportunity for me to come back. For now anyway." She paused, her brow furrowing a bit before she went on. "My father is sick, so I need to be here, to be closer to him." Willow looked over at Garrett, her face serious now. "He has late-stage Alzheimer's. He doesn't really even know I'm back, but it's important for me to be here for him since he's basically all alone now."

She paused again. "My mom was almost fifty when they had me, and my dad was sixty-two. My mom died four years ago, the year after I'd moved to Utah, and my father has been in decline ever since. I'll always regret not having that time with my mom at the end, but my career was just taking off, and I couldn't leave for extended periods of time."

She sighed and took a sip of her wine before looking back at him, the corner of her mouth turned up in a wry smile. "Aren't you glad you asked?"

He was studying her, impressed by her strength and touched by the choice she'd made to come home for her father. He understood her, more than she realized. "My nan suffered from dementia. She and my grandfather raised me back in Washington State. They were the most salt-of-the-earth people you'd ever want to meet. Talk about work ethic; they were farmers—the old-school kind. Gramp taught me everything I knew about heirloom farming before I came to work here in Walland. Finn reminds me a lot of him, actually."

Willow listened, nodding when he mentioned his grand-father. "How did he deal with your grandmother's disease? It's so difficult to lose someone mentally before you lose them physically. I'm still struggling with that."

She felt herself choking up.

Garrett reached down for the wine bottle that he'd set on the stone between them, filling her glass before adding some more to his own. He took a sip before he answered the question, his voice thick with emotion. "He handled it the best he could, I suppose. He wouldn't agree to put Nan in a home, and she got pretty bad at the end. She even went missing for a whole day once, but a search party found her in the back of one of their fields. She was looking for Gramp so they could start the spring planting together. It was November."

Garrett let out a ragged breath. "Gramp died in his sleep less than six months after we lost her. I swear he died from a broken heart. They've both been gone just over three years now. My gramp made me promise I'd take this job right before he died, and he sold the farm because he knew I'd feel obli-gated to stay if he didn't. I always thought I'd make my life in Washington, but I guess my life is here now."

They were quiet after that, each of them lost in thought. The sounds of the tree frogs and crickets were hypnotic, and it was unclear how much time had passed when Willow finally spoke. "I suppose we should go to bed—I mean, get inside. It's getting late."

She looked over at Garrett, who'd been staring right back at her. They stood and walked toward the back door of the guest house. He held it open for her, then followed her inside. When they set their glasses down on the table in front of the fireplace, she could see that he was still troubled by their conversation.

Willow wanted to tell him that it was all going to be OK. She could see the pain in his eyes. She suspected that it was due partly to the memories he'd just shared with her, but she knew that the small blonde woman was also likely the cause of some of his discomfort. If only he knew how little of his energy she deserved.

Willow was pretty sure she'd had too much to drink, because a strange urge came over her just then. Garrett took a breath, most likely preparing to tell her good night, and she officially lost her head.

Closing the gap between them with two small steps, she reached up and placed her hand on his cheek, staring into his eyes. She'd intended only to thank him for the evening, but she found her eyes drawn to his lips, which were now parted in surprise. In a moment of madness, she completely forgot herself and captured his lips with hers. It was the most electrifying kiss she'd ever been a part of, and Willow lost herself in him, allowing Garrett to weave his hands into her hair, deepening the kiss until she felt waves of desire coursing through her entire body.

It didn't take long for them to realize they were both in way over their heads.

Garrett moved ever so slightly, eliminating any remaining space between them. Her mouth was so warm and soft, and her height squared her up perfectly against him. She was confident but shy at the same time, and the combination was intoxicating. Garrett started to pull her closer when he realized something. Kissing Willow was so different from kissing Lindsay.

*Lindsay.*

He stepped back as if he'd been scorched by an unseen match, dragging his hand through his hair as he walked backward. He stared at her for a moment, ashamed of himself for allowing things to get so out of control so quickly. It took everything inside of him, but he knew the timing of this was all wrong.

"I'm sorry. I can't."

Willow blushed deeply, looking stunned, but she didn't answer him, and Garrett couldn't make himself say anything more. He dropped his gaze to the ground before turning and taking the stairs up to his room two at a time, leaving her there in the darkened room to wonder what had just happened.

# CHAPTER

# SEVEN

*Her skin was softer than he'd imagined it would be, particularly that area above her kneecap, the creamy expanse just inside her upper thigh. It occurred to Garrett that he should focus his attention on that spot, so he'd pulled the covers up over his head, intent on doing just that, when he was jolted awake by his bleating alarm clock. Again.*

*Shit. Another dream.*

It was happening way too often, and the most disturbing part was that he knew he wasn't dreaming about Lindsay, like a proper brokenhearted man.

It was Willow who'd been consuming his thoughts, seemingly day and night. What did it say about him that he'd no sooner been rejected by one woman before becoming completely besotted with another? He didn't plan to lie in bed and try to come up with an answer.

Sunday mornings, Garrett usually let himself sleep in, but he still couldn't shake the habit of setting an alarm clock, albeit for seven thirty. He threw back the duvet and climbed out of bed, pausing to stretch and gaze out the giant windows that ran the length of the space. Sunlight was streaming in, but looks could be deceiving and he knew from having watched the news the night before that the morning was a brisk one. He paused for a moment in his boxer briefs, scratching his bare chest as he contemplated the day.

The weather had turned colder quickly that October, and most mornings now, East Tennessee was waking up to blankets of frost. It was hard to tell from the view out Garrett's loft window, but the way the steam from the factory stacks in the distance was being gustily produced, it seemed that Knoxville's Indian summer might be just a memory at this point.

Garrett shivered in the cool air of the expansive room, reaching to grab a sweatshirt he'd discarded the night before. His Sunday-morning routine made him think fondly of his life in Washington. It was the closest he came to enjoying an urban existence these days. He usually went for a nice long run, then hit up the Café 4 for a coffee and some breakfast. He'd spent his childhood with his grandfather, and thinking of those times now made him smile. His gramp was the closest thing he'd ever known to a father, and he'd made sure that Garrett always felt safe and loved. Their Sunday mornings together at the old coffee shop in Seattle were a tradition he hoped he'd have with his own children one day. If he should be so lucky.

It's what bothered him most about the breakup with Lindsay. He'd thought for the past few years that she was his future. They'd talked about babies and how she wanted them too, so to have her reject him the way that she had was still so shocking. Why, then, couldn't he make himself embrace the heartache? When the country singers on the radio droned on about feeling so terrible, his thoughts never went to Lindsay. It was Willow who'd cast some kind of spell over him, and he couldn't shake it, even while he was asleep.

That was going to change. He knew better than to get involved with someone at work, let alone his superior. It wouldn't end well. He'd just have to continue to be a gentleman whenever he saw her, which wasn't very often. He'd even started to wonder if she was avoiding him.

Garrett finished lacing up his sneakers, jammed his headphones into his ears, and, after grabbing his key and a credit card off the counter, pushed the elevator button with the hopes that a very long, cold run and a steaming hot cup of coffee could make him start to forget what he had no right to be thinking about in the first place.

Willow hadn't planned to move back into her family home with her father. But when she saw how comforted he was by having someone besides his nurse around full time, she'd thought better of her finding her own place downtown, at least for the time being.

The first month or so she'd been back had been bittersweet. There were moments when her father was lucid, talking to her in his feeble but seemingly able-minded way. Then, in a flash, he was gone, and she was a stranger to him. It was heartbreaking. She had to introduce him to his nurse all over again, every single morning when she arrived, since he had no memory recall from one day to the next. She'd known it was going to be hard coming home under these circumstances, but it was so much more difficult than she could have ever imagined.

Willow kept her father with her at home as long as she could, but he'd declined rapidly over the last week of October. At his doctor's recommendation, she'd finally agreed to put him in a nearby facility where he could have full-time care.

She'd taken to visiting him most days now, and the night before when she'd stopped by, she was surprised to see that he looked even more frail than usual. The doctors seemed to think he was starting to shut down physically as well as mentally. They'd advised her to be ready at any time. It could be just a matter of weeks.

Her job had kept her busy, and she enjoyed the routine of her new life. Everyone she worked with had been so welcoming, and India and Wyatt were more than supportive of her circumstances. They encouraged her to make time to be with her dad while she could, so most mornings, she arrived at the farm around ten, allowing for a morning visit at his nursing home. Life had a comfortable rhythm for her now, but there was one small hiccup. Actually, he was rather imposing.

Willow had done her very best to avoid Garrett in the few weeks since their encounter in the guest house. She was horrified that she'd allowed herself to make a move on him, and even more mortified that he'd rejected her. She knew how vulnerable he'd been; she'd seen what had happened the night before, which was why she cringed every time she remembered his expression when he'd pulled away from her. The vision returned to her far too often. The man had infected her thoughts, and even with everything she had going on, she couldn't seem to erase the memory.

She'd gotten pretty good at applying her game face the few times she knew she'd have to see Garrett. There were staff meetings once a week, and the occasional farm-wide functions. She could handle it if she had advance warning and she knew there was enough work-related business to keep her distracted. She was grateful that Finn and Susan had taken a short break from their travels, so most of her interaction with the farming staff over the past few weeks had been one-on-one with Finn, not Garrett.

This morning, she didn't have to work, so avoiding Garrett wasn't even on her radar. Her father's assisted-living facility was relatively close to her family home, so on Sundays she usually walked the fifteen minutes or so over to see him, stopping by her favorite coffee shop on the way to get him the hot chocolate he'd always loved. They'd sit together in silence, because at that point, he'd become almost completely nonverbal. He liked it when she held his hand, though. She could tell. It wasn't unusual for Willow to leave wondering if it would be the last time she'd sit with her father.

She'd just ordered and stepped aside to wait for her drinks when the door swung open, and what Willow saw made her heart skip a beat. No one should look that sexy this early on a Sunday.

Garrett was wearing an ancient-looking gray Seattle Seahawks sweatshirt that was darkened with sweat in a V on his chest. He hadn't shaved, and the way the sun lit him up from behind made the hint of russet in his hair and on his face even more pronounced. He reached up to pluck his earbuds out, holding the door for a young woman with a stroller, who gave him an extra-long thank-you. When she'd cleared the doorway, Garrett stepped inside the shop, and that's when he noticed her watching him.

Willow hadn't been able to look away, though she'd tried her best. The barista called her name a second time, more insistently, which snapped her back to the reason she was standing there. She busied herself with lids and a cup holder, but she could feel that he'd walked over and was now standing next to her, waiting to say something.

"Need a hand with that?"

She looked up into his face, just a foot away from her own.

His eyes were even more spectacular than she'd first thought. Such a pale color. They were gray. Gray with a hint of green, actually. *Damn it.* She was flustered, and he was just standing there watching her suffer.

"No, thanks. I've got it. Just getting a cocoa for my dad. It's his favorite. It's kind of our Sunday thing."

Garrett watched her, smiling softly at those last words. "I used to do something similar with my gramp on Sundays back home. I miss that. How's your father doing?"

Willow searched his eyes for any signs of awkwardness, but as he looked back at her, she felt strangely at ease. She wondered if avoiding him for these past weeks had really been necessary after all. "He's not great, actually. He doesn't really communicate much anymore, but I can't help but hope that the time I spend with him brings him some kind of comfort. I'm afraid it's really more for me, though."

She set the drink carrier down, tucking a wayward piece of hair behind her ear. The gesture wasn't lost on Garrett. He'd had to restrain himself from doing it for her.

"I'm sorry to hear that. I know how hard it is. I told you my gran got pretty bad in the end. You do what you need to do to get closure. It's roughest on the family." Had she imagined it or was that a crack in his voice?

She decided to rescue him from the moment. "I forgot that India mentioned to me that you lived in this neighborhood. My father's facility is right around the corner, which is how I discovered this place. It's my favorite. I stop here most days before work now too."

"This place is great. I'm their first customer most week-days." He paused and gestured to his clothes, a rueful smile on his face. "Sundays are my lazy days, though, so I'm a little late to the party this morning."

Willow smiled back. "From the looks of that sweatshirt, you've been anything but lazy this morning."

*Lucky sweatshirt. Hugging that broad chest of his.*

And just like that, things got weird again.

Flushed, Willow picked up her drink carrier and quickly changed the subject. "Well, I guess I'll see you at the staff meeting tomorrow morning? We're entering a pretty fun time of the year at the resort. Thanksgiving, and then the Christmas concert. Lots of stuff to plan. It's probably going to be a pretty busy time for all of us. Which will be good. To be busy, I mean, will be good."

Garrett could kick himself for making her so obviously uncomfortable around him. He desperately wanted to apologize to her for his actions in the guest house, but he couldn't figure out what to say. It confused things even more that all he could think about while he listened to her ramble on was how badly he wanted a second shot at that kiss. He found it impossible to listen to what she was saying without focusing on that full bottom lip of hers.

Willow had managed to regain her composure, and she was moving toward the door to leave.

Garrett rushed around her, holding the door open for her and then stepping outside to say good-bye. "Sure, I'll see you tomorrow for sure. I hope you have a nice visit with your dad." His breath came out in puffs as he spoke.

There was silence for a moment, then Willow smiled and turned to go, but not before looking over her shoulder at him one last time. "Happy Sunday, Garrett."

He felt the knot in his stomach that he hadn't realized was there tighten imperceptibly. Seeing her had certainly made it one hell of a Sunday. "Happy Sunday, Willow."

They did see each other that next morning at the staff meeting, and somehow, things were a little easier between them. Garrett had to remind himself that she was a colleague and that he couldn't stare at her like that when she was talking. And he couldn't stand near her, or he might catch that intoxicating scent of hers. Oh, and he couldn't really focus on her voice, because the slight huskiness would remind him of the sound she'd made when they'd kissed that night in the guest house.

So it really wasn't any easier at all.

But it was less uncomfortable, especially for Willow. She too was hyperaware of everything about Garrett when they shared a space, so she continued to make sure that it didn't happen that often. She had it down to a science. By learning the rhythms of the resort, she was able to know where he was most likely to be at certain times so she could avoid those areas like the plague.

One afternoon, in mid-November, Willow was having lunch with India and Violet in the Dogwood. It was a place she considered "safe," because she knew by then that Garrett usually had lunch at the garden shed while he was working. They'd just ordered and were chatting about India's baby shower the previous weekend when she heard his voice over her shoulder.

"Ladies. Nice to see you all."

She took a moment to steady herself, pasting on a smile before turning to look up at him.

Garrett knew she'd been avoiding him. He'd been letting her. There had been a couple of close calls when he'd seen her going into the dairy or the event hall, and he'd purposely steered clear of her. He was starting to think maybe they'd never talk about what happened, and he wondered if that was the way she wanted it. But he'd walked in today, and Violet had spotted him, so it was too late to make a U-turn without raising her suspicions. He knew better than to get Violet on his case. It was as if she smelled blood in the water, though, her eyes darting between Garrett and Willow as they chatted with India about an upcoming garden tour. Garrett finished the conversation and then said good-bye before moving across the dining room to another table to join a few other garden staffers for lunch.

He chose a seat that faced their table, which didn't escape Willow. She was about to steer the subject back to the babies when Violet wagged her finger and shook her head.

"Oh no. No way. You'd better tell us what's going on between you two, and you'd better start at the beginning, sister."

Willow's eyes went wide, and India laughed in spite of herself as their friend's cheeks bloomed with color.

"Seriously, Willow. Was that good old-fashioned sexual tension we just sensed between you and Garrett? What did we miss?"

Willow glanced across the room without thinking and caught Garrett staring back at her, a glass of water at his lips. He averted his eyes, but not quickly enough. Willow looked back to her friends, and after a moment, she decided to spill her guts.

Once she got talking, it felt good to come clean. She'd been carrying the secret around for several weeks now, not sure if she should be sharing it with anyone, let alone her boss, who just happened to be a good friend now.

India and Violet listened intently as she told them about seeing Garrett and Lindsay on the porch of Woodshed, then she filled them in on the details of their encounter the next night after the first Smoky Mountain Table dinner.

Violet was the first to speak when Willow finished with their run-in at the coffee shop. "I don't care how nice he's being now. He owes you an apology. It takes two to tango, and I have a hard time believing he wasn't giving you some kind of indication that he was interested that night in the guest house, heartbroken or not. And if you ask me? That relationship was dysfunctional for a long time. He was lying to himself if he thought that girl was ever going to be happy living here."

India sipped her sweet tea, crunching on a piece of ice before chiming in. "I don't know, Vi. In the time I've known Garrett, the one thing I can say about him is that he has integrity. I think he was probably conflicted in the moment, and his good guy happened to override his bad guy that night. That's a good character trait, if you ask me."

India turned to Willow. "But there is one way to find out if he's feeling bad about the whole situation. What do you call the one time of year when people get together to break bread and end up talking about the most inappropriate and uncomfortable things?"

Both women looked at her puzzled for a moment before the answer dawned on Violet.

"Thanksgiving." She turned back to Willow, a triumphant smile on her face. "And guess who's coming to dinner?"

# CHAPTER
# EIGHT

Wyatt thought it was ironic that the resort advertised their popular Thanksgiving weekend in Walland as a "hassle-free holiday." He was finding the week chock-full of challenges, particularly as he jumped back from the oven after receiving an unexpected steam facial while checking on the turkey. He wiped his brow and bit his tongue. He wouldn't think of complaining. He'd insisted on taking care of the Thanksgiving brunch they had planned for their close friends so that India could get some rest. She and Wyatt would still have to go over to the barn later that evening to mingle with guests during the official resort dinner, but at least they'd be fed and free to visit.

They were still a couple of weeks from her due date, but the doctor had told them they should be ready at any time, since it wasn't uncommon for twins to arrive ahead of schedule—especially if the mother remained active. That's all he'd needed to hear. Wyatt was determined not only to cook a perfect turkey but to keep both of their own little birds in the oven as long as they could to ensure nice plump, healthy babies.

"Turkey looks good, babe. I'm gonna take it out and let it rest for a bit so I can start working on the mashed potatoes."

He flipped over a sheet of paper he'd printed off from a cooking website so he could review his recipe. "Potatoes have been boiling for at least twenty minutes, and the butter is soft and ready to go in. I think I might actually pull this off."

He peeked around the fireplace. Built into the middle of their home, it opened up on both sides, into the kitchen and family room. India was on the couch, smiling to herself, her feet up on a pillow and hands crossed over her belly. She caught sight of him in his ridiculous "Kiss the Cook" apron, and laughed out loud. She didn't have the heart to tell him he'd planned a dinner menu instead of brunch, and she'd sworn their friends to silence too. They'd all likely spend the afternoon in a food coma after eating the huge spread he'd planned for so early in the day.

"Honestly, I didn't think I could love you any more, but you've done it again. I can't believe you won't let me help you." She crooked her finger, motioning for him to come over. "There is just one thing the three of us need over here, if you wouldn't mind."

The words weren't even out of her mouth, and he was already at her side, kneeling down. She reached up to kiss him softly before taking his hand in hers and setting it on top of her stomach. She watched his face light up in recognition.

"Man, I'm really gonna miss that once they come out. I wonder who's the better soccer player, him or her?" He smiled, taking every bit of that moment to feel his children moving inside his wife.

Suddenly, they both heard the sounds of water splashing out of the boiling potato pot he'd left on the stove. He shot up from his crouched position like a cat and ran back into the kitchen. "Saboteur! Everything was going so perfectly until you distracted me with our wonder twins. Now, if you'll excuse me, I have a five-star dinner to finish."

Wyatt was still trying to figure out how to eject the beaters from the hand mixer when he heard a knock, followed by the front door opening. He walked toward the foyer and saw Rex coming in with heavy bags dangling off both of his arms.

"Help a brother out, man. She's got enough pies here to get us through to the end-times. I'm not sure who she thinks is going to eat them all." Rex glanced over to where India was propped on the couch, and he smiled sweetly at her. "Oh, that's right. A few of them are probably for those hulking babies you're growing."

India grabbed one of the throw pillows from the sofa, hurling it across the room and nailing her intended target in the right temple.

"Damn! I didn't think she was dangerous over there, but I misjudged her." Rex rubbed his head in mock injury.

They were all laughing together when Violet walked in, holding a giant pan of sweet potatoes with two pumpkin-shaped hot pads. "Rex, would you run back out and grab the salads? They're in the backseat. We got everything from the trunk already, I think."

Violet set the potatoes down on the counter, surveying the damage in the kitchen. "Well, this looks festive." It appeared that Wyatt had used every single available pot and pan, leaving a trail of dirty dishes from one end of the room to the other. Violet picked up a dish towel, twirled it into a rope, and swatted at Wyatt's legs, causing him to yelp in pain. "I know you think the cook doesn't clean, but those rules don't apply today, buddy. This is going to be a group effort. Come on, let's at least get some of these pans that you're finished with cleaned up so we have space to set the food out."

She turned the faucet on, filling the sink with hot soapy water while Wyatt started to line up dirty dishes.

"You two had better hurry up in there," India called from the sofa. "Get that lazy husband of yours to help, Vi. This dinner has to be perfect. It's the first time that Garrett and Willow will be in a social setting together since, well, since you-know-when."

Wyatt raised his eyebrows at Violet when he saw that information hit her. "Yep. He told me he's going to try to make things right between them, because he's tired of avoiding her. He feels bad about what happened." Wyatt was drying as fast as he could, trying to keep up with Violet.

"Well, he should. I can't believe he left our girl hanging like that. It really threw her for a loop." Violet scrubbed a little harder, matching the tone in her voice. "He'd better be prepared to grovel. I don't think it's going to be as easy as he thinks. Willow has made him feel comfortable in work settings, but that's because she's a professional. All bets are off when it comes to any kind of personal relationship. She felt totally humiliated by him."

India was up now, having made her way into the kitchen to join the conversation. "Exactly. Let's hope when they get here, we aren't going to be literally breaking bread."

Garrett wished he'd followed his gut and put the hard top on his Jeep. The weather had been so nice the week before Thanksgiving that he just hadn't been able to bring himself to give up his convertible soft top. Now, as he drove out to

Wyatt and India's, he could see that the forecasters might be correct for once. The clouds to the west were low and thick, but it was the color of them that made him believe they might be holding snow.

He flipped on the radio and couldn't find anything but commercials reminding him to get his Christmas shopping done, so he turned it off, listening to the wind whip against the canvas top as he rolled down the road.

He'd been feeling anxious about this brunch all week, maybe even for longer than that. Sure, it had been cordial between him and Willow lately, but he couldn't help still feeling terrible about never having apologized for what had happened. She'd caught him by surprise that night, to say the least.

By the time he'd realized Willow was going to kiss him, it was too late. His body reacted before his head could intervene. Looking back now, he knew he'd probably given her mixed signals by inviting her back for wine. But he'd genuinely thought they were just getting to know each other better. He'd been surprised by her reasons for coming home to Tennessee; the common bond they shared was certainly an unseen twist. But he'd still been hurting from Lindsay's rejection.

Actually, that was only half true. Now that he had some distance from the situation, he recognized that he'd felt a little relief too, but it was unsettling to realize that he'd managed to talk himself into something that Lindsay hadn't wanted all along. To have his entire life plan blown up was what had stung the most. It had left him feeling rudderless.

But honestly, it had felt so damned good to kiss Willow. It was new and exciting, and he'd let himself momentarily forget and had gotten lost in the moment. Before he'd realized what was happening, his hands were woven into her hair, pulling her in to deepen the kiss, their bodies flush with one another. She'd let out that soft sigh, and that's what had snapped him out of it. The sound had been seared into his brain ever since. He'd abruptly let go of her, breaking contact and taking a step back. It wasn't easy. She'd looked incredibly sexy standing there with her mouth open in surprise, a flush across her cheeks and down her neck. He'd messed her hair up just enough to make it look perfect.

He cringed even now as he remembered. She must have been so embarrassed. It's not what he'd intended, and in the time that had passed, he'd felt an increasing urge to set things right. Every time they crossed paths at work, or that day in the coffee shop, she'd been the consummate professional. She was so good he'd started to wonder if it had meant anything to her after all.

He pulled his Jeep into India and Wyatt's drive and threw it into park. He did hope he'd have an opportunity to finally talk privately with Willow today. It had occurred to him more than once that he might've blown his only shot at something with a real woman, one who didn't live thousands of miles away and wanted no part of a life with him. But if he couldn't have that same opportunity now with Willow, he'd settle for their at least being friends.

He'd made it to the front porch with an armful of beer and wine, and was trying to figure out how to turn the door handle, when it swung wide, leaving Rex standing there grinning at him.

"Now we can get the party started. Forget the pies, let's get cracking on the IPA, boys." He carefully extracted the two twelve-packs Garrett had stashed under each arm, freeing Garrett up to carry the bags of wine.

Garrett relaxed a little once he noticed Willow hadn't arrived yet. It would be good to have a few minutes with the group before she got there so he could unwind and not obsess over what to say to her.

"So what are you going to say to Willow?"

Leave it to Violet to make him squirm.

Wyatt came around the counter to step in between them. "Geez, Violet. Give him a minute to breathe, will you? He just walked in. He's going to need at least two beers before you start interrogating him."

Wyatt slapped his friend on the shoulder, steering him away from Violet's prying eyes.

Violet threw a look at India, who just shrugged her shoulders and shook her head. "Mules, remember?"

Willow was still getting used to being all alone in such a huge old house. Every time she forgot something, whether it was her sunglasses, cell phone, or car keys, which was the case this time, it took her ten extra minutes of scurrying around to figure out where she'd left them. By the time she realized they were in the purse she'd just changed out, she was running a good twenty minutes late.

She backed out of the garage now, noticing that there were tiny white snowflakes hitting her windshield. *Great.* People in the South generally went off the rails at the first sight of the white stuff. She hoped unforeseen traffic wouldn't make her even later.

Willow had been anxious all morning. She'd planned to go in to the office earlier that day, but her assistant had called, assuring her everything was fine, which left Willow free to go straight to brunch.

Today was different. India had told her they were getting together as friends; this was social, not business, and Willow was honored they'd included her in such a tight-knit group. She knew Violet and Rex would be there as well.

And Garrett.

She supposed she was as ready for this day as she'd ever be, but a small part of her still hoped that, somehow, they'd get through today without anything uncomfortable coming up. She wasn't sure she could be *that* good of an actress.

She'd just turned on to the road that led to the resort, and was thinking that maybe she should have stopped to grab a couple extra bottles of wine. All of a sudden, she hit a rogue slick spot on the blacktop and felt the car sliding off into a ditch, where it landed with a loud crunch of the front bumper.

Willow couldn't believe it. Throwing the car into reverse, she crossed everything she could think of and prayed her rear wheels could get enough traction to pull her back out. Her Subaru Outback was ten years old, but it had gotten her through plenty of rough Utah winters. She was sure it wasn't going to let her down over a few snow flurries.

It wasn't long before she realized she was going nowhere fast. She sighed as she fished her cell phone out of her purse from the passenger seat. She'd have to call Triple A, but she supposed she should call India first to tell her they should start brunch without her.

# CHAPTER

# NINE

Garrett was in the great room chatting with India when her cell phone rang. It was lying next to her on the table, just out of reach, so when he grabbed it to hand it to her, he couldn't help noticing it was Willow calling. India nodded and thanked him, answering her friend's call with a smile. He was about to head to the kitchen to give her some privacy when he realized something was wrong.

"Oh no!"

Garrett glanced back and saw that India was biting the tip of her index finger, a faraway look on her face. She was obviously trying to figure out how to solve some problem.

"Ugh. No, don't call a tow truck. We have enough guys here; they can come help you out. How stuck are you? OK. The food isn't ready yet anyway, so don't worry about that. Sit tight. The boys will be there in a few minutes. Don't feel bad! I've done it myself."

India ended the call, pushing herself up off the couch to head into the kitchen, which was no simple task, as round as she was these days. Garrett grabbed for her hand to help make it a little easier. Wyatt and Violet were setting the table in the kitchen.

"Well, our favorite local road claimed another victim; this time it's Willow. She's in a ditch a couple miles away, probably the same spot I picked last winter. I'm telling you, there's a little groove there that holds water, and when it freezes, it's like an ice rink."

Wyatt was tempted to crack a joke about how it had never happened to him or Rex, but he caught the glint in his wife's eyes, and that shut him right up.

Violet saw him stop himself and laughed. "Smart man. India, I swear, you've done so much with him in such a short time. I'm still breaking Rex in."

At the mention of his name, Rex stuck his head around the corner, a beer in one hand and a palmful of cashews in the other. He clearly hadn't heard their conversation. "You need me, babe? I was just checking the score. Lions are up by seven with two minutes left in the quarter."

Ignorance was bliss. Violet just smiled at her husband and told him he could go back to the game. "I'd offer Rex, but we brought the family car today. I doubt we'd have much luck pulling her out with our minivan." She looked pointedly at Garrett. "I see you have a Jeep parked out front. You got a winch and a tow strap? That's probably all it will take to get her out."

Garrett had both, in fact. What he didn't have was a strong desire to be alone with Willow before he'd had at least a couple of drinks under his belt, but it didn't look like that was going to be an option. He sighed, running his hand through his hair as he set his beer back on the countertop.

"I'll go help her. Rex can stay here and watch the game. It doesn't sound like it's a two-man job." He walked to the hall table and grabbed his keys, unaware of the look being passed between the two women behind his back. Jumping into his Jeep, he fired it up and headed back down the road to find Willow.

Willow had just hung up with India when she heard a tap on her passenger window, startling her. She bent her head to look out and saw a small elderly man with twinkling eyes smiling back at her.

He was motioning with his hand for her to roll her window down, which she did. "I see you found the slickest spot in the county? Don't feel bad, hon. It happens almost every time it snows around here. You're not the first, and you won't be the last."

He smiled at her, his eyes scrunching up like violet half-moons, making him look even sweeter. "I've got an old truck out back that'll probably get you out of here right quick. In the meantime, why don't you wait inside? My wife'll have my head if I don't let her give you a cup of tea or something."

He jabbed his thumb over his shoulder, moving out of the way so she could see a short, plump woman with white hair standing in the doorway of the farmhouse Willow had wiped out in front of.

While the woman was adorable, the house was magnificent. She couldn't believe this was the first time she'd ever noticed it. She drove that road back and forth every day, but she was usually lost in thought, or using her time in the car to catch up on phone calls.

The house sat back a couple of hundred feet from the road, with a giant knobby old oak tree in the front yard sheltering it and giving it even more character than it had on its own. Willow was enchanted.

"Oh, my friends are coming to tow me out, so you don't have to. Thank you, though. I'm sorry to make you come out in this weather."

It was snowing harder, a light dusting covering the grass and the hood of her car.

"Well, don't just sit there. For my sake if not for yours. One cup of tea?"

His face was so warm and expectant, she supposed she couldn't say no. She reached up and turned her hazards on but stopped short of turning the car off, in case it wouldn't restart for some reason.

"OK, but only because I don't want you to get into any trouble with your wife." Willow paused and smiled at him. "Although she looks pretty sweet to me." Willow extended her hand in greeting. "I'm Willow Armstrong. I work down the road at the resort."

"I thought you might," the man said with a smile. "I'm Fred Thompson. Lived here all my life. But that's about to change, I suppose." They were almost to the porch when Fred turned back and gestured to a sign she hadn't noticed in the front yard.

She gasped, surprised she hadn't seen it before. "You're selling this place? Why on earth? It's incredible!"

She meant it. As they got closer, she could feel her pulse quicken with excitement. It was dreamy. And the property was unbelievable. She could see now that it stretched back behind the house as far as the eye could see.

"Are those fruit trees?" She stole a glance over at Fred, but his face was hard to read. It was clear he was proud of his home, but she could see it was going to be hard for him to leave it.

"Yes, ma'am. This is a bona fide orchard. Wanda and I have owned it more than fifty years."

They were at the house now, where Wanda herself had opened the front door to let them in. Introductions were made, and before long, Willow was holding a cup of hot tea. As she sipped, the couple told her their story. And it was fascinating.

They'd raised four children in that house, all of whom were grown now and living in different parts of the country. They'd started with just a few peach trees for fun, but it had become more than a hobby after a few years. Springtime meant lots of berries; they had corn and other veggies in the summer; and in the fall they grew pumpkins and concord grapes and hosted hayrides, even milling their own cider.

They'd grown their passion into a thriving business. People came from miles to get a piece of the simple life. Willow could tell they both loved it, so she asked them why they would choose to leave.

"Three out of our four kids live in Arizona now," Wanda explained. "If we move there, that means we have a chance to be close to nine of our twelve grandchildren, and we get to say good-bye to the cold weather for good."

Fred shrugged his shoulders. "The decision was easier than we thought."

Wanda smiled at her husband. "Don't let him fool you. This place is his baby. It's going to be hard to say good-bye. We just hope the right person comes along to buy it. Someone who will love it as much as we have and be a good steward of the land. Frankly, I'm surprised I haven't heard from Finn Janssen. He's had his eye on this place forever. I suppose he's been busy enjoying his semiretirement."

Willow was speechless. She felt a little panicked at the thought that this special place might fall into the wrong hands, and she was about to ask them another question when the three of them heard tires crunching on the gravel drive. She looked out the picture window and saw a Jeep parking next to the house. The driver's door opened, and Willow felt her face get red.

Garrett was striding up to the house, wearing a thick, rugged army-green coat and a brown stocking cap. Even covered up like that, she would know him anywhere by the way he moved. His walk was confident, commanding. He was a man who knew where he wanted to go and didn't waste time getting there. She could think of only one time where he'd seemed unsure, and the memory made her blush even more pronounced. She set her tea down and reached up to rub her cheeks and regain her composure.

Wanda smiled and moved to open the door to welcome him inside. "You must be here to help out our damsel in distress?"

She introduced herself and Fred, ushering Garrett inside. Garrett caught Willow's eye, and Willow wished she could turn inside out into a puff of smoke.

No such luck. She took a breath and said hello.

"Thanks for coming to help me, Garrett. I've kept these nice people long enough. If you're ready, I am."

She turned to thank the Thompsons, picking up her cup of tea to carry it into the kitchen. Setting it in the sink, she paused, then asked, "Do you have a timeline for when you want to leave for Arizona?"

She could see that they were a little confused by her question, as was Garrett, who was standing in the kitchen doorway now, studying her.

"I only ask because, well, I guess . . . I mean . . ." She mustered up all of her courage to finish her thought. "Maybe I'm the one who's supposed to buy your place."

It took them only two tries to get her car out. The first time, she'd forgotten to put it in neutral, but, thankfully, Garrett realized it before he pulled very hard, avoiding overstraining the old tow strap. The second time, he eased pressure on the gas, the tow strap extricating the car from the ditch smoothly and without any trouble. The damage to her front end was hardly even noticeable. Willow wondered if she shouldn't actually be grateful for the accident. If it hadn't happened, she might not have noticed the property before it was too late.

Fred and Wanda were delighted that she'd asked about their place, and they also seemed to think it was fate that had brought her to their doorstep. She'd filled them in on her current situation with her father. She planned to sell the family home but not until after her father had passed, out of respect. That would leave her with plenty of money to buy the orchard but little knowledge about how to run it. The Thompsons didn't seem too concerned with that, though.

"Everything has a way of working out, honey. You'll either learn, or find someone who will teach you."

Wanda smiled at Garrett. "You look like you don't shy away from physical labor, young man. I'm sure you'd be glad to help her, wouldn't you?"

Garrett wished he could untie his tongue, which seemed to have worked itself into a knot when he wasn't paying attention. He was unable, so he just nodded his head in agreement, mumbling something about knowing his way around a garden.

*Clever. A real wordsmith, Garrett.*

Willow thanked them for their hospitality, and they exchanged numbers, promising they'd all be in touch after the holiday weekend.

Willow and Garrett were walking out to their cars, which they'd left running in the driveway. Garrett walked ahead to get the car door, but he stopped short of opening it for her. She felt small next to him. Despite the fact that she was tall, somehow it felt like he towered over her, seeming even larger than usual in all his winter gear. His eyes were kind, though, his expression soft.

"Willow, I owe you an apology, and I think this might be my only chance to offer it to you. I feel just awful about that night on the terrace after Smoky Mountain Table."

Willow started to speak, but he shook his head, raising one hand to stop her.

"Please. I just need you to know that it wasn't anything you did. I had just gone through something really terrible, and you caught me at a really weird moment."

As he spoke, it was cold enough to see his breath. The snow was falling steadily now, landing on their shoulders but melting on impact.

The electricity between them was still there.

Willow could feel it, but she knew she would never be foolish enough to act on it again. Besides, there was a very good chance he didn't feel the same thing. Although the way he'd kissed her, she couldn't see how that was possible. She tried to think of something normal to say but couldn't. What came out was a rambling mess.

"I've been cheated on. I get it. It sucks. I should have known better than to take advantage of someone in your situation. Not that I was trying to take advantage. I guess I got swept up in the moment." She looked up into his eyes. "I'm sorry too."

She couldn't understand why he looked so surprised. It certainly wasn't because she'd apologized. She thought he might have been expecting that from her all along.

After a moment, it dawned on her that he hadn't known that he'd been cheated on. Willow had known only because she'd overheard his girlfriend that morning on the way in to her office.

*Oh God.* What had she done?

Garrett looked totally confused and blindsided. "Uh, right. Yeah. My girlfriend had just broken up with me, but why do you think she cheated? Did India say something to you about her?"

Willow had two choices. Tell him the truth or lie to spare his feelings. She knew the latter would be easier, but she couldn't do it to him. It was better to tell the truth. Rip the Band-Aid off for good. She took a moment to choose her words carefully before speaking.

He listened as she told him what had happened that morning after his breakup with Lindsay, his face changing from surprised to sickened to a little bit angry by the end. When she finished, he pulled his stocking cap from his head, running his hand through his curls. He appeared a little wild-eyed, and although the thought horrified her, she found him ridiculously attractive. He looked away for a moment before collecting himself and putting his hat back on. He opened her car door so she could get inside.

"We'd better head back to India and Wyatt's. They'll start to think that we're skipping out on Thanksgiving this year."

He paused for a moment, shaking his head in disbelief. "I have to tell you, I didn't think I'd enjoy today. But after what you just told me, I suddenly feel like I have a hell of a lot to be thankful for. I guess I dodged a bullet this year."

He closed her door, and she watched as he strode back to his Jeep and climbed inside.

# CHAPTER

# TEN

India had been feeling a little off all Thanksgiving morning but hadn't said anything yet to Wyatt. She knew he would over-react and rush her back to the doctor, a drill they'd already experienced twice. The first time it had been gas, which was mortifying, and the second time, they'd told her she needed to slow down and take it easy until her due date, which she'd been doing ever since.

Well, most of the time anyway.

There were her duties for the resort, which she'd mostly handed over to Willow as of late, who had gladly accepted the extra responsibility. They talked daily by phone or in person when Willow stopped by to brief her on everything going on with both staff and guests. They'd become fast friends after spending so much time together and as a result of working so closely with one another. India knew that Wyatt liked knowing there was an extra set of eyes and ears on her when he couldn't always be around during the day too.

He'd become something of a worrywart, especially when he was away from India.

She usually had to wait up at night until Wyatt was asleep before creeping around to finish the punch list she'd hoped to complete before the babies came. She'd been up late the evening before, folding all of the clean clothes and organizing the babies' closets in the nursery. India couldn't believe she'd soon have two tiny people that would fit into those miniature clothes. It amazed her to think about how much had changed over the past two and a half years. She couldn't believe that her previous existence had ever been enough to convince her she was happy. This life she'd made with Wyatt was better than any she could have possibly dreamt of.

She figured she must have overdone it a little last night in the nursery, with all the bending and stretching. If she didn't know better, she'd think she was having Braxton-Hicks contractions again. Her stomach would tighten and then release after a few seconds, but it wasn't painful. That's why she'd spent most of the morning on the couch, hoping the sensation would subside. Rest would do her good, and the brunch was in the capable hands of her husband and best friends.

They'd finally gathered around the table, after Willow and Garrett had returned. India had noticed that they'd both been quiet when they'd walked in, Garrett making a beeline for the fridge and returning with two bottles of beer. He'd handed one to Willow wordlessly before joining Rex and Wyatt in front of the television for the last two minutes of the football game. India had started to ask if everything was OK when Violet recruited Willow to help with the final brunch preparations. Willow had given India a look that said she'd fill her in later. The game had ended shortly afterward, just in time for the friends to fix their plates and sit down to eat.

No one was more impressed with Wyatt's efforts than Rex. His plate was piled high with everything the buffet had to offer. He'd already tasted most of it and was nodding his head in approval, eyebrows raised as he looked at his friend. "I have to admit, I told Violet we might be stopping for a burger on the way home, buddy. I wasn't sure you could pull this off." He took another big forkful of steaming turkey covered in mashed potatoes and lifted it to his mouth. "I'm impressed, brother."

It was obvious that Wyatt was proud of himself. He was still wearing his apron when he sat down to eat, delighted in the surprised but satisfied expressions of his brunch guests. "I'm not just a pretty face, pal. I've got skills you know nothing about."

With that, a big clump of stuffing fell off the bottom of the serving spoon Wyatt was using, landing with a splash in the gravy boat. It was quiet for a moment before everyone erupted into laughter.

"Oh, the irony." Violet just shook her head in mock disappointment.

Wyatt picked up a roll, pretending to get ready to throw it in her direction.

India thought she'd better make a toast before things devolved into a food fight. She took her water glass, raising it up to get their attention. "I'm grateful to all of you for the hard work that went into this meal."

She looked at Wyatt, a soft smile on her face. "I know this was asking a lot of you, but honestly, babe, you never cease to amaze me. Thank you for doing all of the shopping and cooking for today. It wouldn't have been the same without our friends here on Thanksgiving, and you made that happen for me. For all of us."

India leaned over to give him a kiss. The look that passed between them was enough to make everyone blush a bit.

India looked around the table at each of them, these people who were quickly becoming her surrogate family. Her eyes came to rest on Violet, who was sitting next to her. She teared up as she spoke.

"Vi, you've become such an amazing friend to me; thanks for everything today. Those pies should keep me in stretch pants long after these babies are born. I hope I'm half as good at being a mom as you are. Get ready; I plan to ask you lots of questions over the next eighteen years or so."

Violet reached over to give India a hug, her own eyes filled with tears. "You'd better be twice as good, since you'll be outnumbered. Somehow, I suspect you will." She patted her friend's hand. "And Wyatt will be a great dad." She looked over at him, the expression on his face a reflection of how touched he was by her words. "I've always known he would be."

India shifted in her chair, trying to get comfortable before continuing. She looked across to Garrett and Willow, raising her glass toward the two of them. "I'm grateful this year for new friends too. Garrett, you've become like a brother to me since I got here. I feel strangely protective over you, even though I know you can take care of yourself. I'm so glad you're here today, for the first of many holidays together with our little hodgepodge family."

Willow was watching Garrett as he listened to what India had to say. India's words had weight, and he was clearly touched. Willow thought he looked so vulnerable just then. So much so, she looked away, feeling like she was intruding once again. His face was so open, the way it had been when she'd dropped that bomb on him about his girlfriend being a cheater. She wished she had that to do over. She felt awful for hurting him. Surely she could have delivered the news more gently. India's voice brought her back to the present.

"Willow, I know we haven't known each other that long, but I know I speak for Violet when I say we've really enjoyed getting to know you over these past few months. You've made my life so much easier, knowing that our resort is in the very best hands as we prepare to welcome these game changers into the world. Thank you for your capable hands and your open heart. I have a feeling we'll be friends for a very long time."

Willow smiled at India, feeling so grateful to have landed among such wonderful coworkers and friends. They each raised their glasses toward the center of the table, the crystal meeting and ringing out in cheers as the friends prepared to give thanks and share the meal they'd created together.

During brunch, the conversation was lively, and Willow found herself relaxed and engaged with the group. But she couldn't stop thinking about the orchard. She loved the idea of living that close to work. It would be so convenient and would save her a thirty-minute drive each way. She'd taken the information sheet the Thompsons had given her but hadn't had time to look at it yet. She wondered if it was even feasible for her to pursue it. Of course, it all depended on her father's health. That was her priority right now.

"Do you know the Thompsons, by any chance?" Willow asked the group. "My car landed in the ditch right in front of their place. They were so sweet; they even welcomed me in for tea while I was waiting."

Willow glanced at Garrett, who was watching her as she spoke. Something about his gaze was unsettling, so she looked around to see if anyone else recognized the name.

Wyatt was nodding his head. "Yep, sure do. I went to school with one of their daughters. Well, all of them, actually, but Sheila was in my class. Nice family. They've had that orchard for as long as I can remember. My parents used to take me there for hayrides in the fall when I was a kid."

India looked at her husband, surprised to hear this memory of his parents. They'd been killed in a car accident when he was just a teenager, which is how he'd come to be raised by Finn Janssen. He rarely talked about his folks, so it was a surprise that he was doing so now.

Willow took another sip of her wine, an idea suddenly occurring to her.

Garrett had been listening to the conversation too. He was working on his third beer since the meal had started, which India had noticed and knew was out of character for him. Sure, she'd seen him drink on occasion but not so many drinks in such short order. It was clear something was bothering him.

"Willow wants to buy the place," Garrett suddenly announced to the table, lifting his pilsner glass up to his lips for another drag.

All eyes shifted to her now, and she could feel her face getting pink. It wasn't a secret, obviously, but she hadn't planned to announce her pipe dream to everyone at the table so soon. The toothpaste was out of the tube now, though, thanks to Garrett. She gave him a tight smile, turning to address the others. He seemed unfazed by her coolness.

"Well, it is an amazing house, and the property seems really special, but I don't know if it's a possibility for me, considering my situation with my dad."

They were all aware of her father's Alzheimer's, Willow having shared it with them a couple of months ago during a girls' night out after a particularly hard week with her father.

They'd been so supportive, telling her she could step away whenever she needed to in order to tend to his increasing medical needs. They knew he was very ill now, and they were prepared to be there for the worst of it when their new friend needed them most.

In that moment, it occurred to India that this house might just be a perfect next step for all of them. "I think having you so close would be amazing, and it's a lovely old house. They're such sweet people, from what I know of them. I met the Thompsons once too, actually."

Wyatt looked at India in surprise. She nodded her head and continued. "I stopped by last fall on the way back from town and ended up having a lovely conversation with Wanda. She told me all about her family and how they've owned the place for over fifty years. I was surprised to see they were selling when the sign went up a few days ago. I guess that's why they've spent the spring and summer fixing the place up. Wanda showed me the inside. It's been beautifully restored from the ground up."

India was about to add something else when her expression changed.

She grimaced a little, moved her chair back, and shifted around again to try to find a comfortable position before giving up to push herself into a standing position.

Wyatt jumped out of his chair to lend her a hand. "You feeling OK, Indy?"

He'd noticed she'd been squirming during most of the brunch, but that wasn't uncommon these days. They'd eaten most of their meals on the couch lately, where she was more comfortable.

She opened her mouth to reassure him, when she winced and thought better of it. Something was definitely different this time, and from the looks of things, she'd been right to be concerned.

Wyatt looked down at the floor at the same time as India, to where her feet were rooted behind her abandoned chair.

"Is that what I think it is?" Wyatt's face was suddenly as white as the mashed potatoes.

India smiled weakly and tried to keep her voice calm for both of their sakes. "Babe, I can promise you that I didn't just pee my pants. That delightful little puddle means that the button just popped on the biggest turkey of them all." She turned to Wyatt, laying her hand against her husband's ashen cheek. "Are you ready to become a daddy?"

There was a brief hush as everyone absorbed India's question before four other chairs were pushed back in unison, everyone springing into action.

Violet was the first to regain her wits. "OK, people. Follow my directions." She turned to Wyatt first. "You, go upstairs and get her hospital bag. I know it's packed and ready, because we double-checked after the last time you guys went to the hospital. It's on the right side of her closet. It has everything you'll both need. And don't forget your wallet and insurance card. You'll need both to check in at the hospital."

She waited for Wyatt to move, but he just stood there staring back at her, dumbfounded.

India touched his arm to get his attention. "Wyatt, I think we'd better go soon, babe."

He snapped out of it, turning to rush up the stairs before coming back to plant a tender kiss on his wife's lips. "I've got this, Indy. I'm ready. We're ready."

India smiled at him before a shadow of pain crossed her face once again, prompting Wyatt to turn and take the stairs two at a time.

Violet turned to Rex. "You, run out and start the van and get it warmed up. I'm driving them to the hospital. With those deer-in-the-headlights eyes, Wyatt's in no shape to do it, and neither are you." She motioned to the drink in her husband's hand.

Rex set his beer down on the table and reached into his jeans pocket for the keys before hurrying outside to follow his wife's instructions.

Violet finally turned to Willow and Garrett. "Can the two of you stay behind and make sure everything is taken care of here? I hate to leave you with a big mess, but I don't want them to have to come home to this abandoned Thanksgiving feast. Maybe wrap up what you can and stick it in the fridge? And make sure the chef turned off all the burners on the stove and such. Also, when you're done, can you represent them at the official dinner tonight at the barn? You'll need to greet the guests and give the traditional Thanksgiving toast."

Garrett still looked as stunned as the other two men had, but Willow stepped up and agreed that they would take care of everything. India smiled at her new friend and general manager, grateful once again that she'd hired someone so calm and capable.

"If you need a change of clothes, the entire right side of my closet is full of things I won't be wearing for a very long time. Take your pick. Thanks for pinch-hitting for me, Willow."

Willow took a deep breath and blew it out before asking if it was OK to announce why India and Wyatt weren't at the dinner. "I think the guests will be excited to know that the babies are on their way, and it couldn't hurt to ask for a few extra prayers to get you all through this safely. But only if it's OK with you?"

From the touched look on India's face, Willow saw that it was. "Of course. These babies are loved by our staff already.

They've been so kind and generous to our family. Thank you for thinking to share this with them and with our guests, of course. And prayers are welcome, indeed."

India was reminding Violet to try to get ahold of Susan and Finn, who were vacationing in Hawaii for the week, when she grabbed her belly again, clearly feeling the early labor pains intensify. The three women breathed through the contraction together while Garrett stood by feeling completely helpless.

They heard Wyatt coming before they saw him. He had the suitcase in one hand, India's purse in the other, and he wore the new pink Boppy pillow around his neck that India had bought for breast-feeding the twins. "OK, babe, I think I've got it all. Let's go make this a party of four."

The three women cracked up, and Garrett managed to stifle his laughter, but only because he was so stunned by what had just taken place.

Violet led the parents-to-be to the van, leaving Willow and Garrett standing in the doorway watching as the car pulled away for the hospital. When the car was out of sight, they moved inside and closed the door, and then Willow turned to Garrett. Staring at each other for a moment, she finally broke the silence with a long sigh.

"Well, I guess we'd better get started. I'll wash, you dry?"

# CHAPTER
# ELEVEN

The drive to the hospital was a blur for Wyatt, but India knew she'd remember every pothole and bump in the road for years to come. This time the route felt different; she knew for certain she was in labor because the pain was consistent. The forty-minute drive into Knoxville felt like four hours, especially once she realized, with the help of Rex and his watch, that her contractions were coming about every five minutes. Violet was trying to keep everyone calm, but Wyatt could see from the expression on her face in the rearview mirror that she was concerned about getting to the hospital as quickly as possible. He watched as the speedometer steadily climbed every few minutes.

India was right in the middle of another strong contraction when they pulled up to the emergency room entrance of the Parkwest Medical Center. Violet threw the car into park, and she and Rex jumped out to go find someone to bring a wheelchair while Wyatt stayed behind to hold his wife's hand and talk her through whatever came next.

"You can do this, Indy." He rubbed her hands in between his while searching for the right words to say, but he struggled to come up with anything helpful.

He was terrified. His wife was the strongest person he'd ever known, and to see her this vulnerable was unsettling. He knew it was up to him to pull it together and be the person she could depend on.

"These babies must really be excited to meet us." It was a start. *Come on, Wyatt, think.* He tried to keep his tone light and his face relaxed so she wouldn't know how worried he was. "They're gonna be strong, just like their mama."

He watched her face start to relax a little, the pain subsiding for the time being. He reached up to brush the hair off her brow where she'd broken out into a sheen of sweat. He thought she looked so beautiful in that moment. His heart felt like it was going to burst.

"I'm so proud of you, babe. Thank you for giving me this gift. To live life with you would have been enough for me, but to have these babies joining us tonight? I don't have the words to tell you how much I love you."

They were kissing quietly in the back of the van when the hospital doors opened with a whoosh and Violet and Rex came rushing out, followed by a short, plump middle-aged nurse pushing a wheelchair.

"Isn't that how you got into this mess in the first place, Wyatt?" Rex punched his friend lightly in the arm, backing up to make room for Wyatt to crawl out of the backseat of the van.

The nurse and Violet each took one of India's hands, helping her into the waiting wheelchair. The nurse didn't waste any time turning to wheel India back through the doors and into the emergency room, with Wyatt right by her side. It was obvious Violet had made it clear that India's labor was progressing rapidly.

"I understand your contractions are pretty close together, Mrs. Hinch? I think we'd better get you inside and find you a place to have those babies. We've paged your doctor, and I'm sorry to tell you he's out of town for the holiday weekend."

They were moving quickly through the halls of the hospital now.

"There's no need to worry, though. We have an outstanding ob-gyn on call today, and it just so happens he was here at the hospital already, visiting a patient, so he'll meet us up in labor and delivery. He's terrific, and between you and me, he's my personal favorite. I promise you're in the very best hands."

They arrived at the elevator bank, where the nurse came around to push the button, looking at both of them with a kind smile. "I'm guessing that the two of you are about to have a lot to be thankful for this Thanksgiving."

Sarah, the nurse, had made quick work of getting India settled into a bed and hooked up to machines so they could monitor her labor. By the time the doctor came in a few minutes later, it was clear it wouldn't be long before Wyatt and India would become parents.

They'd planned on trying to have a natural childbirth anyway, even taking HypnoBirthing classes, but there was no time for trying any of those techniques now. Before they knew what was happening, India was already pushing; Wyatt grasped her hand and huddled against the bed with his head buried next to hers, reassuring her with tender whispers, even as he struggled to watch his wife writhing in pain.

It was excruciating for him to see her like that. He was wishing he could absorb the pain for her when, all of a sudden, she let out a wail at the same time that the doctor held up their beautiful daughter for them to see for the very first time.

Their son made his appearance a short two minutes later, and then it was all over.

Life as they'd known it was forever changed, and as Wyatt watched his wife cradling their two tiny children, he knew that he was looking at the face of God. He was aware that he would never forget the moment for as long as he lived. He couldn't help feeling that he wasn't deserving of so much bliss. He reached down to stroke the wispy blond hair on his children's heads, in awe as his wife began to feed them both. The look on her face when their eyes met said it all.

"This is all I'll ever need, Indy. 'Thank you' will never be enough." They sat that way for a while, the four of them, in quiet anticipation of everything the future had in store for them. It was India who finally broke the spell once the babies had eaten their fill and fallen asleep at her breast.

"I suppose we should share them with the rest of the world. Why don't you find Violet and Rex so we can introduce Marley and Dylan to the rest of their family?"

Garrett didn't have much experience with large holiday dinners, but he couldn't believe the sheer number of pots and pans and plates that had seen active duty during this one. He wouldn't have been surprised to open the cupboards and find them empty, since it appeared that Wyatt had used every single dish at his disposal. Willow had set about cleaning the kitchen, and after helping her wrap up the food and move everything else to the sideboard next to the sink, Garrett had decided they might as well have a little fun while they worked.

He walked over and grabbed the remote off the coffee table and switched on the sound system, quickly finding a streaming service that was playing country hits. Tim McGraw was singing about his next thirty years while Garrett moved on to his next task of fishing two cold beers out of the fridge. He popped the top on both bottles, walking over to the sink where Willow was still up to her elbows in soapsuds.

She glanced over at him and raised an eyebrow. Garrett leisurely sipped his beer as he leaned one hip against the counter and watched her, the expression on his face unreadable.

"Break time already?" She knew they were almost done, so she felt comfortable enough to tease him a little.

She tried to blow a piece of hair out of her face that kept falling forward over her eyes, but it wouldn't mind her, so she reached up with the back of her hand and wiped it away, leaving a small cluster of bubbles high on her brow.

*Damn, she is beautiful.* He gave her a crooked grin, nodding to the beer he'd set down for her. "Brought one for you too. I'm glad to jump in and help, but you look like you've got things under control for now. So I'm heading up the ambiance committee. Music and beer. It's Thanksgiving, after all."

Willow smiled, drying her hands on the towel she'd thrown over her shoulder. She was about to grab her own beer when Garrett stepped toward her, reaching up to sweep her forehead with the back of his fingertips. She felt her stomach jump in surprise at his touch. He stepped back to where he'd been standing against the counter and raised a brow back at her.

"Sorry. You had some suds on your face." He took a swig of his beer before making a screwed-up face at her. "Might've been a little piece of turkey gravy in there too. At least I hope that's what it was. Hard to tell."

He chuckled as she reached back into the sink for a handful of bubbles, flicking them all over the front of his shirt before taking a long drink of her beer.

It was so cold, and exactly what she needed. She'd been feeling a little skittish working side by side with him in the kitchen, not sure of what to say after having dropped the bomb about his ex-girlfriend. He didn't bring it up, so neither did she. In fact, they'd been working in relative silence until he'd switched the music on.

She looked around, happy enough with the progress they'd made. "At least we got all the leftovers packed up and put away so Wyatt will have something to eat when he gets back from the hospital. I wonder how things are going?"

Garrett shook his head, blowing out a breath, his beer dangling casually from between two fingers. "I can't believe they're having the babies today. It seems like they just found out they were pregnant."

Willow thought he seemed almost a little envious of his friends. He was such a kind person, which made her feel even worse about having told him about his girlfriend's infidelity. She couldn't stop thinking about the look on his face when it had registered. "I'm really sorry about what I told you back at the Thompsons'. That wasn't my place. I hope you'll accept my apology."

The words came out in a rush, and once they'd hit their mark, she glanced up to see what effect they'd had. He was looking at her with a curious expression.

A moment passed before he spoke. "It just caught me off guard, that's all. It's been months since we broke up, but in case you hadn't figured it out by now, most of that—the cheating part anyway—was new information to me."

He finished off his beer, and, not sure what to do with his hands, he moved toward the fridge to grab another one. Opening it, he walked back to where she stood. "If you don't mind me asking, how did you know she was my girlfriend in the first place?"

Willow felt sick to her stomach. She'd dug the hole so deep now, she didn't know if she'd ever get out of it. Taking a deep breath, she figured she'd gone this far; she might as well tell him everything. Her cheeks were stained crimson as she admitted her transgression. "I was exploring the grounds that previous afternoon before Smoky Mountain Table. The light was so beautiful in the garden, I'd gotten out to walk around."

She watched his face for any dawn of understanding, but he still looked puzzled.

"I didn't mean to eavesdrop, I promise. I saw the two of you on the porch of Woodshed. It was, well, a special moment. Or what was supposed to be. As soon as I realized what I was seeing, I turned and left."

She put her hand up over her eyes, wishing she could unsee it for the hundredth time. Willow felt awful that he now realized that humiliating moment had been witnessed. By her, of all people.

When she looked again, his face was so open, so raw. She'd never known a man so unguarded with his emotions. She had the sudden urge to comfort him again, the same feeling that had prompted her to kiss him back in September. She wisely resisted this time, instead waiting for him to speak.

"Well, that explains it. You felt pity for me, so you thought you'd kiss me? I'll admit, if I'd known the whole story, I might have let that go on a little longer." His words were teasing, but his expression was shadowy, hard to read. He wasn't finished with his questioning either. "Is that what it was, really? You felt bad for me?"

He watched her closely and thought he saw something flicker across her face before she controlled it. He knew she wouldn't make the same mistake with him again. She was too proud for that. But she had to feel whatever this energy was between them. It wasn't just nerves. He was sure of that now. She had a kindness he was drawn to, and, realizing now that she'd been so humiliated by him all those months ago but hadn't held it against him because of what she'd seen, he suddenly saw her differently.

"I don't know why I did that, honestly. Yes, I knew what had happened to you, and I felt bad about that. But I think it was more about the vulnerability I recognized in you when we were talking about our families. I felt like we were having a kindred-spirits moment. I'm sorry I overstepped, though. It was such a peaceful evening, and then you throw in the wine and the emotional conversation . . ." She shrugged her shoulders. "I guess I don't have an excuse. I'm just sorry."

They were only a couple of feet apart. Garrett had set his beer down and was listening intently to what she was telling him. He understood now what she'd experienced that night, because he found himself in the interesting position of feeling the exact same way currently. He decided it was now or never.

Her eyes were the color of root beer, and they opened a little wider in shock as he stepped toward her and closed the gap between them. He paused, his whiskered face just inches from hers, and searched her gaze for any signs of rejection.

When he heard her short, surprised intake of breath at his closeness, he stopped thinking altogether.

His hands braced the counter on either side of her, his face tilting ever so slightly so their lips met; the first brush was soft, grazing.

Electrifying.

The second was a bull's-eye.

As the feeling of their first kiss came rushing back, he realized why he'd gotten spooked. It had made him uncomfortable to so easily forget what had happened with Lindsay when he was kissing Willow. What did that say about him? Right now, he didn't care. Now, all he could think about was how grateful he was to have this second chance with her.

They kissed for a while, taking their time with the leisurely exploration of each other's mouths, and before long, he realized their lips weren't the only things pressed together. It was only the persistent sound of a cell phone ringing that finally forced them apart, albeit reluctantly.

It was hers, not his, and she somehow remembered how to use her legs to move to the end of the counter. She reached into her purse to find the phone and answer it, working hard to control her breathing.

Willow answered, and after a moment, Garrett watched her face lose color as she leaned against the counter, bracing herself with one hand. She murmured something about leaving right away before hanging up and looking at the floor in stunned silence. He moved toward her, grabbing her hand in his. She looked up at him with tears in her eyes.

"It's my father, Garrett. He's gone."

# CHAPTER
# TWELVE

People had told India she'd be tired, and she'd laughed. It was part of the witty repartee that other new moms loved to banter about. She'd never wear makeup again; yoga pants would be her new best friend. And the nursing bra. Maybe a better invention than maternity jeans. They were all little gems that first-time mothers loved to bemoan.

They weren't lying about the sleep deprivation, though.

The babies had been home for a week now, after spending ten days in the hospital to make sure their lungs were strong enough to function on their own. It was a safe bet that they hadn't slept longer than two or three hours at a time, although she couldn't be sure about that because she was So. Damned. Tired. Wyatt was doing his best to help her, but they'd been blessed with children that desired their milk straight from the tap, so he was helpless to provide relief to India in the feeding department. Staying on top of the laundry and making sure the nursery was stocked kept him busy enough. He was rendered speechless at how many diapers his children had gone through so far in their short lives. He wondered how people with triplets managed and was grateful that at least he and India weren't outnumbered.

Wyatt was just drying the last piece of the breast pump and then setting it on a towel next to the sink when he heard a soft knock at the front door. They'd taped a note there, warning people not to ring the bell and risk waking India or the babies. He looked down the hall and saw Garrett standing on the porch. Wyatt smiled and quickened his step when his friend raised a six-pack into view. He opened the door soundlessly, motioning for Garrett to follow him back into the kitchen.

"I thought you might be ready for a cold one. I hope I'm not intruding?"

Wyatt pulled two bottles from their sleeves, opened the fridge, and put the rest of the pack inside. He twisted off the tops and tossed them onto the counter, then handed a bottle to Garrett, raising his own in a silent toast. "Your timing is perfect, actually. India just fed the troops, and when I peeked in on the three of them a few minutes ago, they were all sleeping peacefully." Wyatt took a long drag of his beer, welcoming the icy sting as he swallowed. "Everything good at work?"

Garrett pulled out a counter stool and sat down, placing his beer on the coaster in front of him. "Oh yeah, all good. Not much to do in the garden or the shed right now, so I've been helping get things ready for the Christmas concert. It's going to be amazing. Don't worry. Everything is right on track as far as resort operations go."

Garrett was watching Wyatt's reaction to the news and could tell that he was obviously relieved not to have anything else dropped into his lap right now.

"How's fatherhood treating you?"

As tired as Wyatt looked, Garrett knew he'd never seen his friend look more content.

"Honestly? It's a ton of work but mostly for India. She's been incredible. I don't know how she's existing on so little sleep. Watching her with those babies, though . . . I can't believe I get to wake up every day and live this life. It's a thousand times better than I'd ever expected. And I kind of already knew I'd love it."

Garrett grinned. As envious as he was, it was hard to be anything but excited for them. "That's awesome, man. I'm so happy for you. And I love their names. Marley and Dylan. I didn't know you had such great taste in music."

They chatted for a few minutes about the babies before the conversation took a turn. Wyatt had been waiting for the right moment to bring it up. "I never got to ask you; were you able to set things right with Willow at Thanksgiving? I know things got a little crazy, but Violet told me you guys stayed back here together to clean up when we all left for the hospital. Thanks again for that, by the way."

Garrett stood up from his stool, pacing as he talked. "Yeah, I guess you could say that we were able to move past the awkwardness after talking for a while. Then she got the phone call about her father, and since she's taken the last couple of weeks off, we really haven't had a chance to talk since. So we're kind of right back where we started."

Garrett blew out a breath, running his hands through his hair in frustration. "I have a knack for screwing up with her, Wyatt."

Wyatt chuckled, standing to grab a bag of chips off the counter and pour them into a ceramic bowl. "Normally, I'd tell you you're probably overreacting, but it does seem like the two of you are having a hard time finding a rhythm." Wyatt looked pointedly at his friend. "Do you like her?"

"Of course I like her. I mean, what's not to like? She's smart and fun, and she's obviously gorgeous. I think she likes me too, but I'm not sure how to move forward. She's just been through the death of a parent, which I know from personal experience can rock a person to their core. It's hard to tell if I should be giving her space or offering her comfort. I don't want to make a wrong move."

"I don't know that I think offering her comfort would be a wrong move at this point. You said you haven't spoken at all?" Wyatt asked.

"I saw her briefly at yesterday's meeting, which was her first day back, but there wasn't the opportunity to speak in private. I did leave a note on her desk with my condolences, but that's it."

Wyatt nodded. "That's a start. Why don't you stop by her office and create some private time? If you're really interested, ask her out on a date. That's how it works, man."

Garrett knew the onus was on him this time. She wouldn't make a move again until he did. He'd make a point of going to see her the following afternoon when he got to work.

For someone who hadn't lived back in Knoxville for very long, Willow sure had a lot of boxes. Most were full of things she'd packed up when she'd left Utah and had not yet unpacked, but when she'd gone through her parents' house, she'd been surprised at how many things she'd decided to keep. Maybe it was the fact that these items were the only tangible connection to her family she had left, now that both of her folks were gone.

Willow had figured that her family home would sell quickly, but she hadn't expected to be approached before it even hit the market. She'd been packing in the afternoon the week after Thanksgiving when she heard the doorbell. A young man and woman stood there, smiling back at her with hopeful expressions. They were members of the East Tennessee Historical Society and had come to inform her that if she was planning on listing the home for sale, they'd love to have the first opportunity to buy it. Not only was there a desire to preserve the structure because it was one of the oldest in the city, but a wealthy benefactor had hoped to acquire it in trust for the city as a place for local artists to create art for the city of Knoxville and beyond.

Willow was blown away by the idea and found herself agreeing that it was a wonderful option before she could think of any reasons not to.

Now, almost three weeks later, she marveled at how her life had changed so drastically in such a short time. She'd sold the home in a quick-close transaction for more than she'd ever hoped for. In turn, the new owners asked if she could be moved out before Christmas so they could work to have it up and running in the new year. Somehow, she'd managed to pull it all together, and now her car was loaded to the gills with her personal boxes while the moving truck had already pulled away with her furniture and the rest of her stuff.

It was still dark that morning when she parked outside the Café 4 in Market Square for the last time to grab a tea and a breakfast sandwich. She was about to reach for the door handle when it swung open toward her, and Garrett came barreling out, nearly bumping into her.

"Oh God. I'm sorry about that! I didn't see you." He looked genuinely shocked to see Willow standing there. He'd stopped by her office a few times, hoping for the chance to talk with her, but she hadn't been keeping regular hours in the weeks since her father's death. He'd had to settle for leaving her a note.

Now, Garrett backed up, holding the door so she could step inside, out of the cold.

She was just as surprised as he was. She supposed they hadn't run into each other at the coffee shop more often because they kept different hours. Garrett usually got to work before Willow did, and she stayed on later in the evenings after he'd already gone home.

"Still the best coffeehouse in the city." Willow smiled at Garrett. "I'm really gonna miss it. Thought I'd get one more fix before I hit the road."

She glanced nervously at him, hoping to be able to regain her composure. Willow would have felt better about things if there had been time to throw some makeup on that morning. It was surprising he even recognized her so easily with her bare face and stocking cap.

Garrett smiled back. "Amazing I haven't seen you here more often. The coffee is nice and strong, but the people are what keep me coming back. It's one of the things I like most about living in the city." He took a sip from the steaming cup in his hand.

He was having a hard time stitching together a conversation. Her big brown eyes were sizing him up, and he couldn't help thinking that she looked so young and vulnerable in her knit cap. She wore the past three weeks of grief across her face plainly, and he found himself wanting to embrace her, but he resisted the urge.

She took in a breath and raised her shoulders in a shrug before exhaling with a nervous smile. "Well, I suppose it might be the last time you bump into me. Here, at least. My father's house sold pretty quickly, and actually, today is moving day for me."

Garrett raised his eyebrows in surprise. "Gosh. That happened fast. I'm glad to hear that the market is so robust, though. Well, congratulations to you."

"I think I was lucky because of the location of the house," she explained. "It's going to be used as an artists' retreat. A local philanthropist funded the sale so the architectural integrity of the home would remain intact. I'm pretty sure they're registering it with the historical society too, which would have made my dad happy."

They'd shifted together into the short line before the register so that Willow could order her breakfast, but there were still a few people in front of her, so Garrett decided to wait with her.

"Hold on. Are you talking about the old Pineapple property? Over by the Birdhouse? I read about that place in the paper. *That* was your family's home?"

Willow pursed her lips. "Guilty. It's been in my family since the turn of the century. My grandparents lived there before my folks. It's an amazing house, but it's just not me. This opportunity to sell and ensure that it would remain relevant in the neighborhood seemed like the best possible outcome. I'm ready for a fresh start."

Garrett studied her, admiring her strength. It couldn't be easy to let go of that meaningful link to her family so soon after her father's death. "We haven't been able to really talk personally since Thanksgiving. I'm so sorry about the loss of your father."

She was touched. It was true they hadn't spoken, because Willow had taken a couple of weeks off, but her first day back at work, she'd found the handwritten note from Garrett on her desk and was moved that he would take the time to reach out in such a personal way. There hadn't been a service. Her father had wanted it that way. He'd been a quiet man both in life and in death.

"Thank you. And thanks for your note. That was very sweet."

Willow was next in line, so she reached into her purse for some money, but he stepped in and beat her to it, pulling his wallet from his jeans.

"Here, let me. Consider it a moving-day treat." He handed the money to the cashier and motioned for the change to be put into the tip jar before turning back toward Willow. "So where is your new place? Are you staying local?"

Garrett accepted a warm-up from the pretty young barista, who may or may not have been attempting to flirt with him. He didn't seem to notice.

Willow couldn't believe what she was about to tell him. It still didn't seem real to her. It had all happened so fast. "You're looking at the proud new owner of twenty-five acres and an orchard. And a farmhouse. Oh, and a tractor that I have no idea how to drive." She gave him a weak smile. "Got any tips for me?"

Garrett was staring at her slack-jawed. He couldn't believe she'd pulled the trigger on purchasing the Thompson property so quickly. She must've had nerves of steel. "Well, that's some news. Wow. I'm not even sure what to say. Well done. You got yourself an incredible piece of property, that's for sure."

He studied her face, trying to read her expression, but she was guarded now. He thought he noticed her shoulders straighten a little when she spoke next.

"Yeah, I'm really excited about the challenge of it all. I mean, the house has already been completely renovated. It's perfect just as it is, with its gorgeous bones and modern touches. The Thompsons really took great care of it. And there's a second house on the property that you can't see from the road. It sits back along the creek that runs through the rear of the land. I think it's Hesse Creek. It's been renovated too, so I thought maybe we could use it to house the musicians that come in to play in the Great Hall. That way, they'd have their own secluded space with plenty of privacy while they're not performing." She took a deep breath. "But that's just a thought. I still have to run it by India and Wyatt. I haven't wanted to bother them too much while they're still getting used to being parents."

Garrett was impressed. She'd really thought it through. He knew that India would love the idea of having a private space for guest entertainers. Garrett could see why she'd hired Willow. She was forward-thinking and truly had the best interest of the resort at heart.

"I was just up at their place yesterday, but I didn't get to see the babies or India because it was nap time. Wyatt said she's planning on being back for the big Christmas concert. I swear, that woman is a superhero."

He smiled at Willow, raising his coffee cup in a silent toast. "Sounds like you might be cut from the same cloth."

Willow blushed, picking up her tea and sandwich as they turned together to walk toward the door. Garrett held it open for her, letting her exit the shop ahead of him. She could see now that his Jeep was parked a few spaces down the street from her car in the opposite direction. She turned to say good-bye. "Thanks for treating. It's going to be a long day, and this will definitely help jump-start me, especially this early. I guess I'll see you at work when I get back full time on Monday."

Garrett knew he couldn't miss this opportunity. "Actually, if you don't mind, I'd love to stop by after work later and help. I don't have any plans, and it sounds like you're trying to do most of this yourself. I could bring some dinner if you don't already have something lined up?"

He could feel his heart jumping out of his chest. Her answer would be a clear indicator of whether or not she was interested in exploring whatever they'd stumbled into twice now, rather unsuccessfully.

A million different thoughts started to form in Willow's head, many of them involving warnings not to get involved with him, if only because he was her coworker. She knew she should be careful and that it went against her better judgement to get close to the fire with him for a third time. Where would it lead? The thought scared her to death. She opened her mouth to politely decline, but she heard her own voice betray her.

"You know what? Dinner sounds perfect. Can you come by at six?"

# CHAPTER
# THIRTEEN

Willow had worked from the moment she'd arrived at the farmhouse until four thirty that afternoon when the moving truck had finally pulled away. She was grateful that she'd hired such a great crew of guys who were exceedingly patient with her. She had them moving furniture into the house—then right back out of it—all day long. She'd been selective about what she'd brought over from her father's house, but even the few pieces of furniture she'd kept didn't belong in this new house after all. Instead of leaving misfit pieces there to obsess over for months, she'd had the guys load the unwanted furniture into a small Morton building at the rear of her lot. She'd worry about selling it or donating it once she was settled. She knew if her house was empty, she'd be much more likely to get her act together to furnish it properly.

In truth, she probably would have forged on a little later into the evening, but she wanted to jump in the shower before Garrett arrived with dinner. She felt herself flush as she remembered her boldness in accepting his invitation so quickly. She'd woken up that morning, fully intending on immersing herself in this new house and focusing the rest of her attention on work. And here she was, focused only on him.

She'd had plenty of time over the past few weeks to think back to that Thanksgiving evening. Willow had come to the conclusion that there was something about Garrett that frightened her, but not in a physical way. He was the epitome of a gentleman. She could tell that his tenderness was genuine when he'd kissed her. She'd felt the sense of urgency emanating from him, but he'd let her set the pace during their kiss. She'd wondered more than once how far things would have gotten if her phone hadn't rung.

No, her concern was centered deeper than that. She felt like he could see her. Really see her. When she talked with him, his eyes locked on to hers in a way that made her feel completely transparent. She'd never experienced anything quite like it before.

Now, as she stood there remembering, she realized her hand was at her throat, and she noticed the air had gotten chillier, causing her to shiver. Or had it been the memory of the kiss?

Shaking it off, she took the wooden stairs up to her bedroom, happy to see that the one thing that had transitioned beautifully from the old house to the new was a vintage iron bed frame and ridiculously comfortable mattress she'd found in one of her parents' guest rooms. Her suitcase was open on the floor, next to the closet, so she rooted through it to find some clean clothes, settling on a light-wash pair of jeans and a cream-colored sweater.

She showered and dressed quickly, running a brush through her hair before giving up and pulling it back into a ponytail. She was just coming back down the stairs, when she glanced out the window and saw his headlights canvas the gravel as he pulled into the drive. She flicked on the radio, grateful to have Patsy Cline singing about falling to pieces as a distraction. Taking a deep breath, she walked to the door to meet him and was surprised to see him already climbing the last porch step with his arms full of firewood.

*Oh boy.*

Garrett had talked himself out of his nerves on the way over, but they came rushing back when he saw her standing there all lit up from behind by the lights inside her new house. She took his breath away in her simple blue jeans and bare feet, and he had to swallow hard before he said hello. He prayed his voice would sound steady.

"I thought maybe you'd like a fire tonight since it's supposed to be so cold?" He waited while she stepped aside so he could carry the wood through the small entryway.

"Oh, that's great. I think the Thompsons left me the fireplace tools and a starter log, but it will be nice to have these to throw on the fire later. Thank you. Here, let's put them right in here."

Willow led him down the hallway and into the hearth room just off the kitchen.

Garrett glanced around, staring at the empty space that filled the void between them and the fireplace. "I thought you might want to have a fire in a room where you actually plan to hang out? Where's all your stuff?"

He waited for her to point the way, surprised when she looked mortified.

"Well, that's the thing. I got a little overzealous in my decisions about what went into the 'no' pile today, and I guess

I forgot to leave anything for the 'yes' pile. So we might have to stand at the counter and eat if that's OK with you?"

Garrett glanced around again and laughed. He carried the logs to the hearth and set about starting a fire; it caught on quickly, burning brightly and warming the room right away. Standing, he smoothed out the front of his jeans, and Willow was struck by how handsome he looked in the firelight.

"Let me run out and grab dinner from the car. And I might have a solution to our seating problem too." He smiled at her as he strode by on his way back down the hall.

Willow was opening a bottle of red wine and had just started pouring it into two glasses she had unearthed earlier that day when Garrett rounded the corner and came back into view. This time, he had a large picnic basket in one arm and what looked like a couple of dark-green fleece blankets in the other.

"Just because it's the week before Christmas doesn't mean we can't have a picnic here in East Tennessee. The chefs hooked us up with a feast. It's your lucky night."

Willow watched as he set the basket of food down and went about spreading one of the blankets out on the floor in the middle of the hearth room. When he was satisfied that it alone would be big enough, he tossed the other blanket aside and began unpacking the food.

Willow watched him with a smile before she got the idea to reach back into one of her kitchen boxes and fish out a candle she'd seen earlier. She lit it, then carried it over and set it into the center of the spread he was creating before handing him one of the two wineglasses. He stood up from his crouched position, meeting her gaze and raising his glass in a toast.

"Here's to your new home and the fact that you'll never forget that your first meal here was a bona fide carpet picnic."

She laughed as they clinked glasses and took sips of the wine. Garrett extended his hand, inviting her to sit down first before he joined her on the floor. The fire was crackling as they started eating their dinner.

Willow smiled. "Good thing we have access to one of the finest restaurants in the South. I'd hate to invite you over to eat on the floor and then have to serve you some terrible pizza to boot. I'll tell you a secret. I'd eat this fried chicken every single day if I didn't fear dropping dead from a heart attack." She took another bite, licking her thumb and forefinger to emphasize.

Garrett stared at her in amazement. She was so intriguing. On one hand, she was the picture of poise and professionalism at work. She'd commanded the respect and admiration of the staff in the few short months she'd worked there. But the times Garrett had seen her outside of her work role, she was soft, kind. Still strong and confident, but she somehow seemed younger and more open when she wasn't working. He realized he'd been staring at her bottom lip as she made short work of the chicken, and he had to force himself to look away and grab a biscuit.

"So I can't figure out how it is that you don't have a guy waiting in the wings somewhere. How did you escape Utah without a ring on your finger?" He watched her closely for evidence that he was wrong about her being single. He didn't think that he was.

Willow thought carefully about what she wanted him to know and then figured that it wouldn't hurt if she was completely truthful with him at this point. She felt that she could trust him enough to share that part of her past. Besides, he didn't need anyone else lying to him. "You and I have something else in common, besides our family histories. We've both been turned down after a marriage proposal."

She got up and crossed the room, coming back with the bottle of wine to top off their glasses. Crouching back down, she sat cross-legged across from him, waiting for the information to sink in. It didn't take long. Garrett seemed stunned.

"Someone turned *you* down? I don't believe it. You're just trying to make me feel better."

"I wish that were true. You don't know how humiliating it was—well, I guess maybe you do." She looked at him with a sheepish grin. "Oops."

They stared at each other for a moment before both of them burst into laughter. By the end of it, she was lying on the floor, her hands holding her stomach while she tried to catch her breath. He was still sitting next to her, his elbow propped up on one knee, his other hand wiping his eyes from laughing so hard. "I guess it's true what they say about misery loving company. Because I'm not gonna lie, I've never been so happy and relieved to hear that someone else understands my humiliation. Even though it sucks that it's you."

That set them both off again, and it was several minutes before they stopped laughing. Garrett smiled at her when she glanced over at him, but the laughter was gone from his eyes and had been replaced by something else.

"Tell me your story."

Willow stared up at the ceiling for a minute before she spoke. Sitting back up, she found her wineglass and started to tell Garrett about Declan.

"He was a ski instructor up in Deer Valley. I met him a couple of years after I started working at Stein, and we hit it off right away. He's four years older than me, and he'd been helping out as a ski instructor for aspiring Olympic athletes living in Park City. He was fun and so different than anyone I'd ever dated. I feel like I have to be so serious when I'm working, but I could really be myself when I was with him."

She glanced over at Garrett, who was watching her intently. "I've always been a bit of a tomboy, and I love a good adventure. And I thrive in the mountains." Willow shrugged her shoulders. "I guess Declan just fit the bill. Anyway, we'd been dating for a little over two years when I started wondering where the relationship was going. We'd talked about spending our lives together, but I knew Declan was impulsive and not the best planner. So I decided to be a modern woman and do the asking. You can imagine how the rest of the story goes."

Garrett stared at her. "Why on earth would he turn *you* down?"

His expression made her feel strangely vulnerable again, and she instinctively folded her legs into her body, wrapping her arms around her knees. "That's where our stories are different. While Lindsay didn't have the guts to tell you she was seeing someone else, Declan admitted it right to my face. He told me it would be better for me to find out that way than to wonder what I did wrong. He said it was him, not me. That I shouldn't feel bad. Monogamy just wasn't in his genes."

She drained the rest of her wine, setting the glass down in front of her and running her finger along the rim absentmindedly. "That was last winter. In August, I got the news about my father's health, and then this job opened up in September. It was divine timing, for sure. Deer Valley is a small place. Too small for both of us. It was just another reason for me to move on. In truth, I was more devastated about leaving the mountains than I was about losing him."

Garrett reached over and poured the rest of the wine into her glass. His heart broke a little when she looked up and gave him a sad smile.

"Maybe that's why I told you about Lindsay the way I did. The only thing worse than knowing would be not knowing and wondering why she said no. But I still feel bad about hurting you."

She was remarkable. He couldn't believe that she was worried about his feelings in this moment. She was truly selfless. "He was a fool to let you go. I wouldn't be surprised if he realizes that someday and tries to win you back. No mistake of that magnitude could go unnoticed."

It was quiet. The two of them were momentarily lost in their own thoughts, watching the crackling fire and listening to the song change from upbeat to slow on the radio. Blake Shelton and Gwen Stefani were begging for the opportunity to break each other's hearts. Maybe it was the music, or maybe it was the fact that they were both feeling like members of the lonely hearts club. Garrett knew he wanted to make her forget and that he needed to forget himself.

He stood, reaching both of his hands down to her. Looking at him, she accepted and let him take her hands and lift her up off the blanket. They stood there looking at each other for a moment, their hands still intertwined, before he spoke.

"Dance with me."

He searched her eyes for permission, and when she offered him a shy nod, he slowly pulled her close to him. Willow rested her cheek softly against his shoulder and tucked her arm into his in the space between them as they moved to the music.

She could feel the thump of his heart through his shirt, and she shivered despite the room feeling much warmer because of the fire. They were quiet while they swayed together to the final notes of the song, but Garrett was running his thumb along the palm of her hand in lazy circles, providing just enough stimulation to remind them both that this was more than just a casual dance.

The song ended, and another one took its place; this one was slow too but with a more urgent beat. Garrett pulled back just enough to look down into her eyes. What he saw gave him the courage to take the leap. His eyes open, he lowered his mouth to hers. Once their lips met, it was all he could do to keep from pulling the rest of her against him just as tightly. He'd thought to let her take the lead, but that plan vaporized when he felt her tongue graze his for the first time. A primal sound escaped him, and he released her momentarily so that he could shift a little closer. He reached around and slid the elastic out of her hair, tossing it to the floor before stepping toward her again and plunging his hands into her hair to better control their next kiss.

Willow could feel the sensation in her toes. She was glad he'd taken charge, because she wasn't sure she could stand it if he released her anytime soon. Her legs were rubber bands, but that wasn't what held her attention. He'd stopped kissing her mouth and had begun to work his way along her jawline before planting urgent kisses on the side of her neck. The rasp of his whiskers, coupled with the feeling of his incredibly soft lips working that sensitive spot above her collarbone, was pure bliss, and she let her head fall back instinctively so he could have easier access.

His hands were sliding down her shoulders when they both heard a loud knock at the front door.

They stepped apart, looking at each other with twin surprised expressions. There was most definitely unfinished business between them, and Garrett was about to beg her to ignore the interruption, but the person at the door wasn't taking no for an answer.

Willow reached down to grab her discarded hair band off the blanket and throw it back into her hair while Garrett took a lap around the hearth room to find his way back down to earth. Willow mumbled something about seeing who was at the door before disappearing around the corner. Garrett was cursing whomever it was who had interrupted them, when the subjects of his wrath followed Willow down the hall and into the adjacent kitchen.

"We thought we'd bring you some dinner since you've been working all day."

Violet and Rex stopped short at the sight of the blanket and empty wineglasses on the floor.

Violet smiled and raised an eyebrow, lowering the take-out bag she was holding up when she caught Garrett's eye. "But it looks like someone already beat us to it."

# CHAPTER

# FOURTEEN

The four of them stood around the kitchen counter picking at the brownies that Violet and Rex had brought with them. There was another empty bottle of red wine, having been consumed while they talked about their respective days. After chatting for a bit, Willow offered to take them all on a tour of her empty new house.

It was the first time Violet and Rex had seen the inside, since the whole transaction had taken place in about three weeks. Violet and Rex were also surprised that Willow didn't have much furniture, but it was clear that this was going to be a beautiful house once she chose the perfect pieces to make it a home. The Thompsons had used the same interior design firm that had completed all the decor at the resort, so this house could easily be mistaken for an extension of the resort.

The walls were covered in a modern white paneling that was complemented by dark iron fixtures and slate-gray cabinetry in the kitchen. Garrett and Rex got sidetracked in the front room talking about the upcoming NFL playoffs, so Violet and Willow left them behind as they went upstairs to finish the tour. They were standing in Willow's master bedroom when Violet lowered her voice to apologize.

"I'm *so* sorry we barged in on you like that. Geez, it couldn't have been more awkward to come down the hall and see Garrett standing in your living room looking like he just got caught with his hand in the cookie jar. What's going on with you two anyway? Give me an update!"

Violet leaned against the door frame, sipping her wine as she waited for Willow to dish. The blush in her friend's cheeks was the answer she was looking for.

"I don't really know. But *something* is definitely going on." Willow looked at Violet with wide eyes. She bit her lip in contemplation before she spoke again. "He's so damned hot, Vi. I mean, it's like I'm eighteen years old and I have the impulse control of a grease fire. He comes near me, and I want to attack the poor man."

Violet had to work hard not to spit out her wine. "Honey, I think that's what they call chemistry, and it's clear the two of you have it. The question is, what are your plans going forward?" Violet considered her own question and frowned, looking back at Willow. "I guess that's maybe what you were trying to figure out when we barged in?"

Willow was about to answer when they heard the front door open and then close again. They could hear Rex and Garrett's muffled voices now through the bedroom window, indicating that they had gone outside. Willow moved out into the hallway, and Violet followed her down the stairs and out onto the front porch.

Garrett turned toward them from where he'd been standing with Rex in the darkness of the front yard looking up at the house. "We were just going to take a walk around out here and check out your other buildings, if that's OK. But if you ladies are coming with us, you might want to grab a jacket. It's pretty cold once you've been out here for a minute."

Willow ran back inside and grabbed the two green blankets that Garrett had brought in from his car earlier, along with a key from a hook on the wall next to the front door. She wrapped one of the blankets around herself. Once she was back outside on the front lawn with the others, she handed the other blanket to Violet, then motioned for the three of them to follow her.

"Come with me. I want to show you the other little cabin out back. It's where we'll be housing some of the musical guests when they're at the resort to perform, especially if they're traveling without family."

She turned to Garrett, excited that what they'd talked about that morning had quickly come to fruition. "I talked to India about it this afternoon, and she's totally on board. In fact, she wants to put Sawyer Brantley back here when he's in for the Christmas concert this weekend since he's traveling solo."

Garrett didn't know why, but he felt a little prickly at the thought of the handsome rising country music star staying in such close proximity to Willow. The man would have to be blind not to notice her, and some of the things that had been said about him in the tabloids alluded to the fact that he wasn't going to be living in a monastery anytime soon. Garrett knew it wasn't his place, but he made a mental note to keep a close eye on the crooner.

After a short walk, they were standing before a small rustic-looking cabin. Willow slipped the key she'd grabbed into the lock, turned it, and stepped inside to flick on the lights.

It was adorable. There was a queen bed off to one side, covered in red-and-black plaid bedding. Next to that was a wood-burning fireplace and an overstuffed black leather chair draped with a red cashmere blanket. The chair sat opposite a large wooden table covered in coffee-table books, most of them highlighting the nearby Smoky Mountains. The room was lit from a charming antler chandelier that cast a warm golden glow over the entire scene. There was no detail in the space that had been overlooked. Presumably, the doorway on the left led to a bathroom that would prove to be just as impressive.

Rex let out a low whistle. "Whoa, don't take this the wrong way—your house is incredible, really—but *this* is what seals the deal for me. What a cool little pad. Makes me want to get back to work with my band so maybe I'll get invited to stay here."

Violet wrapped her arm around her husband while he stood there dreaming. "Babe, remember. This is for musicians who are traveling *without* their families. You, my love, are a family man. And when we stay on property, we aren't exactly slumming it in the main house." She paused and looked around again before meeting Willow's gaze. "But he's right. This is pretty special. How is it that you have this place totally decked out already, but you ate dinner tonight on a blanket in your real house?"

Willow laughed, pulling the aforementioned blanket tightly around her shoulders before reaching to adjust the thermostat on the wall to begin warming the small space up. "The Thompsons sold it to me furnished. They felt it would lose its charm without these particular appointments, and I have to admit that, as much as I love to decorate a space myself, I agree with them. You can't improve upon perfection."

Garrett was watching her as she admired the space with a look of pride. He couldn't help feeling that she belonged there, on the property. She seemed so relaxed and content. Her confidence and ability to handle such an overwhelming project made her that much sexier. He felt his jaw tighten at the memory of where they had been headed when they were interrupted.

Violet had caught the twitch in Garrett's face as he watched Willow fill them in about her plans for the rest of the orchard. After a few minutes, the four of them walked back out onto the small stone porch and paused under the dim light while Willow locked up.

"I think it's time for us to get back to the troops, Rex," Violet said. "I'm excited to see this place come to life with you in charge, Willow. And if you need any help out in the orchard, I'm sure we can scare up a farmer or two to give you a hand."

Violet moved in to hug Garrett good-bye as she said those last words, then gave him a good-natured shove as she backed away. "We're leaving her with a mess back in the kitchen, Garrett, so make sure you help her clean up before you head for the city." She winked for good measure.

They finished their good-byes, and Garrett and Willow stood in the yard watching while Rex and Violet pulled away, their headlights sweeping across the road as they headed home. It was quiet for a moment before Garrett spoke.

"Well, let me help you with the kitchen, and then I suppose I should get going. I'm sure you're exhausted after your long day."

He glanced over at her in the darkness. The only light that reached them was coming from the windows of her house a hundred or so feet away, but he could still feel that she was nervous. He was too. He didn't want to make her uncomfortable, so he was just about to turn and walk toward the house when he felt her reach out and grab his hand.

"Let's stay out here for a few more minutes. I could stand here and smell that wood smoke forever. If you're cold, you can come in here with me?"

She opened the blanket she had wrapped around her shoulders, sliding it around her to make room for him. He didn't hesitate, stepping closer to her, grateful he'd thought to keep those old fleece blankets in his Jeep. They suddenly seemed a lot more valuable.

Willow was shivering a little from the crisp air, but after a moment, Garrett shifted so her back was resting against his chest, his arms around her. He was sure the wood smoke smelled fine, but it was nothing compared to the scent of her, and he reflexively dipped his face closer to her to drink it in. He felt her shiver again, but he was pretty sure that this time it wasn't from the cold.

The only thing he could compare it to was honeysuckle. He knew the scent intimately, because, as a young boy, he used to pick honeysuckle on his grandparents' farm and then slide out the center to taste the drops of dew inside. The thought occurred to him that her mouth was even sweeter, and just like when he was a boy tasting honeysuckle, he couldn't deny himself another taste now.

Willow felt Garrett change his stance slightly just before his hands gently turned her around to face him. She'd known she wasn't ready for this night to end, but she was still astonished at her own boldness in having asked him to stand outside with her like this. As she looked up at him in the darkness, she felt the first wet, cold flakes of snow land on her cheeks, and she closed her eyes in surprise and delight. She laughed and was about to tell him how much she loved the snow, when she felt his lips softly meet hers.

He'd been right about how she tasted. Like everything he loved most from as far back as he could remember. But it was the softness of her lips that he didn't know if he could live without. Kissing was a privilege, and it was one he wanted to continue to deserve for a very long time to come.

Willow could make a weekend out of this. He could teach a master class in making out. There were a whole lot of men walking around that didn't know how to do it well, but Garrett Oliver most certainly wasn't one of them. His lips were full and warm, and the rasp of his whiskers was just soft enough not to rough her chin up too much, even as he deepened their contact. She felt her stomach flutter when he let go of the blanket, and it slipped to the ground, forgotten, the sensation of the suddenly invading crisp night air adding to the intensity.

It could have been just a few moments, or maybe it was several, until they finally pulled apart, but not before a few last soft kisses were shared. Garrett blew out a breath and reached down to retrieve the blanket. He turned away from her and shook it out, then wrapped the drier side around Willow's shoulders once more.

Wordlessly, they walked hand in hand toward the house, which was practically beckoning them back to its warmth. Garrett opened the door for her, waiting until she'd stepped inside before following her.

It took a moment for their eyes to adjust, but when they did, they could see the flush in each other's faces, and not just from the cold. Garrett summoned all the strength he had to control the overwhelming impulse to scoop her up right there and carry her up the stairs. Willow shrugged out of the blanket, folding it up and laying it over the banister.

"I'll wash, you dry? Isn't that how we do it?" She smiled at him, grabbing his hand to lead him back to the kitchen.

They did just that, making quick work of the wineglasses and cutlery they'd left behind. Garrett knew he could get used to simple evenings like this with her. It was easy between them. But he also realized she deserved so much more. He wanted to show her how a woman like her should be treated, and he sensed that the extra effort would be worth it. Willow was marathon-worthy. She wasn't just a sprint.

They chatted while they cleaned up, laughing at a story Rex had shared about meeting Violet. Garrett smiled as he watched her reach into the soapy sink to unplug the drain, marveling at how she even managed to make that simple task seem dignified. Before he knew what he was doing, he'd walked up behind her and was running his hands down her forearms and into the bubbly water to grab her hands. He tucked his chin to nudge the hair away from her ear, wanting to make sure she could hear what he had to tell her.

"I'm gonna date the heck out of you, Willow." He paused to plant a slow, soft kiss on the side of her neck, grinning when she rewarded him with another shiver.

She glanced at him out of the corner of her eye, releasing his hands to pick up a towel that was next to the sink. "Oh really?" She turned to face him, leaning back against the counter and looking up into his face. "And should I be more than a little worried about that wolfish grin on your face?" She crooked her eyebrow ever so slightly.

*Take it slow, Garrett. Take it slow.*

*Whatever.*

*Slow is for babies.*

He stepped closer to her, grabbing her by the waist and setting her up on the counter next to the sink. Another step, and he was standing between her legs, their gazes level now, each with a challenge for the other. "Well, it would mean some dinners, maybe a dance or two. And a whole lot more of this."

Garrett took her face into his hands again, this time with more urgency. He kissed her like it would be the last time he'd be allowed to do so, and she didn't move to stop him. Instead, she wrapped her legs around the back of him, pulling him even closer and forcing him to let out a low growl in the process. There was a moment when each of them wondered how they would ever stop. The radio was playing a Tim and Faith song, suggesting they do something that neither of them was ready for, but, in truth, it didn't sound like a horrible idea either.

Finally, Garrett managed to untangle his hands from her hair, which he'd somehow worked loose again from her hair tie. As he stepped away, shoving his hands in his pockets, he realized he was in deep trouble. This was going to hurt like hell if it ended badly. But he didn't care. She was worth the leap, he decided, as he watched her slide down off the counter.

He smiled and rubbed the side of his face as he cleared his throat to speak. "So, yeah. That's what I had in mind. You'd better clear your calendar."

# CHAPTER
# FIFTEEN

The next few days went by in a blur, as they often did during the busy holiday season at the resort. There were only two days left until Christmas, which normally would have been grounds enough for the frenetic energy behind the scenes, but this year, there was another reason everyone was buzzing with excitement. That night was the inaugural holiday concert in the newly constructed concert hall, and one of the hottest stars in country music would be taking center stage to perform for guests after dinner. The state-of-the-art facility was constructed to look like it had been there all along, fitting in perfectly with the rustic architecture of the dining barn, which sat just across a gravel drive. Guests who had been lucky enough to experience one of the early performances in the hall that autumn had given it rave reviews.

Wyatt had been keeping an eye on the weather all week, waiting until the last moment to decide whether or not it would be warm enough to use the outdoor amphitheater. He was flipping on the television in his small office in the rear of the building when he heard voices out in the entrance hall. He paused long enough to see the seven-day forecast flash across the screen before grabbing his coffee and heading out to see who was there.

He took a sip but had to work hard to swallow it when he took in what was happening right in front of his eyes.

His gorgeous wife, the mother of his two angels, and the only woman on earth he'd lay down his life for, was blushing furiously while some cretin was looking at her like she was a mouthwatering drumstick, letting his lips linger far too long on the top of India's hand for Wyatt's liking. It was just a flash, but Wyatt had a delightful little mental image of himself dropping the perpetrator on the floor like a bad habit. The thought made him smile. Thank God for his imagination. It had kept him out of trouble so far.

"Wyatt! Come here. I want you to meet someone."

India had managed to free her hand and had the good grace to look horrified at the expression on her husband's face. She knew his smile went only as far as his mouth. These two men weren't going to be braiding each other's hair anytime soon. India linked her arm through Wyatt's, presenting a united front to their guest.

"Sawyer Brantley, meet my husband, Wyatt Hinch. Wyatt, Sawyer was just thanking us for building such a beautiful place for him to play music. He's excited to be headlining the show tonight."

She pinched Wyatt's arm just hard enough to let him know it was time to shake hands and make nice. She might have been a little overzealous, because if she didn't know better, she'd have thought she detected a small wince. Nevertheless,

Wyatt stepped forward, extending his hand, and Sawyer met him halfway.

"There is more beauty in this place than I know what to do with, Wyatt," Sawyer said, then glanced back at India, who looked slightly mortified. He seemed oblivious to the building tension in the room as he continued to speak. "I don't know where to begin." Sawyer dropped Wyatt's hand, flipping his head to perfect his sideswept hair while stealing a look around the rest of the vast open space.

Two female staffers were on the other side of the room preparing stacks of blankets and setting up oversized silver chafing urns for hot chocolate and coffee. Sawyer mumbled something under his breath, shaking his head in obvious appreciation of the attractive young ladies who were smiling shyly back at him.

He was used to being ogled. At just over six feet tall, he was easy on the eyes in jeans and boots and his black shirt, which Wyatt couldn't help but notice was most likely purchased from Baby Gap. It was hard to say what was more irritating: that he actually was a good-looking man or that he clearly knew it.

Wyatt wasn't having any of it. "I know where you can start, champ. Walk with me and take a look at the outdoor space. We would really like to hold the concert in the amphitheater, since it's so unseasonably mild for this time of year. The low tonight is only going to be in the thirties, and from what I just saw on the news, there's not a chance of rain in sight."

Wyatt paused for a moment as they stood outside on the main stage. "I wouldn't want you to be too cold, though, in your T-shirt." He smiled, letting his words dangle before finding their mark, then taking another sip of his coffee and ignoring the death grip that India was now inflicting upon his hand.

Unfortunately, the barb went right over Sawyer's head. The man was obviously too obtuse to know he was being insulted.

Sawyer took his time, ambling around the stage and pausing to admire what would be his view of the audience. Or more likely contemplating the audience's view of him. "This place is so cool, man. I'm feeling it. Let's do this! Outside it is. And no sweat, Wyatt. I've got other stuff I can wear. Besides," he added with a wink at India, "I get pretty hot when I'm performing."

*I will not get in fights. I will not get in fights. I will not get in fights.* Wyatt wrote the sentence one hundred times on his mental blackboard, smiling serenely back at the singer. He was just about to say something when India beat him to the punch.

"Well, I know everyone is really excited for you perform tonight. And congratulations on your CMA award. Awards, rather. That must have been so exciting."

They let him ramble on about the various awards and the Billboard lists he was on before Wyatt decided he'd had enough of Mr. Brantley for one morning.

"Why don't I show you to where you'll be staying? I'm sure you'd like a little downtime to relax before dinner and showtime. It has to be exhausting being you."

The dig went flying over Sawyer's head and kept right on going. *Definitely obtuse.* It was becoming hard to hold a grudge against someone so clueless. Wyatt knew the resort crowd would love him, and he hated to admit it, but he himself had been guilty of singing along to Sawyer's biggest hit in his old green truck a time or two.

The three of them piled into India's SUV for the short ride over to the guest cabin on Willow's property. When they pulled up, it was Garrett they spotted out front, looking like he'd spent the better part of the day mucking out the old barn. His jeans and work shirt were covered in dirt, and he looked surprised to have been caught that way.

"Hey, I didn't expect you guys to be here for another hour or so. I would have been finished by now, but I spent the morning coaxing a couple of stray kittens out from under the floorboard where they'd made a home for themselves. I hope Willow won't be mad, but I think she may have two new barn cats."

Garrett glanced over at Sawyer, who was watching the three of them with growing interest. Garrett stepped closer, offering his hand.

"Sawyer, good to meet you. I'm Garrett Oliver. I work over in the gardens with Finn Janssen. I know I speak for all of the staff when I say we're very excited to have you performing here."

Sawyer reached across to shake Garrett's hand, and they exchanged pleasantries. Garrett could tell that India was anxious about something, because she was talking more than usual as she started to show Sawyer back to the guest house. Wyatt, on the other hand, had been unusually quiet.

Garrett couldn't put his finger on it, but something was definitely irritating Wyatt. He decided to step in and take over.

"If you guys need to go, I can show Sawyer to his place. I was just trying to get this barn straightened out as an early Christmas gift for Willow, but I'm mostly finished."

Garrett turned his attention back to Sawyer. "Once you're settled, I'll get out of here and give you some peace. I have a few things to do before the show anyway."

India and Wyatt agreed to let Garrett take it from there, walking slowly back to their car after Wyatt had delivered Sawyer's luggage to the porch of the cabin with a tight smile. Thanking Garrett, Wyatt jumped in and started the car in silence while India climbed into the passenger seat. Neither of them spoke until they were almost a mile down the road.

India smiled at her husband.

"That's nice of Garrett to help Willow with the barn. Kind of a perfect Christmas gift, if you ask me."

Wyatt paused, throwing India a sideways glance. "You know what I want for Christmas? Besides a one-way plane ticket back to Nashville for Prince Charming back there?"

India laughed, grabbing his hand and pulling it up to her mouth for a kiss. She loved his sense of humor. "What's that, my love?"

Wyatt slowed the car, turning into a drive that led to the private part of the resort. Putting it in park, Wyatt unbuckled his own seat belt before leaning over to unclick India's. He reached up to tenderly push a lock of her hair back from her cheek, smiling when he saw the look on her face. She wore her love for him so plainly. It never got old. He started to speak, but she placed a finger over his lips to stop him.

"You know something? I don't know what you want, Wyatt Hinch, and right now, I don't really care. What I want is to make out with my handsome and slightly jealous husband." She cocked her head to study him for a minute, her face teasing. "Green looks good on you, babe."

Just because they had twin babies at home, a resort to run, hundreds of employees and guests to manage, and the responsibility that came with all of that, it didn't mean they'd ever cut corners when it came to each other.

Wyatt kissed his wife so deeply and thoroughly that, within minutes, they'd both completely forgotten they'd ever met Sawyer Brantley.

There weren't many views that were more lovely than the one that Finn and Susan woke up to most mornings—at least when they were on property, which wasn't often enough for Finn's taste. Sure, he was having the time of his life being married to his best friend, and their recent trip to Hawaii had been a dream come true. They'd spent time on each of the islands and even taken a Jeep to an incredible olive-green-sand beach that was the southernmost tip of the United States. Susan made him feel young again, and even though they were both in their seventies, it didn't mean they had to act like it. Finn couldn't help but think for the thousandth time how foolish he'd been to wait so long to tell Susan how he felt about her. But there was no sense in wasting their time together saying what-if.

Now, as he stood out on their back porch, looking over the white-fence-lined expanse of the horse fields, he felt the same peace that washed over him each time they returned home from a trip. The morning air was cool, but the earth was still warm enough to treat him to a soft blanket of fog rising above the lightly frosted grass, matching the curl of mist from his second cup of coffee. The creak of the screen door behind him let him know that Susan was up, even before he felt her arms wrap around his waist, her cheek resting softly against his back. They stood that way for a few moments, taking in the sounds of the place they loved so much.

It was Finn who finally broke the silence. "I know we've seen some beautiful places this last year, Susie, but I'll be darned if there are any better than this one right in front of us."

He took a sip of coffee, turning to offer her his cup. Taking it, she wrapped her hands around the warm mug, standing next to him as they watched the horses begin to come alive in the pasture with a chorus of soft whinnies.

After a moment, she spoke. "After all these years, there isn't a morning that I stand on this porch when I don't feel lucky to be alive." Susan paused, turned to Finn, her pale-blue eyes questioning. "Have I forced you into a life you don't want, Finn? I know our trips have been incredible, but I sense that you're happier when we're here at home."

She set the coffee cup on the rail of the deck, turning to take his hands in hers. "I knew it would be an adjustment for you not to be in the garden full time this last year, but I didn't realize how much you needed this place to be happy. Have I made a mistake? I just couldn't bear the thought of losing you when we've just found our way to each other after all those wasted years."

Finn smiled at his wife, not quite sure what he'd done to deserve her. "If being with you on the vacations of a lifetime is a punishment, then I'm gonna commit a bunch more crimes, Susie."

He tenderly stroked her cheek, reaching down to place a kiss on her lips, which were still fixed in a slight frown. Stepping back to study her, he knew that she wouldn't settle for anything less than the truth from him. He owed her that.

"I will admit that I miss my office, and it's hard not to stand here and daydream about what we might do differently to make the harvest even better next year. But that is fixin' to be Garrett's domain going forward. He's been pretty patient with an old man who's having a hard time calling it quits. I couldn't ask him to wait much longer when I've already dangled the carrot. Unless . . ."

Susan watched him as he contemplated whether or not to finish his thought. When he took too long, she nudged him with her elbow. "Unless what?"

Finn turned toward her, leaning back against the deck rail with a light in his eyes she hadn't seen in a while. "You know that orchard up the road? The one that Willow Armstrong bought a few weeks ago? I'm wondering if she'd be interested in leasing that back to us. Hear me out. I've always wanted to have fruit trees, and that place has been on my radar for a while. If we hadn't been in Hawaii when it went on the market, I would have tried to convince you to buy it and make it part of the resort. We're lucky she's the one that beat us to it. I stopped to congratulate her on the purchase the other day, and I got this feeling that she knows she bit off more than she can chew, at least in the farming department."

He took a breath, glad to see from her expression that Susan wasn't completely opposed to the idea.

"What if we asked Garrett to be in charge of getting the orchard up and running, to be used as part of the resort? Heck, we're already using that guest cabin of Willow's for our musical acts. And maybe we don't just lease. What if we offered to buy the whole place back from her, with the understanding that she could live there in the farmhouse for the rest of her life if she wanted? She'd have a free place to live and her money back in the bank. It's a good deal for her, and for us."

Susan looked surprised, but Finn knew her well enough to know that the idea was intriguing to her. He decided he'd better seal the deal.

"If she says yes, Garrett can manage the orchard, at least initially, which frees the gardens up once again for yours truly."

Susan sighed, smiling and shaking her head. "So that's it. That's what you've been doing up late these last few nights. I knew your mind was fixated on something. You've got it all figured out, don't you? Tell me why I should agree to let you go back to work full time? What about your heart?"

Finn harrumphed, running his hands down the front of his trademark overalls. "Susie, have you seen me lately? I haven't had a proper meal, at least one that didn't contain the words *gluten-free*, in over a year. I'm in better shape now than I've been in my entire life. You've got me sweating to the oldies most mornings, and I've been a willing victim, for crying out loud. I'm a different man. I know to listen to my body, and I promise you, if I feel the least bit stressed, you'll be the first to know."

He stepped closer to her again, reaching down to rub his nose against hers. "Besides, you're the cutest nurse I've ever had. I'd be a fool not to angle for a little of your bedside manner every now and then. I swear. I'll take it easy."

Susan sighed, taking his face in her hands, this man she loved more than anything. "How can I say no when you put it like that? But it's not me you'll have to win over. First you'll have to convince Willow. And I just hope our young farmer likes apples as much as you do."

# CHAPTER
# SIXTEEN

The full moon was shining brightly that night, casting a warm glow over the concert hall, lending an even more festive atmosphere to the evening. The hall was bedecked with luxurious, timeless decorations. There were full and fragrant plumes of evergreen hanging from the rafters, which were wrapped generously in tiny white lights. A stunning twelve-foot Christmas tree was decorated in the theme of crimson and tin, draped in ornaments that had been hand plucked from antique stores near and far.

The terraced seating in the outdoor section of the amphitheater was a cozy way to experience the biggest names in country music, some of whom had already played there during the venue's inaugural season that fall. At the end of each row were baskets of wool blankets, should any of the guests find the night too chilly.

There were a handful of small cocktail tables clustered closer to the front of the stage, reserved for repeat guests. Truth be told, there wasn't a bad seat in the house. The night air was pregnant with the intoxicating smell of wood smoke, which had become the signature scent of the resort. No matter what time of year guests visited, the same incredible aroma always greeted them.

Bartenders were clustered around a full bar, offering some of the finest wines and whiskey in the world. They most certainly had the favorite whiskey of one Sawyer Brantley, who had a special penchant for Pappy Van Winkle. That particular rare bottle was being stored in a spot under the bar, reserved for their resident artist. It had been unearthed in the impressive wine cellar that began below the great hall and stretched under the driveway to connect to another cellar located under the dining room. The labels on the bottles downstairs would make any oenophile worth their salt beg for a private tour. A fortunate few got their wish.

Everyone had taken their seats, and they were snuggled in with hot toddies when the lights dimmed and the man of the hour strolled out onto the stage. Sawyer sat on one of two stools located in the center of the space, with a member of his band beside him. He started out with a story about how he grew up with country music, and from that moment on, he had the audience in the palm of his hand. But it wasn't until the music started, and the audience was collectively hit by the yearning sound of the steel guitar, that Willow felt Garrett's eyes on her.

He'd been sitting on the outskirts of the amphitheater on a ledge made of rocks. He was waiting for her, ready to see her again. They hadn't spent any measurable amount of time together since the night at her place a few days prior. The handful of times they had bumped into each other at work, it was clear to him that she was just as interested as he was. The current between them was palpable, which made him want her even more.

Now, he recognized her expression as she realized she was being watched, and he knew he couldn't wait any longer. When she smiled at him, he discreetly stood and moved along the back of the crowd. She watched him disappear around the side of the hall and head for the shadows, but not before he beckoned for her to join him with just the slightest nod of his head. He didn't need to do more. She was plugged in to him.

Willow murmured parting directions to the bartenders before excusing herself. She walked back through the interior of the hall toward the front doors and out the other side, into the moonlit night. She was trying to decide whether or not he had indeed summoned her with the same intention she had in mind when she heard him say her name from the darkness.

"Willow."

She shivered in anticipation of his touch, aroused by the mere sound of his voice and despite the fact that she wore an oversized sweater that was more than sufficiently warm for the weather.

She turned and waited for her eyes to adjust to the darkness. She could see him now, just barely, in the faint glow of the leftover moonlight that was busy flooding the other side of the hall. Garrett was leaning back against the building, watching her again. The shiver traveled her body now, propelling her toward him. Her mind was trying to figure out what to say, but her body had other ideas.

The space between them seemed to disintegrate when she got close enough for Garrett to reach out and pull her into his embrace. He wasn't interested in a hug. His kiss had a purpose, and it was to let her know she would be busy later. Willow knew she would remember the moment for a long time. It was the time she'd been kissed by a man who solely had her pleasure in mind.

Garrett's initial urgency had given way to a slow exploration of Willow's bottom lip, which he was gently biting and sucking on, causing her to question whether or not she still had legs and feet.

They were vaguely aware of the music floating over the rooftop and meeting them where they were entangled in one another, existing in their own private space. The sexy strains of the guitar sent a charge through them, and despite the fact that Garrett could feel himself losing control, he couldn't have cared less. He slid his hands down her arms and, finding the edge of her sweater, pushed his way underneath, skimming his palms lightly against the warmth of the bare skin on her stomach. Her flesh responded immediately, rising up in goose bumps.

Willow felt her senses explode, and the sound that escaped her throat was his undoing.

Garrett reached down and picked her up so she could wrap her legs around him. Turning around, he pushed Willow up against the barn, still holding her as their mouths met with renewed interest. It wasn't clear how long they were lost in each other, but in time, another song ended, and the applause from the audience brought them back to earth.

Willow uncrossed her ankles and released her grip on him, sliding down the front of his body, which confirmed her suspicions about his state of arousal. To his credit, Garrett knew they both had obligations yet that night, so he stepped back, raking his hand through his hair, trying to gain some shred of composure. Willow commended him for even trying. She still had no use of her lower extremities, and she was leaning against the building looking like she'd just lost a pillow fight at a sleepover.

"My God." It was all she could think to say.

Garrett chuckled, backing away into the shadows once again, winking at her wickedly as he went. "I'll see you later, Willow."

She stood still for a moment, wondering if it had really even happened, before turning to go back into the concert hall the way she'd come.

Sawyer was riding a high, just as he always did when performing. The audience feedback was always like a drug to him, and tonight was particularly rewarding. When he played stadiums and arenas, the spectacle and the lights made it difficult to see the faces of the fans. Tonight, though, in the small venue, the adoration from the audience was tangible. It fed him, and he felt like he could do anything. But he had one particular thing in mind.

He'd seen her earlier that day getting out of her car at the farmhouse just as he was pulling away from his cabin to come over for the sound check. She was stunning, all long legs and masses of dark hair, elegant even in her simple black dress. He'd asked the driver who she was, surprised to find out he was staying on the personal property of the general manager. What a perk. A few questions later, and he'd known her name and that she was single. Perfect. He'd make sure to stop by and introduce himself later.

Sawyer had looked for Willow during the concert, anxious to judge by her expression whether or not she was a fan. He scanned the crowd for most of the show, but it wasn't until late in his set that he finally spotted her. She was exquisite, dressed simply in black jeans, boots, and a sweater that was a little too loose for his taste. He'd have preferred to be able to

admire her hot little body once more. On a positive note, he
didn't know how she'd managed it, but she looked like she'd
just been for a roll in the hay. Her face was flushed, and her
hair was loose and slightly more disheveled looking than it
had been that afternoon.

It all worked for him.

He tried to catch her eye, but she was busy tending to the
needs of the guests, so he left it for later. A few more songs
and a Pappy Van Winkle or two, and he'd be able to do no
wrong.

Lady boss didn't know it yet, but this was going to be her
lucky night.

Willow managed to cut out of the concert early and head
home. She wanted to ensure she had time to herself before
Garrett arrived. She knew that he'd come to see her at the
house, and even now she flushed at the thought. Kicking off
her boots and socks, she padded barefoot through the first
floor, lighting candles here and there. She blushed as she
climbed the stairs to light a few in her bedroom, chiding herself for being such a prude. She knew what she wanted with
him, and she'd waited long enough.

She put out a bottle of Macallan 18 and two rocks glasses,
remembering that he'd mentioned liking Scotch and recalling
the faint taste of it in his kiss from earlier. Her hand instinctively went to her mouth, the feel of his lips against hers still
so fresh.

Willow had just synced Pandora to her speaker, choosing
a country love-song station, when she heard a knock at the
front door. She flipped her hair upside down and shook it out
before flipping it back and giving her cheeks a little pinch.

There. She was ready to embrace her inner vixen. She smiled coyly as she swung the door open, ready to tease him a little before letting him in.

But it wasn't Garrett who was waiting there for her. Sawyer Brantley was standing three feet away on her porch, his guitar in one hand and a bottle of amber-colored liquor dangling from the other. Willow instinctively reached up to smooth her hair and stepped shyly to hide her bare feet behind the door. It didn't seem to faze him one bit.

"Well, I wasn't sure you'd be up for company since the autograph session ran so long, but I'm glad to see I was wrong."

Sawyer cleared the threshold, stepping past her and into the front hall. Looking around, he noted the music and the candles before returning his gaze to Willow, taking her in from tip to toe. He all but licked his lips appreciatively, then turned to set his guitar in the corner by the front door. He held up the bottle, nodding down the hall toward the kitchen. "Mind if I scare up a couple of glasses? I grabbed the good stuff on the way out, and it'd be a shame not to share a glass with the general manager of this fine establishment."

Willow felt herself relax a bit, relieved that Sawyer just wanted a drink. She'd spend just enough time with the man so as not to be rude while still allowing time to get ready for Garrett. She was sure she could get rid of him in time.

*I'll have to grin and bear him.*

*It.*

*Whatever.*

"I'll grab the glasses, and we can sit here in the front room. Make yourself comfortable. That couch is new; it just arrived yesterday. Let me know what you think." Willow rambled as she rushed down the hall to the kitchen, coming back with the same two glasses she had set out for her and Garrett. Retrieving the bottle from where he'd carelessly set it on her new wooden coffee table, she poured two small glasses, then returned the bottle to the table with a coaster underneath it this time.

She handed Sawyer his glass, and he took it willingly. He was now comfortably ensconced on her new sofa, with no signs of leaving anytime soon. She felt a panic bubble up in her, praying he'd finish his drink and leave. She tried to appear casual as she sat down on the other end of the sofa, as far away from him as she could get.

He noticed, and a dark grin spread across his face. "You don't have to be afraid of me. I don't bite. Unless you want me to."

He raised his glass in a silent toast.

Willow felt sick to her stomach. She stood to walk to the door, hoping he'd follow her. "I'm sorry, Mr. Brantley—Sawyer. Please forgive me, but I was expecting someone else tonight."

Willow turned around to explain, only to find that he'd followed her to the foyer, assuming she was headed for the stairs.

He stroked her cheek confidently as he spoke. "Oh, I can be whoever you want, Willow. It's Willow, right?"

He lunged forward to kiss her, and she suddenly snapped out of her shocked state and reached out to slap him. He caught her hand in midair, his eyes looking back at her darkly now. "Hey, that's not usually my thing, but if you like it rough, who am I to say no?"

Sawyer shoved Willow up against a nearby wall, forcing his leg between hers. He crushed his lips against hers, a kiss so different from Garrett's, they didn't deserve to be in the same classification.

Willow was twisting away from him then, unable to say anything but no, over and over again. Suddenly Sawyer was being pulled off her, and it was over. She fell to a heap on the lower steps, holding on to the banister and trying not to black out.

Wyatt had been right. Sawyer Brantley was a total douche bag. Garrett had wanted to like him, since his music had gotten him through the breakup with Lindsay, but it wasn't possible. The guy was the definition of self-absorbed. Garrett had stayed during the autograph session, just to make sure everything went smoothly. From the guests' perspective, it had been a perfect evening. The concert was incredible, and the weather had cooperated as promised.

Sawyer had been more than willing to take pictures with his adoring fans, suggesting they hashtag their photos *#sawyertakestennessee*. That was Garrett's first clue. This wasn't a hashtag kind of crowd, but it was clear that Brantley was hoping for a media bump out of the night. Concerts at the resort were just the opposite. They were intimate and exclusive affairs, which was why guests were willing to pay a premium to attend and artists were excited about the privilege to perform.

Garrett had also stayed behind to offer Sawyer a ride back to his cabin, since Garrett was headed to Willow's anyway. But as the signing was winding down, Garrett had gotten to chatting with two couples who'd wanted to pick his brain about starting heirloom gardens at home. Before he knew it, it was almost midnight, and Sawyer was nowhere to be found. Figuring he'd gotten a ride from someone else, Garrett climbed into his Jeep and headed down the road toward Willow's house. He killed the lights as he swung into the drive, surprised to see one of the resort golf carts parked there. He was trying to figure out who would have driven it all the way from the resort when he glanced up at the house and watched through the front picture window as Sawyer got up off the couch and started walking toward the foyer.

Garrett jumped out of his Jeep, racing up the front steps and coming to a halt just outside the door in disbelief. Brantley had pushed Willow against the wall, where they were kissing. Garrett was stunned still, but only until he realized that Willow was trying to get away from Sawyer. He burst through the door, and, grabbing the back of Brantley's Baby-Gap-looking T-shirt, he threw him to the ground.

Garrett instructed Sawyer to stay there while he scooped Willow into his arms and carried her up to her room, laying her gently on her bed before pulling the covers up around her. She had her eyes squeezed shut, but he knew she was conscious and well enough for him to go back downstairs to chat with Mr. Brantley.

Sawyer attempted to blame the whole thing on a misunderstanding. It quickly became clear to Garrett that, as narcissistic as Brantley was, he'd mistakenly assumed that Willow had been setting the scene for a rendezvous with him. Sawyer apologized profusely before backing out the front door and slinking off into the night like vermin in the direction of his cabin. Garrett doubted the singer would forget this humiliation. He hoped not anyway.

Garrett took the stairs two at a time in an effort to get back to Willow. She had turned away from the door, and he could tell by the soft shaking of her shoulders that she was crying. He wasn't sure she wanted him there, and he didn't know if he should even ask her. Hesitating in the doorway, he had decided to leave her be for the night when he heard her muffled voice ask him a question that changed everything.

"Will you stay with me, Garrett?"

# CHAPTER
# SEVENTEEN

He didn't answer her right away, unsure of what she wanted or needed from him. He'd had the urge to climb into bed beside her and wrap her up in his arms and never let her go, but somehow he'd stopped himself.

Willow sensed his hesitation, so she rolled over to face him again, her eyes shimmering with leftover tears, which she wiped away with the back of her hand. Their eyes met for a moment before she lifted the duvet, inviting him into the bed beside her.

Garrett kicked his boots off and shrugged out of his jacket at the same time. In two strides he was at her bedside, where he paused for a moment before climbing in. He wanted to be respectful and not smother her after what she'd just been through. But once he was next to her, she scooted right over to him, snuggling her head into the crook of his arm and laying her cheek against his chest. He folded her into him, kissing her head and stroking her hair, not able to get close enough no matter how hard he tried. It wasn't arousal he was feeling. This emotion was much more powerful, and it scared him. He couldn't imagine what he would have done if he'd arrived any later.

"I'm so sorry, Garrett. I thought it was you at the door. I shouldn't have let him in, but I was afraid to be rude because of my position here. And then he saw everything I'd done to get ready for you, and he got the wrong idea, but . . ." Her words trailed off. "I'm so lucky you got here when you did."

She let out an involuntary shiver at the thought of what could have happened if he hadn't.

Garrett sat up, bringing her with him, holding her by the shoulders so she was looking squarely at him. "That is the last time I ever want you to apologize for what happened. To anyone. This wasn't your fault, Willow. This was a case of someone who is very bad at reading a situation correctly, and him feeling entitled. I promise you, he won't make that mistake again."

He stared at her, seeing relief flood over her face, but it still wasn't enough to wash away her lingering embarrassment. She shook her head, though, and he agreed to let it go, pulling her close again as they both sank back into the pillows.

Willow could feel his powerful heartbeat calming her by the minute. She started making lazy circles on the top of his chest, feeling his heart rate increase ever so slightly. He reached up and clasped her hand in his, raising it to his lips to kiss it. He smiled at how easy it was to be there with her.

"So, you mentioned that you were getting ready for me. How did you know I'd be coming over? Are you psychic?" He felt her smile against his chest and knew they were going to be OK.

"Well, I guess where I grew up, a guy doesn't kiss a girl like you did earlier and then just leave her to twist in the wind. Besides, you did say you'd see me later. It's later, right?"

She lifted her head to read his expression. He was smiling at her with those kind eyes of his. But he was still holding back, she could feel it. She knew he was worried about her. She decided then and there that she was going to hit the rewind button on this night, refusing to let Sawyer Brantley ruin such an important evening. "Stay right here. I'll be back."

Willow sat up, throwing the covers aside and smiling shyly at him as she walked toward the door. When he looked at her that way, she couldn't help feeling sexy. She was giving him her best flirty face when she tripped over one of his boots, catching herself on the doorway and narrowly avoiding falling on her face. She glanced back at him and saw that he had pulled the covers up over his mouth to hide his laughter.

"Oh, go ahead and laugh now, Garrett. Because when I get back up here, things are going to get serious in a hurry." Willow crooked her eyebrow and flipped her hair over her shoulder as she turned the corner and headed downstairs.

Now she had his attention.

He grinned in anticipation, folding his arms behind his head to wait for her return. She was one hell of a woman. She was soft and vulnerable one minute, but he knew she could kick his ass in a heartbeat if she needed to. He'd never been so turned on.

He didn't hear her coming, but then there she was, turning the corner, careful this time to avoid his boots, which she paused to playfully kick against the wall. In her hands, she held two highball glasses and a bottle of Scotch. The small radio from downstairs was tucked under her arm.

She gave him a sassy look before setting the glasses and radio down on the dresser. She uncapped the Scotch and poured them each two fingers, then walked a glass over to where he lay motionless, watching her every move with interest.

"Try to relax," she teased, noting his carefree position. Willow took a sip of his drink, pausing to swallow it before holding the glass just out of reach so she could gently lean down over him to brush her lips against his. Only then did she stand up and hand him the drink, which he didn't seem to have much interest in anymore.

Crossing the room, she fired up the radio, which was on the country station she'd chosen earlier. Chris Young's voice filled the room. She was taking a sip of her own drink when she felt Garrett behind her.

"We never finished that dance, did we?" He offered his hand, which she took.

They moved together to the sultry song for a few beats before she spoke again. "Truth or dare?"

She pulled away from him just enough to read his face. He looked serious, but there was a twinkle of amusement in his eyes. He'd play.

"Hmm. Truth."

Willow grabbed her Scotch, taking a sip and then offering one to him, which he accepted. Setting the glass back on the dresser, she looked up at him with those liquid brown eyes. "What's your fantasy, Garrett?"

He felt his resolve slip. It seemed impossible for him not to devour her on the spot. He took a breath, then blew it out hard before he answered. "If I'm being honest, Willow, I can't remember any original thought I've ever had prior to this moment."

He stepped toward her, and she thought he was going to kiss her. "This has to be pretty damned close to anything my monkey mind has ever been able to cook up."

Instead of kissing her, he swept her hair over her shoulder, dipping his head so his mouth barely hovered above her neck. He trailed a few soft kisses from her collarbone up to her ear, where he paused with the slightest nip of her earlobe to whisper a question. "Truth or dare?"

Willow forgot they'd been playing the game. Her body was made of liquid, and she felt a little dizzy from the sensation. He continued his teasing, kissing his way around the back of her neck now, holding her against the front of him while he did. She let him, ignoring the roaring in her ears.

"I'm waiting." Garrett wasn't letting her off the hook.

Sighing, she turned to face him again. The heat between them was crazy.

"Dare." She raised her chin in defiance.

He was ready. "I dare you to let me show you how a woman like you should be cherished."

She closed her eyes in response to the raw honesty of his words. She took a moment to let the sentiment wash over her, and before she could think of a reason to say no, she found herself staring back into his eyes and silently nodding her head.

Garrett studied her expression for a moment, so she whispered the word for emphasis, positive that she meant it.

His lips found hers, their mouths working in tandem to communicate everything they were feeling. It was Garrett who pulled back first, checking her face once again for any hesitation. The nod she gave him was almost imperceptible, but it was enough. He reached for the hem of her sweater, lifting it slowly up over her head before dropping it to the floor. He untucked his own shirt, reaching to take it off, but she brushed his hands away.

"Let me."

Watching her graceful fingers make quick work of the buttons on his shirt was hot. He shrugged out of it, letting her then lift his T-shirt over his head.

"My turn."

He reached for her again, unbuttoning her jeans and walking her backward to the edge of the bed. He sat her down, working to slide her legs free, trying hard to ignore the matching black bra and panties she had on underneath. She was a goddess, and for the slightest moment, he wondered if he deserved her. When she slid back up onto the bed with a mischievous but shy smile, he decided that he did.

He rid himself of his own jeans, then climbed up toward her, hovering over the top of her when he got there. If he didn't know better, he'd have thought there was an actual magnetic charge between them, his body wanted hers so badly.

Willow reached up, splaying her palms across his chest and toying with the smattering of hair for a moment before turning her palms and sliding them down his torso and wrapping them around the sides of his hips. When she pulled him down onto her, he broke. They were an unorganized tussle of legs and hands, touching every part of each other, unable to get close enough.

Faith and Tim were singing "I Need You," and the timing couldn't have been more perfect.

This wasn't a want anymore. It was a need. Garrett needed this woman, and not just physically. He was in love with her. It hit him like a twelve-foot tidal wave. He finished undressing her, and then himself. There were a thousand things he could have told her right then, but as he was poised above the center of her, they said everything they needed to with their eyes. Neither of them blinked as he slowly entered her, turning them from two halves into a whole.

Garrett managed to hold still for a split second before his body took over. They moved together as if they'd done so hundreds of times before. He was careful to take it as slow as he could, but he must have been doing something right, because it wasn't long before he felt her shudder, and he knew she'd be meeting him at the top.

When they finally made it there, they were together in every sense. Garrett was murmuring things to her, things that made her feel so beautiful and cherished. They didn't pull apart afterward, instead adjusting to lay on their sides, facing each other.

The kisses were tender now as their breathing slowed and their bodies recognized the late hour. Willow smiled at him, watching as he started to drift off to sleep. His face was even more handsome when he was relaxed that way. She allowed herself to reach up and gently stroke the soft whiskers on his cheek, surprised when his eyes opened and found hers.

They stared at each other, so much between them still unspoken, but it was clear that they had managed to meet in the same place. Garrett was sure he would never get sick of feeling her hand against his cheek. He turned ever so slightly to kiss the tips of her fingers, reaching up to brush the hair that had fallen around her shoulders behind her. She shivered at the sensation of his hand trailing along her bare shoulder.

She smiled. "It was better than I imagined it would be."

He wasn't sure he'd heard her right. He propped his head up on his elbow. "I'm sorry. Are you saying you imagined how this would be between us? Wow, I'm glad I didn't know I had expectations to live up to. Talk about pressure."

Willow giggled, turning around so he was spooning her. "Any expectations I had were eviscerated, believe me. I never knew it could be like this."

She could feel him smiling at that, and she turned to look over her shoulder. She could see that he was proud of himself, and she laughed at the honesty of his expression. "Would you like me to move so you can sit up and pound your chest?"

They laughed together, and she nuzzled into him.

Willow wasn't ready for the night to end, hoping they could stay together in the hazy afterglow of their first time together a little longer. In a few hours it would be dawn, and they'd never have this first night back.

Willow slid out of his embrace, reaching down to the floor to find Garrett's T-shirt. Slipping it over her head, she got out of bed and headed toward the bathroom, stopping at the window. "Garrett, it's snowing!"

She stood there watching the big fat snowflakes drifting through the moonlit night. Garrett couldn't believe how beautiful she looked standing there in his shirt and nothing else. She turned, grinning at him.

"Let's go for a walk! When are we going to get this chance again?"

Garrett shook his head and laughed, but he tossed the duvet aside and reached down for his jeans to slide them on. He walked over to look out at the snow, which had dusted the lawn with a blanket of white. He spotted the golf cart and had an idea.

"If we're going to do this, I'd better bundle up, because we're going to take that golf cart back to the resort. I can't believe that idiot drove it over here. He's lucky he wasn't killed. The middle of the night is the only safe time to return it, so this is a perfect opportunity. I'll drive the cart, and you follow me in the Jeep. We'll leave it by the garden shed. I want to show you something anyway."

He dipped down to give her a long, lingering kiss. She started to turn toward him, the spark reignited just like that, but Garrett stepped back. "If we don't leave now, I'm never letting you out of here. Find that horrible sweater, and let's go."

He slapped her teasingly on the behind, sending her into fits of laughter as they fumbled around to get dressed.

It had seemed like a good idea, but by the time they'd made it to the garden shed, Garrett could barely feel his hands and face. The fields were covered in a blanket of snow now, which hadn't been forecasted. It was magical, though, glowing in the moonlight.

He was unlocking the shed when Willow walked up next to him. He gestured for her to go inside first before following her and closing the door behind them.

It was still chilly inside, but Garrett felt a million times warmer than he had five minutes before. He found a pack of matches and struck one, then lit the small kerosene lantern that was sitting on the workbench.

Willow looked around the cozy space. She'd been in here only a couple of times, and never at night. There were bowls of seeds stacked all over the place and baskets of root vegetables that had been dug out as recently as a few days ago. It had an honest, earthy smell that appealed to her.

Garrett was unwrapping something from a piece of burlap, slowly revealing a small tree, which he set on the end of the workbench, a proud, shy smile on his face. "I was going to wait for Christmas, but this seems like the right time to give this to you. Willow, meet your very own apple tree."

He handed her a small framed document. She held it up next to the lantern.

Willow Twig Apple: The origin of this apple is rather obscure but generally believed to have arisen in Virginia in the mid-1800s. The tree is very attractive, with a drooping appearance similar to willow trees. A medium to large apple, conical in shape, and sometimes slightly ribbed. Smooth yellowish-green skin blushed with dull red stripes and splashes. The yellowish flesh is coarse, crisp, and juicy. Ripens in October and an excellent keeper, remaining fresh and firm until March or later.

Willow looked up at Garrett, who was watching her read.

"I think it sounds like you. Rare, very attractive, and an excellent keeper. Seemed like the perfect gift for a one-of-a-kind woman. It took some searching, but I finally found one."

Willow had her hand pressed high against her chest. She couldn't believe how thoughtful he was. She opened her mouth to thank him, but she couldn't find the words. She walked toward him and reached up on her tiptoes to kiss him.

They caught fire again, just like that.

He picked her up and then placed her down next to her apple tree on the workbench.

Garrett found another way to warm them up in a hurry.

# CHAPTER
# EIGHTEEN

Willow woke up on Christmas Eve morning to the peaceful sounds of a UPS truck roaring into her driveway. She'd gotten only a couple hours of sleep. Not only was she exhausted, but her body felt like she'd been doing yoga for forty-eight hours straight. She stretched like a cat, reaching over for Garrett and finding nothing but cool sheets. She lifted her head to spot a note on his pillow, along with a single apple on the nightstand. Smiling, she grabbed the note and opened it.

> *What a perfect night.*
> *Ran home to change, but I'll see you soon for breakfast.*
> *Don't forget about the meeting with Finn and Susan at ten.*
> *Hope Santa brings you what you want tonight.*
> *XO,*
> *Garrett*

She sat straight up in bed, searching wildly for the clock, which had somehow ended up on the floor upside down. Leaping out of bed, she grabbed it and cried out when she saw it was already 9:16 a.m.

Willow was rushing into the bathroom when she heard a knock at the door. Throwing on her robe, she hurried down the stairs to find the UPS guy standing on the porch. When he saw her, he indicated he needed a signature to leave her the envelope he was holding. She signed quickly, glancing at the return address as she shut and locked the door behind her. It was from her father's attorney, which was strange. She thought she'd dotted all her i's and crossed her t's in regard to finalizing his estate planning. Anyway, there was no time to look at it now, so she tossed it on the foyer table for later. If she didn't hit the shower immediately, everyone at the morning meeting would know what she'd been up to all night. The thought made her blush.

And incidentally, she knew exactly what she wanted from Santa.

Bluegrass Christmas music was playing softly when Garrett entered the barn. He could smell the beginnings of what would be an unforgettable holiday meal that evening for the guests of the resort. The Christmas goose was in the oven, and all sorts of savory aromas wafted out to greet him.

Chefs were busy in the kitchen, but the dining room was empty for now, since breakfast was served in the Dogwood and handled by a separate team of chefs. The barn was used only for dinners and, in this case, the morning meeting with upper management.

Garrett felt his stomach growl and realized he was ravenous from his long night. He headed for the coffee station that was set up in the demonstration kitchen where they would be meeting. He was adding three packets of sugar to his cup when he felt someone clap him on the shoulder.

"Merry Christmas, Garrett." Wyatt gestured to the large black coffee in his friend's hand. "Long night?"

Wyatt could tell from Garrett's exhausted face it had been, but he didn't get much in the way of an answer. He decided to break the news about that morning's excitement. "Don't know if you've heard yet, but Sawyer Brantley couldn't get out of here fast enough this morning. The bell staff got a call just after midnight saying he had a family emergency and that he needed them to call him a car to take him to the airport. I guess he had a jet waiting for him there at two in the morning to head back to Nashville."

Wyatt paused, watching for any indication that Garrett knew about the middle-of-the-night drama. Either his friend had a great poker face or he truly didn't know anything. Rumor had it Garrett's Jeep was parked at Willow's house when the bellman went to help Brantley transport his luggage to the car.

Which was newsworthy, regardless.

Either way, Wyatt was happy to be rid of the singer, and from the look on Garrett's face, he wasn't terribly sad to hear about Sawyer's departure either.

"So what did you do last night after the concert?" Wyatt innocently took a sip of his own coffee, trying to look nonchalant while he waited for the answer.

Garrett was about to tell him what he could do with his question when they heard the others enter the barn. "We'll finish this later, wise guy," Garrett mumbled under his breath, leaving Wyatt snickering behind him.

Finn and Susan were walking toward them with India, who was pushing the babies in a double stroller. Once they'd all said hello and settled in, Wyatt reached down and picked up his daughter, then turned to Garrett.

"Would you like to hold the most beautiful girl in the world, my friend? Go on. She won't bite. She might projectile vomit, but it's no biggie. It's like when a bird poops on you. It's good luck."

Garrett threw Wyatt another sideways glance before gingerly taking Marley in his arms. Looking down at her, he couldn't believe how small and perfect she was.

Wyatt had picked up his son and was staring with reverence at Dylan. He never got tired of gazing at his miracles. "I make pretty nice babies, don't I?"

Garrett had automatically started mimicking the bounce that he saw Wyatt doing, the two of them swaying together to a bluegrass version of "Deck the Halls." It was at that moment that the door to the barn opened with a whoosh, and Willow rushed in toward them, slowing her pace when she saw the men holding the babies.

India smiled at her friend and then shrugged her shoulders, secretly pleased at the look on her friend's face. Something was different between Willow and Garrett now. She'd bet on it. "Look at these two, Willow. My husband is busy taking credit for 'his' beautiful babies while tormenting poor Garrett with tales of vomit and leaky diapers."

Garrett's head snapped up at that last part. "Whoa, no one said anything about leaky diapers. Whose turn is it to hold Marley?" He turned to Willow, his eyes pleading.

They all laughed, and after she set her bag down and took her coat off, Willow was happy to take the beautiful baby girl so that India could have a break during the meeting.

They spent the first few minutes going over the holiday rundown for the next several days. Aside from the festive dinners, there were usually sleigh rides to coordinate and ice-skating on Walland Pond, but only if the weather was cold enough. The late-night snow was a good sign, and the temperature that morning was unseasonably cold with more snow in the forecast. Snowshoeing was offered too, and for guests who preferred staying inside, it was a safe bet that the Farmhouse Spa would be a popular destination over the next week.

Once Christmas and New Year's were over, the resort entered a quiet period, switching the focus from decadent feasts to wellness and resolutions, along with workshops like the photography week where Wyatt and India had met almost three years ago. Violet and Rex would be teaching that once again in March.

"This brings me to the real reason I wanted to meet with you all today," said Finn, looking around at the group of young people who he admired so much. His eyes came to rest on Willow.

"Young lady, I've told you how happy we are that you bought the Thompson orchard. We're so grateful to you for letting our musical guests stay in your cabin too."

Finn paused, looking from Wyatt to Garrett. "Although I hear this last fella was a bit of a horse's ass."

"Finn Janssen!" Susan looked mortified, but Finn just kept on going.

"That's even more of a reason to consider what I'm about to propose, Willow."

India reached over to take Marley so that Willow could concentrate on what Finn was saying.

"The Thompson property is one I've had my eye on for years. The only reason I didn't make a play for it is because we were in Hawaii when it went on the market, which I never thought was possible. I've talked to Fred Thompson since the sale, and he told me that the only reason he didn't contact me is because he knew that I'd want to run the place like I ran the gardens here, and he knew that Susie expected me to slow down."

Finn looked over at his wife, who grabbed his hand, nodding for him to go on. This had to come from him.

"I would never ask you to give this property up if it's really your dream, and I may be wrong, but I suspect you fell in love with the house, and the orchard just happened to come with it. It's a lot to think about, and the workload is tremendous."

He turned to Garrett. "Here's where you come in, Garrett. I know I've told you that the resort gardens will be yours to run when I'm officially retired, but that's just it; I don't think that's going to be as soon as you hope."

Garrett put his hand up, wanting a moment to clarify but not wanting to interrupt. "Finn, I promise you, I've got all the time in the world. I'm not sitting around waiting for you to be put to pasture. Heck, if I'm being honest, I was shocked you'd agreed to the whole idea so willingly. I know you still have so much more to give, and I'm happy to be around for as many seasons as you'll continue to share your knowledge with me. Being your second fiddle is a better job than most men will ever have running their own place."

Finn reached across the table and shook Garrett's hand. "Son, you're a credit to your grandparents. They raised you right, which also confirms that my instincts were spot on about you. We need you in our foxhole. But I'm about to suggest something that might come as a surprise to both of you."

He glanced back and forth between Garrett and Willow. "Willow, we're wondering if you'd consider selling the orchard to us so that we could officially make it part of the resort? You could live in that house until you have gray hair and grand-kids, for all we care. Consider it yours. We love having you close and know you're going to be a longtime member of our work family. But this would protect you, and protect the resort, from a paperwork standpoint. It would also allow for us to have an official stewardship over the orchard."

Finn looked back to Garrett, and he could see the big picture was dawning on him now.

"That's your department. Garrett, we would like to propose that you be chiefly in charge of running and managing the orchard, and the other fields and crops on the property."

Finn took a deep breath before finishing. "Selfishly, that would give me my purpose back and allow me to manage the fields here, with the help of the rest of the garden staff, of course. I'd love to work closely with you, Garrett, on getting started, because I agree that we can learn a lot from each other. Your grandparents had knowledge of apple growing in Washington State that I know you'll share with us here. I really think it's a win-win. So what do you say?"

Finn sat back, relieved to have the asking behind him. Finn liked to have his hands in the dirt much better than he enjoyed being the pitch man at a staff meeting.

Willow didn't know what to say. She was exhausted from little to no sleep, and a huge decision felt like more than she could tackle just then. She looked over at Garrett to see how he was handling the news, but he was just staring back at her, taking the lead from her.

She must have looked as stunned as she felt, because Susan stood up to come and sit next to her on the sofa and take her hand. "I know it's a lot to consider, Willow, and we certainly don't expect you to decide immediately. Take time to think about it, and we'll circle back when you're ready to discuss it."

She smiled warmly at the girl, hoping what she would say next would help and not hurt the cause. "We'd actually like to ask one more favor of you, if you'd consider it?"

Willow nodded, waiting to hear what came next.

"You might be aware that we have a pretty big presence at Aspen's Food and Wine Classic in Colorado every summer. Finn and I have just closed on a second home there so that we'll have a base when we're in town for the festival, and obviously during other times of the year. We'd really like to expand our professional footprint out West, so we're looking to acquire another property in Aspen. Ideally, it would be set out of town on some land, to be used as a place to host guests of ours who would like to have the Walland experience in Aspen, both during Food and Wine and year-round. We plan to call it Walland House. We think that you'd be the perfect person to help us select the property, based on your performance here so far. You know our aesthetic better than anyone besides Wyatt and India, but they have their hands full right now. Finn and I have been traveling so much, it feels good for us to be home right now. Would you do us the honor of heading up that project for a few weeks in Aspen? It's a quiet time of year here, so between India and myself, we can hold down the fort. Here's the catch: you'd be leaving the second week of January. You're welcome to take someone with you if that sweetens the deal? And then perhaps you'll be ready to discuss the proposition that Finn mentioned when you get back. What do you say?"

India couldn't help herself. She was excited about this opportunity for her friend. "Oh, Willow, don't say no! If you've never been to Aspen, you'll absolutely love it. And you'll be going at a great time. The holidays are just ending, so it will be a little quieter, but there is still plenty to do. It's a winter wonderland."

India turned to Susan, a twinkle in her eye. "You never cease to amaze me. I knew you guys bought the house there, but I had no idea about these new plans! What a wonderful way to expand our brand, and in such a special place. When did all of this happen?"

Susan laughed, shaking her head in disbelief. "Would you believe me if I told you it was just over the past couple of days? I guess I've been taking Finn on too many vacations, allowing for a lot of time to daydream. Now he's rubbing off on me. Who knows what we'll come up with next?"

Garrett was watching Willow, anxious to hear what she would decide to do. He knew it was an incredible opportunity for her to establish herself as an important member of the team, but he couldn't imagine three weeks without her after what they'd just shared. As if she could read his mind, she looked at him, a silent question in her eyes that he wished he could answer.

Willow was trying to figure out how to ask Susan and Finn the only question she cared about in that moment. She knew that, by doing so, she'd be laying her cards on the table in a way that terrified her.

*This is what it must feel like to skydive,* she thought, right before she asked the question.

"I'll go to Aspen, on one condition. How would you feel about me taking Garrett with me?"

The room went so quiet you could have heard a pin drop.

# CHAPTER
# NINETEEN

If she didn't know better, Willow would've thought that the waitstaff was whispering about her and Garrett all during Christmas Eve dinner. She realized she was just being paranoid, because they'd all agreed that morning that, even though the proverbial cat was out of the bag within their inner circle, it would be better for everyone if this new relationship remained as private as possible.

Finn and Susan had been surprised to learn of the romance between them, but they were very gracious about it and even seemed to enjoy being in cahoots about keeping it a secret for now.

Willow had just said good-bye to the last guests of the evening, wishing everyone a Merry Christmas as they headed off to their accommodations for the night. She was taking the time to check out the reservations book for brunch the next morning when she felt her phone buzz in her pocket.

It was Garrett, letting her know he was waiting outside for her. He'd left a couple of hours ago, saying there was something he had to take care of before he called it a night. She hadn't had much time to wonder what he was up to; she'd spent all of her free time during dinner making sure to visit with each and every family that had chosen to spend their holidays in Walland.

She said good night to the staff and wished them all a Merry Christmas, since she herself had the day off tomorrow and wouldn't be working. Pulling on her coat and grabbing her bag, she stepped out into the driveway.

Garrett was waiting beside his Jeep to open the door for her. His wipers were busy tending to the snowflakes that were falling as if on cue on this perfect Walland Christmas Eve. She had the urge to brush the flakes from Garrett's hair, but she caught herself at the last minute, just in case anyone could see them from inside the barn.

Once they were in his Jeep, Garrett pulled down the road, stopping in front of the automatic gate at the edge of the property. He reached over to grab her hand, bringing it to his mouth for a kiss. "Have you finished your Christmas list yet? Only a couple of hours until Santa arrives."

He loved to tease her, knowing she'd reward him with that smile.

"I think it's safe to say I've already gotten my gift this year. I can't believe you're coming to Aspen with me! I mean, it was slightly mortifying to have to ask that of Susan and Finn, who clearly had no idea we were—well, whatever we are, I guess." Willow looked at him shyly. "And you know Wyatt is never going to let you hear the end of this. He looked like he had about a dozen things to say to you but had the presence of mind to mess with you later, out of earshot of his wife."

Garrett laughed at the memory of his friend's stunned face. He would get the business from Wyatt, that was for certain. But he could care less. He was going to Aspen with Willow for three weeks. Merry Christmas, indeed.

"You're right. This is kind of the best Christmas ever."

They pulled into her driveway, and the house seemed especially dark. Only the porch lights were on. The yard was covered in snow, and the storm had picked up in intensity since they'd left the barn a few minutes earlier.

"That's weird. I thought I left the foyer light on, and I almost always leave my bedroom lights on too. I must have really been in a hurry when I left this morning."

Willow could see Garrett smiling as he walked around the front of the car to open her door for her.

He took her by the hand, leading her up onto the porch. Reaching into his pocket, he pulled out a necktie, holding it up for her to see. "Don't take this the wrong way, but I'm going to need you to put this on. Like a blindfold. I have a little surprise for you. I know we aren't doing gifts, but this is different."

Willow stared at him, dumbfounded. When had he had time for this? Today had been a blur, and neither of them had gotten any sleep last night. She couldn't make her mind understand. "OK, if you want me to put it on, I trust you."

She took the tie, wrapping it around her eyes and fastening it behind her head. Garrett grabbed her hand and led her through the front door and down the hall. She could hear music, and the room was warm, so she figured he must have lit a fire. But when he lifted the blindfold from her face, she couldn't believe her eyes.

There in her still-empty hearth room stood a beautifully lit and decorated real Christmas tree. It smelled incredible. She was right about the fire too, which was crackling in the hearth. Under the tree, he had recreated her bed from upstairs, her fluffy white duvet and half a dozen pillows spread out on the floor. The bottle of Scotch and two glasses were sitting nearby.

She turned to him, and he couldn't help thinking this is what she must have looked like as a kid. She was flush with excitement, squealing and grabbing him around the neck.

"Oh, Garrett, this is incredible! I mean, I can't think of a better surprise! I've never spent one Christmas without a tree, even a little crappy one when I had my small place in Park City. This year, there just wasn't time. How did you manage this?" She was alternately kissing his face and turning back around to admire the scene before her.

Garrett was touched by her delight. He knew she'd be surprised, but he had no idea the tree would be that meaningful to her. "I've had my eye on that tree for a while, thinking it would be a real show-off at Christmas. I asked last week over at the Great Hall if they had any leftover decorations, and they did, so I squirreled those away in your barn. Tonight, I left early, chopped down the tree, and spent the last couple of hours trying to provide you the memorable Christmas Eve you deserve."

She was still now as she listened to him explain the time and energy he'd spent on her before they'd even shared last night. He was an incredibly thoughtful man, and she knew how lucky she was to have met him. She stepped forward, pressing herself against him and grabbing his hands at his sides. "I can't tell you what this means to me, Garrett. No one has ever treated me with such kindness. I'm so grateful to have this memory with you. It's another night I'll never forget, and I hope that you won't either."

Garrett bent down to rest his forehead against hers. "I'm the lucky one, Willow. You gave me a second chance after our misfire in August, and I can promise you I won't need a third. I can't wait to spend time with you in Colorado, but if I'm being honest, I can't think about much more than right here, right now."

He captured her mouth with his, feverishly running his hands up her arms and into her hair, where he was better able to control the kiss. He felt her shrugging out of her coat, letting it drop to the floor, so he did the same without breaking from her. Their hands made quick work of the rest of the clothing that was a boundary between them, and before long, they stood bathed in the glow of nothing but the Christmas tree lights. The fire had burned down to a low flame at that point, but there was enough heat between them that the chill in the room went unnoticed.

Garrett stepped back to look at her, letting out a low whistle of appreciation. "You are a vision. Really. I'm not worthy."

The old Willow would have been self-conscious under a gaze that intense, but Garrett's smoldering eyes just made her feel even more beautiful and confident. She allowed herself the luxury of appreciating this man who stood before her in all his glory. His body was magnificent, chiseled in all the right places from his hard work in the gardens. He had the V that started at his hip bones and directed her to the core of him, which was letting her know that he wanted her with everything he had.

Garrett scooped her up into his arms before gently setting her down on the blankets and pillows he had spread on the floor. He picked up the duvet cover and wrapped it around his back, and, with a wicked look on his face, he swooped down over her, covering them both with the feathery coverlet.

The things he did to her under those goose feathers would paint her dreams long after that night. He made her feel like a woman. A powerful, confident, sexy woman. She'd already been to the edge and back when he finally joined with her, the two of them finding their rhythm once again in the wonderland he'd created for them. They watched each other as the crescendo built, and at the moment of their climax, they felt connected to each other on a soul level.

Garrett shifted slightly so they were lying side by side, still staring at each other in awe. He reached up to stroke her hair, letting his fingers trail down her cheek, shoulder, side, and coming to rest on her hip bone. It was a long time before either of them spoke.

Willow wanted to know everything about this man. "What's your best Christmas memory ever—not including this one?"

She kissed him deeply in order to punctuate her question, in case there was any doubt that this took the prize.

Garrett rolled onto his back, folding his hands behind his head to think for a moment. "There isn't really anything that comes close to this." He shot her a sideways glance. "But if I had to choose a second, I'd say it was the year I got my BMX bike."

He was smiling up at the ceiling at the memory.

Willow stared at him for a minute before she burst into laughter, sitting up to reach for the bottle of Scotch. She poured them a glass to share before turning over and propping herself on her elbows to take a sip and stare once again at the tree. "Men really are simple creatures, aren't they? A BMX bike? That's your second place to this? Well, I guess I should be glad it wasn't a pet snake or something."

She giggled again, bending her knees and crossing her ankles behind her as she sipped at the Scotch.

"Hey. Are you gonna share that or what?" Garrett sat up and swatted her on the rear end, reaching for the glass, which she willingly handed to him.

"So what's your second-favorite memory?" He was having a hard time concentrating with her looking so relaxed and beautiful. And naked. But he fought hard to focus.

Willow knew her answer without a doubt. "It was the year my parents told me what they'd gone through to have me."

Garrett studied her thoughtfully.

"I was twelve years old when they told me, and I remember feeling so loved. My mother spent the better part of her thirties and forties trying to get pregnant, only to suffer miscarriage after miscarriage. She delivered two of my siblings stillborn at full-term. Most people would have quit, but they fought to have me. Those people went through hell to be my parents. Finally, at forty-nine years old, my mother had the daughter she'd always wanted. Anyone can have a baby by accident, but do you know how loved you feel when you're raised by two people who made a conscious decision to push through every obstacle put in their way? Every Christmas, I'm reminded of that conversation we had, and the incredibly loving parents I was blessed with."

Garrett was blown away. "You are something else, Willow Armstrong. I've never known anyone quite like you. I only wish I'd met you years ago. I can't imagine that kind of parental love or devotion. My mother was a drug addict, and she never even knew who my father was. She fought my grandparents' decision to move me from Seattle to their farm, but in truth, she couldn't have cared for me the way she needed to. She overdosed when I was nine. I was very fortunate that my grandparents were willing to keep me and raise me, even though it took me well into my teen years to stop resenting them for keeping me from my mom."

Willow could see the pain in his eyes as he spoke, and it broke her heart. "I'm so sorry, Garrett. Addiction is a horrible disease. You must know that your mom wanted you too, in her own way, but she couldn't have done right by you in that condition. Thank God your grandparents were caring enough to intervene—they probably saved your life. Don't beat yourself up for not knowing that as a child. The way you turned out, they obviously did right by you, raising an amazing man. I'm grateful to them."

Garrett pulled her close, both of them fighting the exhaustion that had been building over the past thirty-six hours. They fell asleep that way, snuggled together under the tree in her farmhouse. The last conscious thought Willow had before drifting off was that she loved this man. Whatever her plans for the future turned out to be, Garrett Oliver would be a major part of them.

She knew he was awake the next morning because she felt him gently stroking her back. She cracked one eye open to peek at him and was rewarded with that smile of his. She felt her stomach clench. She could get used to this. He'd been propped up on one elbow watching her, but now he rested his head back down on the pillow so they were face-to-face.

"Merry Christmas."

She smiled at him. "Merry Christmas to you."

"So, what are we?"

Willow crinkled her brow questioningly. "What do you mean?"

Garrett had stopped rubbing her back, reaching his hand up now to stroke her cheek. "Last night, you said 'whatever we are.' So, what are we? I mean, I have an idea, but I'd love to get it in writing this morning if you have a pen around here somewhere."

Willow laughed. "Are you asking me to officially be your girlfriend? Do I need to check yes or no? Because I'd definitely check yes." She turned on her side, nuzzling closer to him and placing a kiss on his neck. "I could get up and find a pen, or you could just take my word for it and let me show you."

Garrett decided that paperwork was overrated. He took his sweet time unwrapping the best present he'd ever gotten.

# CHAPTER
# TWENTY

They spent the rest of Christmas morning together puttering around in her kitchen. Garrett surprised Willow with his culinary skills, whipping up two simple omelets and toast while Willow sat at the counter watching him work. It helped that he was barefoot and wearing only his jeans, his face a little extra scruffy since he didn't have any of his personal items with him. She thought how nice it would be if they could spend the rest of the day together too, but she knew he'd need to leave to get cleaned up and changed.

"You know, I've never seen your place in Knoxville. Didn't you tell me you're in the Sterchi Lofts? I've heard they're so cool. When am I going to get a look at your world?"

She admired him openly as he walked toward her carrying two plates, one of which he set down in front of her, leaning over for a kiss while he was in the neighborhood. She ran her hands up his bare chest, not able to resist when he was so close. The eggs weren't as hot when they finally turned their attention back to their food.

"Funny you should mention my place. I was just thinking about inviting you over for New Year's Eve. I'm on the top floor, so I have a pretty good view of the fireworks they set off in Market Square. I could make you dinner, and we could get into a nice bottle of wine and see what happens."

Willow laughed, but she thought it sounded perfect. "I'm so glad you don't want to go out for a big night on the town. I guess this is a good time to tell you that I'm a bit of a homebody. Not that I won't go out occasionally and let loose, but New Year's Eve is amateur night in my opinion. Mingling with the drunk masses isn't my idea of a great time. But it's an important night. Let's dress up anyway."

Willow had gotten up that morning and thrown Garrett's flannel shirt on, and now, as she sat at the counter with her hair in a topknot and her feet tucked under the stool, he thought she'd never looked more lovely. "Damn, girl, if you look this good first thing in the morning, I can't wait to see you all dressed up."

He reached over for another kiss, which she happily gave him.

They finished breakfast and were cleaning up when he decided to pick her brain. "We haven't really talked about what Finn is proposing to do with your orchard. What do you think about all that?"

He watched her as she dried the dish he handed her and set it back in the cupboard above her head.

She shrugged her shoulders and threw the towel over her shoulder, leaning back against the counter to look at him. "I don't know what to think. I mean, it was love at first sight with this place. I know it's a lot of property, but all I see when I look at it is potential."

She sighed, dropping her head to study the floor. "But I'd be lying if I said I wasn't a little overwhelmed at the thought of being in charge of it all. Maybe it's a gift that they want to buy it for the resort. I guess it makes sense too, since they are already using the guest cabin. But for the first time in a while, owning this place made me feel like I wasn't so rudderless. It was good to set down roots for a change. It's hard to say if agreeing to sell it, even if I do get to still live here, would diminish that feeling of security."

She bit her lip, waiting for him to say something, but he was quiet, letting her talk. She walked around and sat back down at the counter, continuing her thought. "The idea of you running the orchard is certainly appealing. But is that what you want to do? I don't want you to feel trapped into being around me twenty-four seven. I mean, I finally land you as my boyfriend, and now you're forced to work right outside my front door? It seems like that might be a whole lotta Willow time for you."

Garrett chuckled as he walked over to sit next to her and reached to pull her stool closer to him, his knees on either side of hers. He looked directly into her eyes. "I'm fine with Willow time. In case you hadn't noticed, I'm borderline stalking you at this point. I mean, I broke into your house to put up a Christmas tree last night. If that didn't have you calling the authorities, I think we're in a pretty good place."

He rested his palms on her knees and tilted his head down to recapture her gaze. "I want this decision to be yours, Willow. This is your place, and it affects you much more than me. I meant what I said when I told Finn that I'm just happy to wake up every day and get to do what I love. It doesn't matter where I do it. Here is what I propose. Let's go to Aspen. Get lost in the mountains, help Finn and Susan however we can. Make love. Yep, definitely make love. And at the end of the three weeks, you'll know what's right. If not, then don't make a decision. They aren't going to fire you for not being ready to decide something so monumental. One day at a time, OK?"

She rose from her stool, leaning into him to embrace him. "Thank you for that. You're right. It will keep, for now."

Wrapped in her arms, Garrett could visualize a reality in which they never left that house again. But he knew they should probably get out and do something. He dropped a soft kiss on the side of her neck before sitting up to look at her. "I have an idea. It's rare for us to have snow on Christmas Day. Let's bundle up and go snowshoeing. I should run home and get changed anyway, so I can grab some warmer gear while I'm there. I'll be back by noon, and we can head out and enjoy the day together. What do you say?"

Even though she didn't like the idea of missing out on two hours with him, Willow thought it sounded like a great way to spend the afternoon.

She stood at the door a short while later, watching him brush the snow off his Jeep while he warmed it up. Waving good-bye as he pulled away, she shut and locked the door and was turning to walk upstairs when she spotted the UPS envelope on the counter where she'd tossed it the day before. She grabbed it, pulling the cord to open it on her way up to the bathroom. She reached in to start the shower and glanced at the paperwork while she waited for the water to heat up.

The shower had almost run cold by the time she got over the shock of what she'd just read.

Garrett didn't waste any time getting in and out of Knoxville. Before he could talk himself out of it, he'd packed a small duffle bag worth of clothing that would get him through a few days, just in case he got invited for a sleepover in Walland. He didn't want to presume, but he couldn't think of a reason why they shouldn't be together as much as they wanted to, especially since they'd be spending three weeks out West very soon.

He'd just thrown his bag into the backseat of his Jeep and was pulling out of his building when his phone lit up. It was Wyatt, calling to wish him a Merry Christmas. They chatted for a few, and it was decided that Wyatt, India, Violet, and Rex would join Willow and Garrett for snowshoeing, and then they would all go back to Wyatt and India's for drinks afterward.

Garrett knew Willow wouldn't mind, but he shot her a quick text when he stopped at the store to pick up a bottle of wine to take with them to Wyatt's place. Within moments she'd answered him, agreeing to meet everyone at the garden shed in an hour, where Garrett had several pairs of snowshoes stored.

By the time he pulled up, everyone else had already arrived, having dropped the kids off to be with Finn and Susan for a few hours. Garrett had to stop himself from walking over to Willow and letting her know how much he'd missed her during their two hours apart. Instead, he simply smiled at her, wondering why she seemed distracted. Maybe it was just awkward for her to express her feelings openly in front of their friends. There would be time for that, so he didn't give it much thought.

They spent a good two hours hiking around the property, joking and laughing with each other. It was an easy group, so Wyatt coined them the Six-Pack. They chatted about taking a trip together sometime, without directly addressing the newest relationship among them. It was so obvious that Garrett and Willow were crazy about each other, so it was hard not to talk about it. They were taking their gear off at Wyatt and

India's when Rex couldn't hold his tongue any longer. The four of them were finished and standing by, watching as Garrett's hands lingered on Willow's leg as he helped her out of her snowshoe.

"Vi, I never thought we'd be the old married couple in the group, but watching these two circle each other has got me thinking we might need a date night pretty darn soon. I'll have what they're having, for sure. Come on, just kiss her already, Garrett."

Willow burst out laughing when Garrett shot up from his seated position, holding his hands out at his sides, in a posture of innocence. "What, you can't pick on Wyatt anymore because he's sleep deprived and his reflexes aren't that quick, so now I'm your new punching bag? Bring it, Rex."

The women were cracking up now, especially at Wyatt's wounded expression. He fancied himself the funny man of the group and didn't take kindly to the knock on his comedic prowess. "Whoa, leave me out of this. Besides, my wife is about to have her six-week checkup, so things are looking up around my house, boys. Literally and figuratively."

India rolled her eyes and jokingly mouthed the word "no" to the girls when Wyatt turned his back. They made their way into the family room, laughing all the way. The guys flipped on the television, and Wyatt went to work building a fire while the ladies moved into the kitchen to see about snacks and drinks.

They chatted about the kids, and Violet had them both laughing when she told a story about Sadie trying to wrap her baby brother in paper and bows so that Santa might deliver him to another family. She was making it known lately that she preferred being an only child and the sole receiver of all parental attention.

Willow took a deep breath and decided to confide in her friends. "Speaking of only children, I got some interesting news this morning. Turns out, I'm not one."

Willow waited for her news to sink in. When it was clear she'd stunned them into silence, she continued. "Well, I might not be. My father's attorney sent me a letter saying he'd heard from a woman who says she had an affair with my father over two decades ago. She doesn't have a claim, per se, but she has an almost-twenty-seven-year-old son who just might. His name is Logan."

Violet had just uncorked a bottle of wine, so she quickly poured Willow a glass, handing it over. "Oh, honey, I'm so sorry. That must have come as a shock. How will you know if the claim is a legitimate one? Will they do DNA testing or something?"

Willow took a swallow, nodding her head. "They've already done his test, so once they get mine, they'll have one of the most respected labs in the country analyze the findings, per my father's attorney's request. The problem is, it can take three to four weeks to get results. And here is where it gets interesting. Logan lives in Colorado Springs. Can you believe it? I couldn't help myself. I called him this morning, and we got to talking. He wants to meet me when Garrett and I are in Aspen, and I said yes."

She bit her lip, waiting for them to respond.

India spoke first. "Do you think that's a good idea? I mean, I'm sure he's nice, but I'd hate for you to get attached to him and find out the claim is bogus. That would be uncomfortable. Honestly, though, I don't know if I would have done things any differently. I'm an only child, so I get it. The idea of having a sibling after all these years must be intriguing."

"Have you told Garrett?" Violet asked.

"Told me what?" He was standing at the threshold of the kitchen, having come looking for Willow.

Willow stood up to walk over to him, smiling, and took his hands. "Don't worry. I'm not married, and I don't have a deadly disease that I know of. But what I may have is a brother."

India raised her eyebrows at Violet, and they both stood up. "We'll give you two a minute."

The women grabbed the drinks and food and scooted around Willow and into the family room.

Garrett was staring at Willow with a puzzled expression. "I thought you said you were an only child? I don't understand."

Willow led him over to the kitchen table and sat across from him, not letting go of his hand. "This is news to me too. I received a letter yesterday that I remembered to open when you left this morning. I'm as stunned as you are. I've been told my entire life that I'm an only child. But there's a woman who is claiming that my father also had a son. The product of an affair with her that happened decades ago."

She explained the DNA test and how she'd come to invite Logan to meet her in Aspen. Garrett listened to her with interest, but there was no judgement in his eyes. When she was finished, he spoke. "I would hate for you to get your hopes up, Willow. I mean, why didn't they come forward when your father was alive? I don't want to be pessimistic, but I'm glad I'll be there with you when you meet him. Promise me you won't get too attached until we see what the DNA test has to say?"

Willow knew Garrett was right; her head told her so. But in her heart, she knew that even though Logan might not be a blood relative, her curiosity was overwhelming, and he would be too close to them in Colorado not to at least meet each other. If he was anything like her dad, he couldn't be a bad person. She'd proceed with caution but give him the benefit of the doubt.

"Agreed. And in case I haven't told you in the last two hours, I'm glad you'll be there with me too."

He peeked around the corner to be sure they wouldn't be caught before he leaned in to take her mouth with his. He didn't want her hurt. Ever. But he could see it in her eyes. She needed this man to be her brother, in the same way she needed her house to ground her.

He wondered if either of those things would end up working out.

Garrett did his best to make her forget it all with his kiss.

# CHAPTER
# TWENTY-ONE

The next few days flew by, and New Year's Eve arrived, bringing with it much warmer temperatures. Wyatt and India had put Marley and Dylan into their slings that morning and were taking a walk around the property, happy to see guests out and about enjoying the sixty-degree day. The creek was up, thanks to the melt-off from a few days prior, so the guides had a few brave customers who were willing to fly-fish in the chilly water. Wyatt and India stood hand in hand, watching the poetry of the fishing lines as they danced over the current before landing in the gurgling waters in search of trout.

The babies were finally settled into a routine, sleeping most of the night, even though they were just six weeks old. The biggest coup was that Wyatt and India had finally gotten them to sleep together in their own crib—in their own room. Which, in Wyatt's mind, was good for business. He looked at his wife as she watched their guests, marveling again at how gorgeous she was in the morning light. The fact that she was a mother now added another layer to her beauty. She had a newly acquired quiet confidence, and nothing seemed to rattle her too much, even when she had a right to be overwhelmed. He felt the now-familiar swell of love for her as he studied her.

Their connection was powerful, so of course she felt him staring. She turned to look at him and smiled back when she saw his expression. It felt so incredible to be loved by him. Wyatt was a one in a million, and she still woke up every day grateful for this life that she'd stumbled into. She leaned over to touch his face, which was extra handsome this morning with his faint shadow of whiskers. His crystal-blue eyes remained open when she kissed him, as they often did.

He didn't ever want to miss a second of their life together.

India had some news for him, but she wanted to pick just the right moment. They resumed their walk, heading back in the direction of their house. She must have been smiling to herself, because he squeezed her hand to get her attention before he spoke.

"What are you thinking about? You seem extra happy this morning. Don't get me wrong, I love it when you're like this. I feel pretty damn great myself about getting six uninterrupted hours of shut-eye last night."

He reached down to kiss his daughter's downy head, talking to her in a baby voice. "That's right, Daddy's little angel is showing her brother how it's done. I knew Dylan would fall in line eventually." He glanced at his son, who was wrapped up in the sling that India was wearing. "We all surrender, son. Might as well get used to it now."

India giggled, thinking how true it was. Their son had held out as long as he could, the lone crier at precisely two in the morning, every morning, until just two days ago. It was as if he knew the six-week mark was upon them and it was time to be a big boy and sleep through with his sister. It had been a game changer. India felt like a human being again, and although she knew it certainly wouldn't be their last parenting hurdle, she was glad to be moving past the sleep-deprivation stage. Really glad.

They were back home now and had taken the babies out of their slings to lay them down on a blanket on the family room floor, where they kicked and cooed to each other, as if they were happy to be home.

"I'll get us some coffee. Why don't you crack those front windows and let a little of that fresh air in here?" India headed off to the kitchen while Wyatt did as she'd asked. He flopped down on the couch, flicked the TV on, and had just tossed his ball cap onto the coffee table when he saw something come to life on the screen that made him freeze.

"India, come quick. You won't believe it."

Jack Sterling was a meteorologist by trade, a bullshit artist by nature, and the man that India had left at the altar three years ago, just a couple of months before her fateful first trip to Walland that spring. Jack and Wyatt had survived a nasty run-in that spring when Jack had shown up at the resort for an event with his new girlfriend, renowned chef Laina Ming. He'd discovered the budding relationship between Wyatt and India and had taken it as a personal affront. India's ex-fiancé had taken over hosting the third hour of *Good Morning America* about a year ago, where he was a perfect fit for interviewing narcissistic actors and musicians. Birds of a feather. That morning, he was sitting across from Sawyer Brantley, and Wyatt was astounded that the television set was big enough for the two of them.

"Oh God." India had walked back into the room, her hands frozen at her sides, her face white. They watched together as Jack interviewed Sawyer, the two of them seeming to be the best of friends. It wasn't until the very end that Wyatt and India remembered why they never watched morning television. Jack took subtle swipes at them any chance he got, like any scorned man would, and there was blood in the water now.

"Sawyer, weren't you just performing down at a resort we both know well in Tennessee? Tell me about that experience." Jack showed his teeth, but it could hardly be classified as a smile. Not a genuine one anyway.

Sawyer rubbed the back of his neck, a distasteful look on his face as he spoke. "Yeah, sometimes you have to play those smaller venues, but I try not to if I can help it. It can get a little uncomfortable to have to ward off people that don't understand that you're just there to work. The guests were great, actually. It was a couple of female staff members I had a problem with."

He leaned over to slap Jack, his new bro, on the arm. "But, hey, occupational hazard, right?"

They chuckled together, Jack shaking his head in amusement. "Isn't it, though?"

The interview was over, but even if it hadn't been, Wyatt had heard enough. He clicked the television off, staring at the blank screen left behind. "We were having such a nice morning. *Why* did I turn that idiot box on?" Wyatt sighed, glancing over to where his wife stood waiting to see how he'd react. He decided to mess with her a little to lighten the mood.

"Babe, could you do me a favor and get United Airlines on the phone? I need to make a quick trip to New York, but I promise I'll be back before the ball drops."

India looked at him, her face not buying it. "Settle down, hothead. Don't give those dummies a shred of your energy. Besides, you're going to need it."

Wyatt looked at her, puzzled.

This was the perfect time to break the news.

"I had my six-week checkup yesterday. I asked them to get me in a little early, because I was hoping to have a special date with my husband tonight, providing I got the green light. Which I did. Unless you're too angry?"

Wyatt stared at her for a minute before leaping off the couch to do a little happy dance. "Hot damn, India. I'm as happy as a pig in a peach orchard. Forget those bozos. It's full steam ahead for Daddy tonight!"

He looked down at his babies, pausing midwhoop to look questioningly at his wife.

India laughed, reading his mind. "They're staying with Grandma Susan and Grandpa Finn tonight."

The doorbell rang just then, so she glanced out the window. "Speak of the devils."

She paused on the way to answer, pressing against him and tucking her hands into the pockets of his jeans, wiggling her fingers. His mouth dropped open.

"You, my friend, are about to begin almost twenty-four uninterrupted hours with your wife. You might want to grab a PowerBar."

Kissing him, she turned to walk toward the door, looking back over her shoulder with a wink. "Happy New Year, Wyatt."

Garrett was off work that day, so he'd spent the night before in the city, making it easier to shop and get ready for their evening together. Willow had worked in the morning, then spent the better part of the afternoon trying to decide between two dresses. She had a black sequin number that was pretty and festive enough for New Year's Eve, but she was trying to figure out if she was brave enough to wear a winter-white dress; it was a simple and classic cut but very fitted and super sexy. She went for it and chose the latter, finishing up the outfit with a pair of nude Louboutins that made her legs look a mile long. She'd spent the night before exfoliating every inch of herself and applying self-tanner so she'd have a healthy glow, despite the season. She'd painted her nails black to contrast the dress.

It was still unusually warm when she left the house to drive to Garrett's, but she'd thrown on a cashmere wrap anyway to keep the chill out. He'd given her directions about parking in his space in the gated lot, and she knew she was in the right place when she saw his Jeep out on the street. He'd wanted her to text him when she got there, but she was in the space before she knew it, so she grabbed her overnight bag and went inside. She found his name and hit the buzzer next to it. After a minute she heard a click and opened the door, then made her way to the elevator.

She had butterflies in her stomach on the way up, but they were nothing compared to the way her stomach dropped when the doors opened and she saw him standing there waiting for her.

He was wearing a fitted dark-gray suit with a crisp white shirt and a black-and-gray-checked Burberry tie. Willow was happy to see he'd kept his signature dusting of facial hair intact. He looked hot. H. O. T.

"Why didn't you call me? I would've come down to help you. Here, let me have that bag." He took it from her, watching as she shrugged off the wrap she'd been wearing.

He froze in place. She was extraordinary. The dress hugged her in all the right places, and her legs would give any supermodel a run for their money. He was speechless, but only for a moment. "I've never seen anything more beautiful in my life, Willow. You are the stuff dreams are made of. I should know. You've been starring in mine for a few months now."

He leaned it to kiss her softly, stepping back for another look.

She blushed, rushing to return the compliment. "I wouldn't kick you out of bed for eating crackers either. I mean. Wow. I hope you gave the guy that made that suit a great tip."

He laughed as they walked through the door and into his loft. She was blown away by the space. It was almost all floor-to-ceiling windows on two of the walls and exposed brick on a third side. A true loft: she could see his kitchen, living room, and bedroom all from where she stood. The space was furnished simply in a masculine way that was very Garrett. There were candles lit on almost every available surface, and soft music played in the background. She smiled when she thought of how he must have spent the day cleaning up and preparing it for her to see for the first time. And whatever he was making them for dinner smelled incredible.

"What's on the menu? It smells delicious."

She tried to ignore the way he was still looking at her like she was the main course. She felt a blush rising up her chest in anticipation.

"Ribs."

He cracked up when her face fell, and he knew she was wondering how she was going to manage that in her white dress.

"I'm kidding! Do you honestly think I'd make you eat ribs in that little number? Although, I have to admit, I would like to experience that meal with you eventually. It sounds pretty sexy, actually."

She slapped him on the arm playfully, near enough to drink in his familiar scent. He was all man, and tonight, in his suit, she thought he looked stronger and more powerful than ever.

They had a relaxing dinner, which started out with a caprese salad and finished with a beautiful fillet and sweet potato. Garrett poured them the rest of a rare bottle of Abreu wine he'd been saving for a special occasion, and they moved to the couch to wait for the fireworks. They mulled over the things they wanted to do while they were in Aspen, each of them looking forward to exploring the hiking trails in particular.

Playing with her hair, Garrett listened to her talk excitedly about what kind of property she was hoping to find. He tucked a strand of hair behind her ear so he could better see her profile. He couldn't stop staring at that irresistible spot just below her jaw, where the skin was extra creamy and soft. He leaned in, gently nipping at her there, knowing he'd hit the mark when he heard a soft sigh escape her lips. Billy Currington seemed to confirm it, crooning about how, once again, he must be doing something right. He grabbed her hand, helping her up from the couch and into his arms so they could sway together to the sexy song.

Halfway through the song, they heard the fireworks start to go off, but instead of watching them, Garrett looked to Willow for an unspoken agreement, and when he got it, he grabbed her hand and led her over to his bed. Willow climbed up onto the bed, turning to face him while up on her knees, grasping his face in her hands as he stood at the foot of the bed before her. Garrett kissed her intensely, making quick work of the zipper at the back of her dress while she desperately fumbled with his tie and buttons. Once she'd freed him from the shirt, she allowed herself a more leisurely exploration of his chest and torso, finding her way to his belt. Undoing it, she pulled it out in a quick motion and dropped it, the buckle falling to the hardwood floor with a thud, giving her a shiver.

Garrett had managed to get her out of the dress, and Willow was now standing at the foot of the bed beside him in nothing but her white lace panties. He couldn't remove his own pants fast enough. He'd planned to take it slow with her, but all he could manage in that moment was to pick her up again, and, with Willow's legs wrapped around him, he flung them both down onto the bed together. Every time she moaned, it sent him closer to the edge, until he could wait no longer.

When the calendar flipped from December to January that year, they were there in Garrett's bed, as close together as two people could be.

The fireworks were only a footnote.

# CHAPTER
# TWENTY-TWO

The days leading up to their trip had been busy ones, leaving little time for Willow and Garrett to spend together. There was packing to be done, and preparations needed to be made to ensure that they could each comfortably be away from work and home for the rest of the month.

Garrett managed to pull it all together in time to stay with Willow at the farmhouse the night before they left. Wyatt and India stopped by in the evening to say good-bye, bringing with them drinks and takeout from the barn. The four of them sat around the kitchen table, excited to see some of the tear sheets that Willow had received from their realtor in Aspen on potential properties that were currently available in the area.

India picked up a stack and shuffled through a few before finding one that literally gave her goose bumps. It sat on eighty-three acres outside of town a few miles, off Castle

Creek Road. It had a huge main house on the land that would be perfect as the hub, along with several other outbuildings with lots of potential. She held the paper up, waving it at the rest of them. "What about this one? It's amazing! I think it's exactly what Susan has in mind."

She glanced back at the paper, then paused, her face suddenly crestfallen. "Well, I guess I got ahead of myself. The price tag is about double the budget. The realtor must have put this in the pile by mistake."

India moved to fold it in half and set it aside, but Willow stopped her, reaching for the paper to slip it back into her folder. "It couldn't hurt to take a look at it anyway. Maybe they'd be willing to parcel off some of the property. Besides, the agent told me it's kind of a famous property in Aspen. I feel like it could be perfect for what Susan has in mind. Indulge me. Let's at least take a look at it, even if only to get some ideas. Besides, it's the first time in generations that it's even been on the market."

Garrett smiled as she spoke. One of the things he admired most about Willow was her confidence. And she had great vision, whether it was for the orchard and farmhouse here in Tennessee or this new property out West. He was excited to watch her work, and he knew that she'd end up hitting it out of the park for Susan and Finn. He reached under the table to squeeze her hand in a show of support.

India smiled too, the gesture not lost on her. She saw so much of herself and Wyatt in the two of them, and being around this new romance was infectious. She'd miss them when they were in Aspen. It gave her an idea. "I don't want to infringe on your time in the Rockies, but I just had a thought."

Willow was intrigued, wondering what her friend considered "infringement."

"What if we flew out and met you in Aspen for the last four or five days of your trip? Wyatt and I are going to have to get out there sooner than later to see the place you've chosen anyway. This seems like a great way to mix business and pleasure. We'd have to bring the kids, of course, but we could stay in town at the Little Nell. It's one of my favorite hotels in the world. Honestly, it would be nice to have access to room service and housekeeping for a couple of days."

Wyatt clapped his hands, rubbing them together before pointing at himself with both thumbs. "You're looking at our home's housekeeping and room service, and this employee will be glad to have a few days off by then. As long as it's OK with you guys if we crash the party?"

Willow and Garrett didn't need to think about it. They loved hanging out with Wyatt and India and agreed readily.

"You'll get to meet my brother too," Willow blurted. She caught herself, noticing the worried look her friends and Garrett exchanged.

"Logan, I mean. That's his name. We obviously don't know the DNA results yet, but we might by the time he gets to Aspen. It's going to be close. He mentioned that he's traveling before that, so that last Friday is the earliest he can join us. You'll have been there for a couple of days before that, but I'm glad you'll meet him. I trust your judgement."

It was getting late, and Garrett and Willow had an early flight that next morning, connecting through Chicago. So they said good night, promising to have staked out the best restaurant in town for a big night out by the time Wyatt and India arrived at the end of January.

The bluebird skies of Colorado were showing off for them
when Willow and Garrett finally landed at Pitkin County
Airport in Aspen. They were astonished by the number of
private jets lining the outskirts of the runway, which was very
short and wedged in between two mountain ranges, making
for some rock-and-roll landings when the weather wasn't
great. Fortunately for them, Garrett and Willow arrived on a
clear day, but there was a big storm off to the west, promising
to dump up to eighteen inches of snow on the small ski town
within the next forty-eight hours.

Garrett collected their luggage while Willow got their
rental car squared away. The airport was small, so before long,
they were in their SUV headed toward town. Susan and Finn's
new place was in the coveted West End neighborhood, within
walking distance to everything. As they drove around the only
traffic circle that stood between them and downtown, Willow
pointed off to the right, showing Garrett where the dream
property that India had fallen in love with was located.

"That's the road you take to get up to the Maroon Bells
visitors area. The views are supposed to be magnificent.
On a clear day, the mountains make a mirror image on the
lake below. I guess it's the most photographed spot in all of
Colorado."

Garrett pointed to the left, indicating she should take the
next turn onto Fifth Street. "I've seen a picture of it. I had
a buddy in college whose family spent vacations nearby in
Snowmass, and he had a print of the Bells in his apartment."
He grinned at her. "Right next to his poster of Bob Marley."

They laughed as she made the final turn onto Francis
Street, looking for the address that Susan had given her. She
didn't really need it, though. The neighborhood was a collec-
tion of houses representing many different styles, but she'd
have known this one belonged to Susan even if she didn't

have a house number. It looked like something straight out of Walland.

The outside was classic white clapboard, trimmed with black zinc windows and a dark-gray tin roof with lots of peaks. It was a farmhouse, but in the most modern sense of the word—the perfect combination of wood, stone, and metal. There were two rockers on the front porch next to an over-sized black front door that was framed by two gas porch lights. The yard wasn't large, with a Zen-looking stone wall framing the front. The house sat back off the street just enough to provide privacy from the equally posh houses that flanked it.

Willow pulled the car into the heated drive, winding back behind the house and parking underneath an ample portico that attached to a glass catwalk leading from the main house to what looked like a guest apartment. She put the car in park, and they turned to look at each other.

Garrett grinned. "This is gonna be tough to take."

He loved seeing the anticipation on her face, knowing she was ready to kick off this adventure. He unclipped his seat belt, reaching over to slide his hand under her hair and around the back of her neck. "In case I forget to tell you, I had a really great time with you over the next three weeks."

He kissed her softly, feeling her smile against his lips at the old movie reference. Pulling back, he opened his door and jumped out, coming around to her side to get her door for her, like he always did. "Come on, let's get started!"

Willow walked toward the back door, digging through her purse for the keys, while Garrett got their luggage from the car up to the back porch. Willow unlocked the door, and once they were inside, they kicked off their boots and dropped everything by the door to go explore.

They emerged from the mudroom into a large open living space. Off to one side, there was a sunken family room, luxuriously furnished with oversized, extra-deep white couches and dark wood accent tables. Willow recognized a couple of Sloane Bibb art pieces, a large trout and an acoustic guitar, both created from his signature vintage metal materials. This one incorporated several old car parts, including a speedometer that made up the bridge. Willow was a big fan of the Alabama folk artist and would know his work anywhere.

There were black leather stools tucked under a white marble countertop and a huge wall of windows on the north side of the space that showcased the gorgeous mountain views. Every detail had been perfectly executed. Willow shouldn't have been surprised, having noted the way Susan operated over the past several months. She didn't do things halfway, and this house was no exception. It was architectural eye candy.

Willow was standing next to one of the giant down-filled sofas, about to suggest they head upstairs to look around, when Garrett playfully tackled her, spilling her over the armrest and into the softness below. She squealed in mock protest but didn't make a move to escape. They lay there together, wrapped up in each other with their eyes closed in silence, exhausted from the long day of travel. They hadn't slept much at all over the past two weeks, and in that moment, they felt every missing wink. With Garrett stroking her hair, it didn't take long for Willow to fall asleep. Garrett wasn't far behind her.

*I must be dreaming.*

Garrett didn't remember falling asleep, but waking up next to Willow was unforgettable. She must have unbuttoned his shirt at some point, because she was toying with the hair on his chest, softly stroking his skin back and forth, waiting for his eyes to open. He played possum for a few moments, wanting to memorize the sensation, but he knew if he didn't put a stop to it, they'd be participating in some very rude behavior on this very new, very white couch.

Willow smiled when he finally snuck a peek at her. She'd known the exact moment he'd woken up. She'd felt his entire body stiffen in response to her touch.

"Hi."

"Hi, yourself. Do you always feel free to have your way with innocent sleeping people?"

"Not usually, but you were irresistible. When you're dreaming, you do this thing with your jaw, and it makes a little grinding sound. That's what woke me up. So it's your own fault, really. Was I supposed to just lie here and watch you saw logs for another two hours?"

Garrett glanced out the window and saw that it was almost dark outside. The couch had grabbed ahold of both of them and wouldn't let go.

"Two things: That was a fast couple of hours. And I do not snore."

She was about to disagree, but he wrapped her up in his arms, flipping her up and over his chest to pin her to the back of the couch. He buried his head in her hair, and his mouth found her neck, loving the sounds that emanated from her when he nipped at the smooth skin there. They fooled around that way for a few minutes, until they couldn't ignore Garrett's stomach growling loudly.

He pulled back to look at her face, and they both burst out laughing. "Did I mention that I could eat?"

"I'm so glad you said something. I'm *starving*. I was starting to wonder what you'd taste like with a little barbecue sauce."

Garrett sat up on the couch to ponder the idea. "Hmm. We can try that later, but I was thinking more along the lines of ordering a pizza or something. Or speaking of barbecue sauce, I saw a rib joint when we turned off the main road. It's literally walking distance from here, and you're not wearing a white dress, so how about I carry the luggage upstairs and then let you unpack while I run and get us some grub?"

Willow threw her leg over him, straddling him while she gave him a big fat kiss. "Sexier words were never spoken. I'll take a full slab. Fries. Extra sauce. And coleslaw too if they have it. Any respectable rib joint will."

Garrett sat there with his jaw hanging open as Willow climbed off his lap, standing to rub her stomach.

"Chop-chop! Those ribs aren't going to fetch themselves! I need them to get in my belly!" She walked over into the kitchen. "I'll contribute by opening up that cabernet that someone so graciously left for us. If you hurry back, I'll leave some for you."

Within the hour, they were sitting side by side at the kitchen counter, their hands covered in sauce, each of them working on their second glass of wine. Garrett was wearing a paper napkin like a bib, and he'd been cracking her up for most of the meal. The experience of watching her eat those ribs was everything he'd imagined and more. He was convinced that she could look sexy taking the garbage out.

"So tell me what the game plan is for tomorrow." Garrett reached over to grab her hand, sucking the barbecue sauce off her fingers one at a time while he waited for her answer.

It was hard for Willow to remember why they'd even come to Colorado in the first place.

She let him finish but refused him when he reached for her other hand. "Well, for starters, we have to resist each other for a few daylight hours so we can manage to leave this house." Her kiss punctuated that statement. "We do actually have an appointment to meet with the realtor at ten, so we can sit down and prioritize which properties to see first." She paused, a strange look on her face. It seemed like she wanted to add something else but didn't for some reason.

"What? Are you worried you won't pick the right house?" He could see the wheels turning as she tore open a wet nap and finished wiping her hands clean.

Finally, she answered him. "No. That's just it. I'm afraid I'll find the perfect house and want to stay here and live in it."

She glanced over to see how he felt about that but couldn't read his expression.

"I love the mountains. I forgot how much. I knew coming here to Aspen would be a slippery slope, because it would remind me of what I'd left behind in Park City to go home to Tennessee. The job there was divine timing, and then I met you, which tipped me into staying, even before we got together. It's like I knew I needed to know you. I wouldn't change our stop-start beginning for anything. It makes this—what we have now—so much more amazing. You were worth the wait."

Garrett stopped her with a finger to her lips, leaning in to whisper in her ear. "I really, really like you too, Willow."

She shivered, leaning back to look him in the eyes. "But here's the thing, Garrett. I can't ignore the feeling that I'm eventually supposed to come back to the mountains. So house hunting here could be a dangerous endeavor, even if it is supposed to be for the resort."

Garrett listened, smiling at the last part. "I don't think you need to worry about being tempted by the properties you're going to see tomorrow. I think that place that India loved was eighteen million dollars, and I'm certain this place we're sitting in now was close to double digits too." He wanted to address the other point she'd made. "As far as living in the mountains, I get it. I understand being inexplicably drawn to something."

She blushed at the look he gave her.

"Maybe as a compromise, you could arrange to travel back and forth, helping to run Walland House once they finalize all the details." There was a pause as he turned to face forward, not looking at her. "I'm not sure where that leaves us, though. I don't know if you guessed this, but farmers aren't usually drowning in job offers. I'm never going to be a pauper, thanks to the sale of my grandad's farm, but the homes you're talking about here are a little out of my price range. I've got a great gig in Tennessee. I don't know that I could find the equivalent in or near Aspen. Not that you invited me into your hypothetical life anyway." He gave her a rueful smile.

Willow took a deep breath and turned to face him head-on. "What if I wanted to invite you? And I told you that I have a job in mind for you? A really good, really lucrative job."

He looked confused.

"That package I got from my father's attorney? The one with the information about Logan? There was a second letter inside, finalizing the details of some other news I got right after my father died."

He watched her, waiting. She bit her lip and then closed her eyes as she spilled her secret.

"Garrett, would it freak you out if I told you I'd recently inherited twenty-five million dollars?"

# CHAPTER
# TWENTY-THREE

Garrett stared at her for so long, Willow wasn't sure he'd heard her. She was about to repeat herself when he sputtered back to life.

"I'm sorry. Did you just tell me that you are a multimillionaire? I thought you used most of the money from the sale of your house to buy the orchard? How did you stumble into an extra twenty-five million? That's not exactly cup-holder change."

Willow raised her eyebrows, expelling a breath while shrugging her shoulders. It was a lot to digest, even for her, and she'd already had a couple of weeks to sit with the idea. She was rich. Filthy rich. She just wasn't sure what it meant for her future.

"I didn't see it coming either. When I met with our family attorney to read my father's will last month, I got the surprise of a lifetime. I had no idea, but it turns out my father was the original founder of the StayOver hotel chain. I thought he just worked for the hospitality management company that owned the chain. I always assumed that he was one of their executives. Money wasn't an issue, growing up, but I really had no idea the true depths of our wealth. My dad made it seem like he had a normal nine-to-five job, which is what he wanted me to think, I guess. He chose for us to live rather modestly, aside from our house, which was already in his family for generations, because he wanted me to grow up to be a hard worker like he was. The attorney told me that my dad built the entire hotel chain from the ground up. He said that if my dad hadn't sold it when he did, my inheritance could have been in the triple digits by now. Not that I'm complaining. I have no desire to manage a hotel chain. In fact, until this Aspen trip came up, I wasn't sure what the heck to do about this sudden windfall."

Garrett had been watching her, drinking his wine as he listened. "So you come by the hospitality business honestly. That's crazy. And your dad never let on?"

Willow shook her head, clearly exasperated. "No, I promise you. It is weird that I ended up in hotel management too. My father never talked about his work when he was home. It was all about family when he came through the door at the end of the day. I'm embarrassed to admit now that I really never understood what he did for a living. I just had a vague understanding that he was in upper management in the company. *His* company, as it turns out."

Garrett had gotten up and was opening and closing drawers in search of a corkscrew. Willow figured out what he was looking for and reached over the counter, grabbing it from beside the sink where she'd set it earlier. She handed it to him, and he made quick work of uncorking a second bottle of wine.

"Well, I'm not sure how I feel about dating an heiress, but I guess I can make an exception."

He topped off her glass before refilling his own, raising the wine in a toast. "Here's to my hot, rich girlfriend and to the adventures ahead of us. I hope that you find what you're looking for here in the mountains, Willow, and if I'm lucky, maybe I'll get to be a small part of it."

Willow touched her glass against his, then took a sip before adding her own toast. "And here's to my hot, witty, not-exactly-a-pauper boyfriend, who makes every day that I'm with him the grandest adventure of them all."

She walked around the counter toward him and set her wineglass down. Standing before him, she reached up to place her hands on either side of his chest, her expression serious. "As tempting as all of this is—the mountains, the ability to call my own shots and live here—I don't know if I have it in me to make those kinds of decisions if it means losing this. Losing you. I hope that doesn't scare you, Garrett. I'm just being honest. You really matter to me."

Garrett's expression had grown darker somehow, and Willow felt a little overwhelmed by the look in his eyes. He responded by ducking down for a kiss, but the way his lips claimed hers this time telegraphed a sense of desperation. He plundered her mouth, fervently trying to get his message across with actions rather than words.

Suddenly, he was moving with her, his hands on her hips as he walked her backward toward the steps leading upstairs. They stumbled upward, still grasping at each other, fueled by a different kind of urgency now. At the top of the landing, Willow broke the kiss, moving her mouth around the side of his jaw and down to his neck, biting and sucking on him there.

She could feel him scanning the hallway wildly, trying to decide which bedroom to guide her into. He settled on the closest door. He'd guessed right. It was the master bedroom, where she'd unpacked earlier when he'd gone out for dinner, and, thankfully, she'd drawn the shades. Willow felt him steering her through the doorway, but now her hands were busy, having found their way back underneath his shirt.

Before she could remove it for him, he reached down and pulled his shirt decisively over his head, the sounds of a popped button or two scattering, forgotten, across the hardwood floor. She buried her face against his bare chest, laying kisses from one side to the other, drinking in the intoxicating scent of him. He was so warm, and all she wanted was to spend the rest of the night as close to him as she could get.

But she was craving a shower, which wouldn't be a bad way to kick off the festivities. "As much as I love where your head is right now, how would you feel about rinsing the travel day off of us first?"

She'd worked her way around to the back of him now, trailing her fingers across his back and shoulders with a feather-soft touch, planting kisses here and there as she went. She felt him shiver in response.

"A shower, huh? I sure hope you're thinking coed. Because if not, then no deal. I'm sorry, but I'm not letting you out of my sight, woman."

He took her hand, leading her into the adjoining bathroom. Opening the shower door, he reached in to start the water, making a few adjustments before closing the door and turning his attention back to her. "It's a steam shower. Not that we'll need the extra heat."

The way they rid each other of the rest of their clothing proved that.

The light in the bathroom was dim, but Willow could see his face, thinking that his expression was a bit dangerous, but in the best possible way. He opened the shower door.

"Ladies first."

She stepped in, feeling the sting of the hot water as it traveled over her body. Leaning her head back, she allowed the water to drench her hair. Even without looking, she could feel his eyes on her. She peeked and could see him still standing there at the shower threshold, the steam enveloping him, making him appear dreamlike. She smiled inwardly, enjoying the feeling of her womanly power over him. Making the most of it, she lifted her hands and let them travel the length of her own body, then back up again, pushing the extra water out of her eyes and face before turning to look at him.

"Are you just going to stand there, or are you coming in?"

The door closed with a decisive snap behind him, and then his mouth and hands were on her.

It was not a leisurely exploration.

Finally, when Willow wondered again how she was still standing, he reached behind her, picking up the shampoo bottle she had unpacked and set on the shelf. Squirting something that smelled like sunshine into the palm of his hand, he turned her around, gently massaging her hair into a lather. She could feel his body close behind her, the soap creating a slippery film between them. His fingers worked against her scalp, rubbing and kneading, the feeling luxurious and yet somehow forbidden. When he was satisfied with his work, he turned her back around and lay his hand tenderly behind her neck, carefully dipping her head back to rinse the suds away. She was about to pick her head back up when she felt his lips brush her breast.

The sharp intake of her breath drove Garrett wild. He took his time, until he could feel that she was primed and ready for him. She gasped as he lifted her leg, wrapping it around him as he entered her in one powerful stroke. Maybe it was the steam that made it hard to breathe, but he suspected that it was more than that. Her face bore an expression of complete surrender that made it hard for him to hold back, and eventually he couldn't. They peaked together, for the first time overwhelmed not just by the physical sensations but by the emotions that neither of them could ignore.

Afterward, he wrapped her in one of the giant white towels he'd found under the sink and took a second one for himself, slinging it loosely around his own hips. He leaned against the counter, watching her work her way through various lotions and potions, applying some to her face and some to her hair.

"Is it weird that I could get used to watching you do this?"

She laughed, taking an inch of the toothpaste before offering him the tube. He accepted, and they brushed their teeth together in contented silence. She finished first, stepping into the closet to find something to wear to bed.

Garrett wasn't worried about pajamas, so he walked over to the antique iron bed, dropped his towel, and climbed in.

A moment later, he felt sorry for what used to be an old favorite of his. The soft, broken-in University of Washington sweatshirt that he'd always loved more than anything was completely outmatched. It had gone from nothing special to the luckiest piece of fabric on earth, draped over his freshly scrubbed girlfriend. He couldn't imagine what this image would do for the marketing department at the university.

Turning down her side of the covers, he welcomed her into bed. She clicked the lamp off, and they snuggled into each other, thoroughly exhausted. Sleep came like a thief in the night.

The skies were gray and the clouds low when they woke the next morning, the impending snow just a few hours away, according to the morning news. They bundled up, Willow making sure she had all of the corresponding papers for the properties they planned to see that day while Garrett stepped outside to warm up the car. Once she'd locked up, they jumped in the car and headed toward the Sotheby's office in town to meet the realtor. It wasn't far, located on a small pedestrian street in the downtown area, so they arrived shortly and parked nearby. Willow couldn't believe her eyes when she glanced across the street and saw who was waiting at the crosswalk.

Garrett's ex-girlfriend Lindsay was arm in arm with a tall, handsome man with salt-and-pepper hair. She'd been looking up at him and smiling broadly, before glancing across the street and noticing Willow staring back at her. It took Lindsay a moment before it dawned on her who Willow was with, but it finally clicked right about the time Garrett turned to see what had caught Willow's attention, his eyes landing on his now-stunned ex.

They'd been holding hands, so Willow felt Garrett tense up when he realized it was Lindsay. The light turned green, and Willow gently tugged his hand, indicating they should continue to cross the street as planned, bringing them face-to-face with the couple. Lindsay's voice was overly cheerful, considering the circumstances, causing Willow to inwardly wince.

"Garrett! What are you doing here? Oh my gosh. I can't believe it's really you."

She made a move like she might hug him hello, but Garrett stood his ground, a tight smile on his face. "Hi, Linds. You're looking well." He was sick to his stomach, because not only was she looking well, she was looking pregnant.

Very pregnant.

He wouldn't allow his mind to do the math.

Lindsay instinctively placed her hand across her protruding belly, smiling serenely. "Thank you. I'm due in the spring. We just found out we're having a boy."

There was an awkward silence before Lindsay remembered herself.

"Garrett, this is William, my fiancé. Will, this is Garrett." She paused for a moment before adding the detail that hurt most of all. "You've met, actually. Will worked at the ad agency where I interned last summer. He was at the party I took you to when you visited last spring."

Willow could feel the *physical* sensation of that information sinking in while Garrett was processing it. After a beat, to his credit, he recovered as well as he could.

The men shook hands with hurried greetings, and Lindsay turned her attention to Willow.

"I know you. You're Garrett's boss, right? From Tennessee?"

Lindsay seemed to finally notice then that Garrett and Willow were holding hands, her eyes darting back to Garrett questioningly.

Willow felt him squeeze her hand reassuringly as he answered. "Lindsay, this is my girlfriend, Willow. And yes, we work together in Tennessee. We're here in Aspen to work too, as a matter of fact, and we have an appointment in a couple of minutes, so we really have to get going. It was nice to see you."

Lindsay looked at Garrett sadly but shook her head knowingly. Will didn't seem fazed at all by the unexpected meeting, checking his watch with mild disinterest.

Lindsay uncomfortably prattled on. "Oh, of course, we won't keep you. I'm sure you're very busy. William has a place here, so we're just in town on a little babymoon."

She paused for a moment, her eyes softening as she looked at Garrett. "I'm glad to see you looking happy, Garrett."

Lindsay looked at Willow, her smile slightly strained. "Willow, it was nice to officially meet you. You've got a good one here. Take care of him."

Willow smiled sweetly back at her. "I sure do, and I sure will. Happy New Year to you both."

The four of them drifted away from each other, Lindsay and William disappearing quickly around a corner.

Willow wished she could turn back the clock and change it so she and Garrett hadn't run into them, but that was impossible. She stole a glance at him and could tell he was rattled. Willow wasn't sure she could say anything that would make it better, so she simply reached over to hug him. He pulled her close, kissing the top of her head as he held her for a minute, collecting his thoughts.

"You know what's strange?" He released her and started walking the way they'd been headed, grabbing her hand as he spoke. "It doesn't feel like I thought it would. Seeing her again. I mean, it's a little weird that she's pregnant, and that she most likely was when she came to Tennessee to break up with me. I don't even want to try to figure out when that happened. What good would it do me? But she looks happy. Happier than I ever made her. And the real kicker? I'm happier now too."

He paused just outside of the Sotheby's office, grabbing Willow's other hand in his. "I don't know if I was ever really in love with her, Willow. That's clear to me, seeing her today. I know that because I don't feel at all heartbroken. And now I have perspective."

There was so much more to say, but he stopped himself.

Willow squeezed his hands, smiling up at him. His eyes were soft again, not stressed anymore. She could tell that the encounter had brought him a sense of peace, and for that she was glad. She reached up for a quick kiss. "I can't help but feel like I'm the lucky one. Everything happens for a reason, right? That's what I tell myself anyway. Now let's get in there and hope the universe guides us toward the right property for Susan and Finn. Strangely, today it feels like we have luck on our side."

# CHAPTER
# TWENTY-FOUR

Sasha, the realtor that Susan and Finn had used when they'd purchased their house in Aspen, had planned to show Garrett and Willow dozens of properties. On paper, a few of the places possessed potential, but it seemed like each of them had at least one thing that kept it from being the perfect fit. They decided to look at an option that Sasha thought could at least be modified to fit their needs.

The property that Willow had been most anxious to see was the one that India had flagged the night before they'd arrived. Unfortunately, Sasha broke the news that it had gone under contract over the holidays.

So much for good luck.

"There is a beautiful home on the lot right next door to that ranch, but it's only on six acres."

Sasha let that sink in, trying to gauge Willow's response to determine whether or not she should schedule a showing.

Six acres wasn't really big enough for what Susan had in mind, but Willow wondered if they should look at it anyway, simply because of the location. It was less than ten minutes from town, which was what Susan had indicated she wanted. She and Finn had bought their house in town primarily for personal use but also to host special guests if they needed to. This second property was going to be used as more of a retreat. There would be a shuttle available to take guests into the heart of the action, but Walland House should feel remote while still being accessible.

Garrett was studying the paper that Sasha had printed off and handed to him while Willow weighed the idea of scheduling the smaller property for a look.

"Willow, I think you might want to take a peek at this place." Garrett walked over to her, handing Willow the paper and then watching her expression while she read it. He knew what she was thinking. And he knew she'd schedule the tour.

"Let's schedule an appointment. Why not?" Willow was quick to answer.

Sasha picked up the phone to call the listing agent while Willow glanced over at Garrett, who was trying not to appear too pleased with himself. He didn't say a word, just gave her a quick wink, listening as Sasha arranged for them to see the home that afternoon.

They'd spent that morning at two very different properties. One of them was a huge log home on seventeen acres, which was plenty big enough. Unfortunately, it was set close to the road, with most of the property spanning out behind it. Even though traffic was light, Willow and Garrett agreed that the log structure didn't really fit Susan's aesthetic.

The second home was closer to Snowmass than Aspen, which meant the possibility of bad traffic during the busy ski season or festivals throughout the year.

It was almost three o'clock when they finally stopped for lunch at a popular natural, organic restaurant in town called Spring Café. Sasha dropped them off, promising to circle back in an hour to get them for their four thirty appointment after she checked in at her office and made some phone calls.

Garrett got the mushroom-lentil burger, and Willow chose the coconut vegetable curry bowl. They sat down at a counter facing Spring Street. The snow was just starting to fly, and they watched as people rushed by, bundled up and carrying shopping bags full of whatever they would need to hunker down with during the impending storm.

Between bites of food, they chatted about what they'd seen so far. Willow knew it was early in the search, but she couldn't help wondering if the right property even existed. "I can't believe that ranch sold. Such unfortunate timing for us. I was really excited to see it. I know it was over budget, but I just had this weird feeling that it was going to be the one. So much for my instincts."

Garrett finished the last bite of his burger, wiping his mouth and leaning back in his chair, contented. "I wouldn't worry. We've only seen two places, and there are plenty more where they came from. Besides, aren't you a little bit excited about seeing this next place?"

He smiled at her, rocking his chair back on two legs while he studied her, waiting for an answer.

Willow smiled back. He looked so handsome in his gray sweater, which was almost the same color as his eyes. He looked really happy too.

"I'm curious. Why did you think I'd be interested in this house in particular? I mean, the lot isn't nearly big enough, and the house is definitely too small for Walland House. Why are you so excited about it?"

Garrett let his chair fall back onto all fours, leaning forward with his elbows on his knees to look at her. "I don't think the property is right for Walland House either. But I do think it's perfect for *Willow's* house. And I think you do too. I saw it in your eyes when you looked at the spec sheet."

He wasn't wrong. She'd been shocked when she'd seen the picture. It looked almost exactly like her farmhouse in Tennessee. It was eerie. The only difference was, this house was newer and had slightly more modern touches, including the tin roof and other trimmings.

"It's crazy, right? You think it looks like my house? I couldn't believe it when you handed it to me. But still. You're not suggesting that I look at this place for personal reasons? Are you trying to get rid of me?"

He laughed, leaning forward to kiss her. "Nope. I guess I'm just warming to the idea of my girlfriend being a mountain momma." He pulled the straw out of his drink and began to chew on the end.

Willow just shook her head, laughing. "I'm not going to start yodeling anytime soon, so don't get your hopes up. But I guess it wouldn't hurt to look at it. It might give me some ideas for the Tennessee farmhouse, if nothing else."

By the time Sasha came back to get them, the snow had picked up in intensity, and the wind was howling. "This is a good old-fashioned Rocky Mountain snowstorm," she told them. "The next few days are going keep the ski shops busy. Locals love to ski powder."

The roads were covered, so Sasha drove slowly through the roundabout, turning the car toward Castle Creek Road. A few minutes later, they were making a left onto an unmarked road, then easing the car down a long lane flanked by twin snow-covered aspen groves. After a couple of hundred feet, they came to a clearing and stopped.

There it sat, Willow's architectural soul mate.

In person, it had an energy that was hard to ignore. Even with the driving snow, they could see that the house was lit up, every window seeming to beckon for them to come inside. There was a curl of smoke rising up from the chimney, and although it appeared that the front path had been freshly shoveled, it was quickly disappearing again under a swirl of snow.

They rushed up the walkway, pausing on the covered porch to stomp their boots on the mat while Sasha opened the door and alerted the listing agent of their arrival.

They were surprised when it was the owner who appeared in the hallway, urging them to come inside.

Garrett instantly recognized him but tried hard to play it cool. He looked different without his trademark cowboy hat, but it was definitely him.

Sasha obviously wasn't expecting to see the multi-platinum country star that owned the place. "I'm so sorry. We had an appointment with Brent at four thirty to see the house. We'll come back another time."

"Oh no, I told Brent to stay home with this crazy weather. It's fine. Come in and take a look. My wife and the girls are still in town, so it's just me, and I'll stay out of your way unless you have questions."

The singer turned his attention to Willow and Garrett, and they introduced themselves. He couldn't have been nicer or more down-to-earth, and before long, he and Garrett discovered that they had mutual friends in the Nashville area. After chatting for a few more minutes, the man opened the hall closet to grab a North Face jacket. Pulling it over his impressive physique, he said his good-byes, then headed outside to plow the driveway in an attempt to keep it clear for his wife and daughters' eventual return.

The front door slammed shut behind him, leaving Willow and Garrett to shake their heads over what had just transpired, then set about touring the house with Sasha. She excitedly led them down the hallway into the kitchen and hearth room. The space was modern but decorated in a contemporary mountain style that made it feel warm and cozy. There was a fire in the hearth, making the rooms feel even more inviting.

"They've owned this property for a while, but they're currently building a new place up mountain since their girls are getting older. They wanted more room for extended family when the time comes."

She turned to face Willow. "This is a really special home. They designed it to be very environmentally friendly, and every single material used is the best of the best. I didn't mention this before: this is technically a pocket listing. It's not even on the market yet, but I'm close with Brent, the listing agent, so he called me about it this morning. It's going to go fast, believe me. It seems like the owner liked you both, though, so maybe that will count for something."

Sasha told them they were free to look around while she waited in the front room. They made their way upstairs, where they found a common area and four bedrooms fanning out in different directions. They each had en suite bathrooms, and the master even had a small sitting area with a fireplace in the corner.

Willow stood for a moment, looking out the huge back wall of windows.

"It looks like a snow globe out there, doesn't it? With the aspen and pine trees? What an incredible view to wake up to." She sighed. "This is a dream place. But I don't know . . ."

Garrett walked up next to her, slipping his hand into hers. They watched the snow swirl for a minute before he turned to look at her. "Willow. This is your house. It is. You can't deny it. It's fate that it isn't even listed, and yet here you are, feeling like you're standing in your own bedroom. So what's holding you back?"

Willow knew there were a million reasons she should run the other way. She had no business buying more property when she'd just bought the orchard. And how insane would it be to have a place in the mountains when she didn't even know how often she'd be able to visit?

She took a deep breath and finally answered him. "This is terrifying, Garrett, but I guess nothing is holding me back. Which is why—as crazy as this sounds—I think I'm going to make an offer on this house."

The snowstorm raged on for the next two days, putting their Walland House search on hold. But true to her word, Willow made an offer on what she and Garrett had started jokingly referring to as "Farmhouse West." They were sitting in the family room of Susan and Finn's, trying to guess what the counteroffer might be, when Willow's phone rang. Glancing at the screen, she saw that it was Sasha. Taking a deep breath, she nodded to Garrett for reassurance before answering. "Hello? Yes. Hi. Yes. OK. Uh-huh. Wow. OK. I'm just surprised. Wow. OK. Yes. Sure. I do. OK, thanks, Sasha. Talk soon."

Willow ended the call, her face unreadable. She stood up and walked over to the kitchen, disappearing behind the counter for a moment in search of something.

Garrett wasn't sure what had just happened. He hesitated to ask, but then his curiosity got the better of him. "So. What did she say? Was the counter really high?"

He waited, and when Willow didn't answer right away, Garrett stood up and walked toward the kitchen. Willow popped back up from behind the counter, a bottle of champagne held above her head in triumph. "It wasn't high at all. They didn't counter—they accepted the offer as is! It's official, Garrett. I'm the proud owner of not one but *two* farmhouses."

She'd been working to free the cork from the champagne bottle while she talked and finally succeeded with a resounding pop.

Garrett reached behind her, grabbing two glasses from the cupboard. Willow hastily poured them each a glass, which they clinked together in a toast. "I'm so happy for you, Willow. It's an amazing house and a special property. Cheers to your farmhouse fetish."

Willow laughed, setting her champagne down so that she could hop up on the counter, where she sat facing him. Crooking her finger, she motioned for him to step closer, which he did, setting his own glass down. He placed his hands on the counter on either side of her, leaning in so they were just inches apart. "Yes?"

She searched his eyes for any indication of how he might be feeling about this turn of events, but he was hard to read. She needed him to hear this. "I'm obviously excited about this property, Garrett, but I want you to know what it represents for me."

She leaned in to kiss him softly before continuing. "I want this to be the house I have my family in, whenever that might be. That's what I felt when I was standing in the bedroom. I could feel the love that's been infused into that place, and I want that someday. So I rolled the dice. For now, I don't know what is going to happen in Walland, but I'll admit, I'm inclined to take Finn and Susan up on their offer of buying the orchard since my long-term future isn't going to be there. It's going to be here."

She paused, afraid but anxious to tell him what she was really thinking. "I feel like my future is with you, Garrett. When I close my eyes and picture what a life could look like here, I can't get a clear image that doesn't include you by my side. I don't want to scare you, but we promised we'd always be honest with each other. So maybe you should tell me now if you don't—"

He didn't let her finish but instead covered her mouth with his. The kiss spoke volumes. He was all in. Still, he knew she needed to hear him say it. After a time, he pulled back, resting his forehead softly against hers.

"Willow, I'm totally in love with you. I think I have been since you smiled at me during that first meeting in Walland. I felt it in my toes, but I didn't recognize what it was. Here's why. Seeing Lindsay here in Aspen made me realize that not only do I love you but that you're the first woman I've ever really loved. So if you think telling me that you see a future with me is going to scare me, you're crazy. What terrifies me is the thought of living my life without you in it."

Willow closed her eyes, soaking in his words. He'd already made her feel those things, but hearing him say it was more powerful than she could have imagined. "I love you too, Garrett. And I'm so excited about where we go from here. The fact that you're here with me and that we found that house together, I don't think it's an accident. I love you, and I want to move forward together with you. Here, or in Tennessee—wherever we end up, it doesn't matter as long as we're together."

Garrett wrapped her up in his arms, their hearts beating together in sync. "Now we just need to hurry up and find a place for Susan and Finn before we end up exiled here, like it or not."

Willow leaned back to look at him. "I don't know. Exile with you sounds like a very nice idea."

# CHAPTER

# TWENTY-FIVE

The next two weeks flew by in a flurry of paperwork to finalize Willow's new purchase, wedged in between dozens of showings in search of Walland House. Sasha had exhausted all of her listings, and although they still hadn't found a property that ticked every single box, they had come across two that had potential.

Wyatt and India were arriving that day, so Willow and Garrett had scheduled second showings of the contenders for the following afternoon. Fortunately, there was a break in the nearly nonstop snowfall, so the airport had reopened the day before, allowing Wyatt and India to fly directly into Aspen. At the last minute, they had decided to leave the babies home with Susan and Finn rather than bring them during cold and flu season. As excited as India was about having a few days alone with her husband, she was already missing her babies when they touched down in Colorado. The thought of the twins reminded her that it was almost time for her date with the breast pump.

"I swear, if those babies don't have enough milk after all of my hard work over the last month, then I don't know what to do. Honestly, at one point, I thought I might turn inside out."

Wyatt chuckled, lifting their bags into the back of their rented SUV. He found a scraper in the backseat and went to work brushing off the foot of snow that covered the vehicle while India stood outside keeping him company and rubbing her hands together to stay warm.

"I think it's safe to say that our babies are in good hands with their grandparents. And seeing as we had to purchase a deep freezer just to store your ample milk supply, they'll be set for weeks."

India crafted a snowball from what was left on her side of the windshield, tossing it squarely at Wyatt's shoulder, where it exploded, covering the whiskered side of his face. "Oh really?"

He had a wicked look in his eye now, causing India to squeal and duck behind the car. It didn't matter. Wyatt had used the scraper like a hockey stick to flip an entire sheet of snow over her, leaving her covered from head to toe.

"You'll pay for that, Mr. Hinch."

India shook off the snow and jumped into the passenger's seat, reaching over to start the car to warm it up. After a few moments, they were headed out of the airport and toward town. India called Willow to let her know they were on their way, and after a few minutes of chatting, she hung up and turned her attention back to her husband.

"Willow made a reservation for the four of us tonight at J-Bar. She sounds really happy. I can't wait to hear all about the last couple of weeks."

Wyatt reached over to grab her hand. "I'm happy to be here with you, Indy. Aspen is such a cool town. I've only been here a few times for photography gigs back in the day. It's going to be nice to spend some time in this beautiful place with my sweetheart. And without Marley and Dylan around to sabotage me, I'm not gonna lie: I like my chances."

India laughed, happy to be experiencing Aspen with Wyatt. She'd been here a couple of times to ski when she was in college, staying with a friend whose parents had a condo in town. It was exciting to think about Susan and Finn's plans for expansion here. The clientele in Aspen was similar to guests of their resort in Tennessee, so India knew that Susan would bring her Midas touch to whatever she created there.

They pulled into the drive corresponding to the address they'd been given, and Wyatt let out a whistle. "She doesn't pull any punches, does she? This place is incredible. Feels like we're still in Walland—with three feet of snow thrown in."

India agreed, but she wasn't surprised. Susan's vision was unmatched, and her taste in both houses and furnishings was impeccable. They'd made their way up to the front porch when the front door swung open and Willow and Garrett were there to greet them, huge smiles on their faces.

Garrett pulled on his boots and headed out to help Wyatt unload the car before carrying the luggage upstairs to one of the guest rooms. India and Willow made their way into the family room, curling up on the couch to catch up.

"You're sure it's not going to cramp your style to have us staying here with you guys? We were more than happy to stay at the Little Nell," India told her.

Willow shook her head. "No way, especially now that you don't need the extra room for the kids. Besides, if anyone should be moving to a hotel, it's us. We've loved staying here, but I'm feeling weird about my—Logan—coming and staying in the guest apartment. You guys should have this place to yourselves while you're here."

India grabbed a blanket off the arm of the couch, wrapping it around herself. "Now what fun would that be? I'm planning on having a big fat dinner tonight at J-Bar, then coming back here to put sweats on and play cards in front of the fire. Sounds like a perfect way to kick off a working vacation, if you ask me."

Wyatt had just come back downstairs, taking a running leap and vaulting himself over the back of the couch to plop down next to India. He reached for her blanket, squirreling himself underneath it, head and all, causing her to squeal with delight.

"Wyatt! Buy me a drink first!"

The four of them laughed while Garrett moved into the kitchen to start a pot of coffee. Once they had four steaming mugs, they settled in to talk about the property search. Willow had already told India that they were set to head out the next day to see a couple of places, but India was curious to hear more.

"So I can't wait to see the two properties tomorrow. Do you think there's one we'll like more than the other?"

Willow sighed, cupping the hot mug with both of her hands, waiting for it to cool down before taking a sip. "Well, I was hoping to be blown away by something, but honestly, neither of them lives up to that ranch that you and I loved. I wish we'd never seen the flyer, because the bar was already set so high coming in. That said, I do like one of the properties we'll see tomorrow, and think it could work, but it definitely needs some updating, and there aren't really any secondary buildings like Susan was hoping for, so those would have to be built. On the bright side, the price is right within the budget, so let's see what you think."

"And the other place?" Wyatt knew his question was likely rhetorical, because Willow wouldn't be wasting their time if it wasn't worth seeing.

"It's nice too, but it's a little farther out than I think Susan had in mind. And Sasha seems to believe that the owners aren't going to budge on the price, which is hovering at the high end of what we agreed on. But it's definitely a pretty piece of land, and the house and outbuildings are lovely."

"Nice. Well, let's wait and see tomorrow. We'll keep an open mind." India smiled. "Maybe we should get an early start. I know we asked for afternoon showings originally, when we thought we'd have the kids with us, but do you think Sasha could try to bump us to morning appointments instead? I'd love for you and I to have a chance to shop a little in the afternoon before Logan arrives on Friday. We'll try to stay out of your way once he's here."

Willow stood up and reached across the coffee table for her phone. "Let me call Sasha and see what she can do. I'm sure it will be fine. It's been pretty quiet in town on her end, so I'll bet she can switch us to the morning."

She dialed Sasha's number, putting her hand over the speaker as she finished her thought. "And as for you disappearing once Logan gets here? Don't worry about that. I thought I might take him skiing on Saturday morning, but I'd love to have a chance for all of us to hang out Friday afternoon if you guys are open to that."

Sasha answered just then, so Willow stood up to walk into the kitchen.

While she was gone, Wyatt lowered his voice to ask Garrett, "Do you think she's ready for this visit? She seems like she's already decided this guy is her brother. Did the results come yet?"

Garrett rubbed the back of his neck absentmindedly. "No, not yet. I'm a little worried about it myself. I'd hate to see her set herself up for a heartbreak. They've talked on the phone a couple of times since we've been here, and she's already pretty attached to the idea of having a sibling. I sure hope he's legit."

India was about to add something when she looked over Garrett's shoulder and saw Willow walking back in to join them, a nervous smile on her face.

"Well, I have some news, friends."

Garrett stood up to walk over to her, grabbing her hand in support. "Is it the DNA test? Did you get results?"

She shook her head, leaning in to bump her shoulder against him sweetly. "No, not yet. But I'm not worried about that right now. I'm more concerned with how we're going to talk Susan and Finn into spending a large amount of money on the most perfect property in Aspen. Guys, the sale of the ranch fell through, and it's going back on the market, as of Friday morning. Sasha told them we're interested, so they're giving us a courtesy day tomorrow to come take a look and decide if we want to move forward."

The smile on her face was contagious. "Guys, the ranch is back in play!"

They decided to go ahead and look at the other two properties the next morning, since the ranch couldn't be shown until noon. Willow had been right. Both were nice in their own way, but neither of them was quite right. They stopped for a quick lunch at Justice Snow's in the historic Wheeler Opera House building before finally setting out to see Highland Ranch. Sasha gave them the nuts and bolts on the ride over.

"So, Highland Ranch was the first ski lodge here in Aspen. It was built in the 1930s, in the Bavarian style of lodges of that time. Everything you'll see in the main lodge is original, from the hardwood floors to the big white stone fireplace in the center of the room. There are three bedrooms in the main lodge and another two bedrooms in an adjacent bunkhouse that has its own kitchen and wood-burning stove."

Willow was so excited she could barely sit still, but she was also nervous. She and Garrett hadn't yet told Wyatt and India about how she'd bought the farmhouse next door to the ranch. She'd been waiting for the right moment during dinner the night before, but it had never presented itself, and she still wasn't sure how to explain why she'd felt compelled to move forward with the purchase in the first place. As they lay in bed together after dinner the night before, Garrett had told her that it was her news to share when she was ready and that she shouldn't feel rushed to do so. She would tell them at the perfect time.

Willow turned her attention back to the ranch as they made their way around the traffic circle and headed up Castle Creek Road once again.

"Did I read that there is an artist's cabin too? And what about water on the property?"

Sasha glanced in the rearview mirror, nodding her head. "You have done your homework! Yes, there is a painter's cabin that overlooks Castle Creek, which runs through the property. There are also several small ponds, creeks, and gorgeous meadows. It's really a spectacular setting, particularly in the summertime when the mountains framing it in are still snow-capped. There are also several places on the property where you have direct access to the national forest, and the property even comes with adjudicated water rights."

Sasha turned the car down a driveway that sat less than two hundred feet beyond Willow's new home.

India was in the passenger seat next to Sasha and had peeked down Willow's drive when they'd passed, noticing the "Sold" sign out front with Sasha's name on it. "What's the story with that property next door? You just sold it, I see. To a family and not a developer, I hope?"

Sasha was quiet for a moment, glancing again at Willow in the backseat before answering carefully. "Yes, it recently changed hands, but the new owner is quiet. You won't have any problems there."

They traveled down the drive another quarter mile or so and finally emerged into a clearing surrounded by mountains. There, set back on the banks of a rather generous lake, was the lodge.

It was unassuming but exceedingly charming. India thought it looked like something out of a European alpine village. To the left of it was the bunkhouse, obviously built later but in a similar style. There was a large classic barn off in the distance. Sasha told them that the painter's cabin wasn't visible from where they were standing but that she would drive them down to it after they'd toured the main house.

As if on cue, they could hear elk bugling in the distance while they walked from the car to the lodge, the untouched snow crunching under their boots.

The interior was everything they'd hoped it would be. Guests who stayed here would truly feel like they were a part of something special and unusual—not just a trip to Aspen but an experience. It was clear that the architects had kept the spectacular surroundings in mind when they'd drafted the original plans for this eighty-year-old structure. The windows were oversized, framing the beauty of the mountains and meadows perfectly. The massive stone fireplace was the anchor of the space, and India and Willow discussed how they could already visualize guests gathered around with their afternoon tea or glass of wine. It would be a retreat the likes of which would be impossible to recreate anywhere else.

It was perfect.

It was Walland House.

Within the hour, and after Wyatt had snapped dozens of photographs to upload to his laptop and send back home, it was decided that they would go back and call Susan and Finn to give them the hard sell. They all agreed that no other property could ever match this one and that it would only enhance the brand they'd been building as a family for over forty years in East Tennessee. This very special place would be the bridge to carry their brand westward.

On the way out, India gestured once again toward Willow's new property, asking Sasha to pull in for a moment so she could see the proximity of the house to the ranchlands. The way the farmhouse was situated on the lot, they figured it sat about a hundred yards or so from the boundary of the ranch, which mildly concerned Wyatt and India. They persisted, wanting to know more about the new owners, since they'd be rather intimate neighbors.

As they got out of the car for a closer look around, Willow decided it was time to fill them in. "Guys, I can assure you, the owner of this place is going to be a great asset to the ranch."

India looked at her curiously, watching as Willow nervously shifted her weight from one foot to the other. "How can you be so sure, though?"

Willow smiled weakly, encouraged by Garrett's gentle squeeze of her hand. "Because I'm the owner." She stuck out her hand. "Nice to meet you, neighbor."

# CHAPTER
# TWENTY-SIX

After the initial shock wore off, India and Wyatt couldn't have been more pleased to hear that Willow had purchased the farmhouse. They all agreed that it would be the perfect scenario if only Susan and Finn would agree to buy the ranch. Once they got back to Sasha's office, Wyatt uploaded the photos he'd taken and emailed them to Susan. He and India called Susan to explain the crazy events of the last twenty-four hours, and to talk her through the images. After hearing about the ranch and seeing the pictures for herself, Susan consulted with Finn, and together they agreed to put in an offer. Even though it was more than they'd intended to spend, they could put some other projects on hold for a couple of seasons to make it happen.

The four of them had a celebratory early dinner at Mezzaluna before the girls set out to do a little shopping, leaving the guys behind to have a beer at the bar while they waited.

India linked her arm through Willow's while they leisurely window-shopped down Galena Street as the snow started to fall in the early-evening light. "You minx! I had no idea you were in the market for property here in Aspen. You're just full of surprises, aren't you?"

Willow laughed, shaking her head. "I promise you, I wasn't looking. But I've always had a thing for the mountains, so it was like sending a kid into a candy store letting me come here. Especially in light of recent events."

Willow glanced at India, who had stopped walking and was studying her curiously.

"Which recent events? Did you decide to sell your orchard to Finn and Susan? Is that why you felt like you wanted to reinvest here?"

Willow sighed, stepping underneath the awning outside the Prada store in an effort to stay dry. "No. I mean, yes. I think I've decided that I am going to sell them the orchard. But that's not why I bought the farmhouse here. I wouldn't leave you in the lurch like that, just up and quitting without warning. I love my job, and I see a future with the resort." She paused and took a deep breath before continuing. "India, I recently came into some money from my father's estate. A rather large amount. My buying this farmhouse was purely an investment, I promise. I'm committed to the resort and to you so I'll figure out a way to make it all work. Maybe for now, I can only come here on vacation. I don't really know. I can't explain it other than to say I think my long-term future might be here."

The snow had let up a little, so they started walking again, turning the corner to head back toward the restaurant.

"You know I came back to Tennessee because of my dad, right? I had no idea he would be gone so soon, and I couldn't have imagined how not having family in Knoxville anymore would make me feel so unanchored. Garrett has changed all that. India, I'm completely in love with him, and he feels the same way. We want to be together. Which makes this whole situation all the more confusing."

India stopped again, reaching out to hug her friend. "I'm so happy for you, Willow. For both of you. Wyatt and I can see that the two of you have something special. Everyone can feel it when they're around you. I'm so glad you both got out of your own way."

They laughed, pausing before reentering the restaurant to get Wyatt and Garrett.

"Don't worry about the orchard or the farmhouse or any of it for now. You've got a huge day ahead of you tomorrow, meeting Logan. Focus on that for the time being. Besides, I have a feeling it's all going to work out exactly as it's supposed to. Somehow, it always does. We can't push the river."

Logan Matthews felt like he was walking into some pretty great expectations. It wasn't every day he took a road trip to meet a sister he'd never known he had. He'd lived twenty-seven years believing he was an only child, until a phone call from his estranged mother about a month ago had changed all that. He usually let her calls go to voice mail, dreading any kind of interaction with the woman who'd given birth to him, but when she redialed him three times in a row, he'd finally answered. Janice Matthews was the most selfish woman he'd ever known, and that was being generous. He knew that whatever she had to talk to him about would ultimately benefit her in some way. So when she told him he had a sibling, he knew there had to be some reason she wanted them to meet. He just hadn't figured it out yet.

Logan had carved out a nice life for himself as an Expert Ranger for the Pikes Peak Ranger District just west of Colorado Springs, Colorado. He loved being part of a group in charge of protecting and managing a quarter of a million acres in the Pike National Forest, making sure visitors respected and appreciated the hundreds of miles of trails and nearly one million acres of public land in the area. His job was to keep visitors safe while they explored the wilderness, and he felt such a sense of purpose doing it. He had the best office in the world.

He'd been living in the Springs for only about two years, having moved out West from Pennsylvania, where he'd graduated from Hawk Mountain Ranger Training School, a search-and-rescue school operated by the state's wing of the Civil Air Patrol. He'd joined the Air Force right out of high school, uncertain about what he wanted to do with his life and without a father to help guide him in the right direction. His mother hadn't been much help either, too busy trying to land herself another future ex-husband. She'd already been through three at that point in his life. Their relationship was strained enough that Logan was surprised if he heard from her more than two or three times a year. When she did call him, it was with her hand out.

Logan had earned his first cadet stripe in record time, discovering his love of all things outdoors along the way. Working through the ranks, he moved from third to first class within two years and had eventually earned his Expert Ranger status, awarded to him by the unanimous approval of current Expert Rangers.

He'd just returned from a winter survival school held on a section of the Appalachian Trail, where he'd helped instruct other cadets on how to conduct search and rescue in cold-weather environments with little to no equipment. He'd spent an extra week with some of his buddies, hiking a stretch of the trail, which thanks to its northernmost position and the winter season, they'd had all to themselves.

Now, as he turned off I-70 into Glenwood Springs, the last major town standing between him and Aspen, he was grateful for the working heater in his old Ford Bronco. They'd gotten a lot more snow up in the mountains than in Colorado Springs so far that winter. Every time he traveled into the mountains, he was blown away by their beauty, and he found himself wondering why he didn't make it a point to come more often.

He'd spoken to Willow a few times on the phone, and they'd had great discussions, but she'd warned Logan that her friends were cautiously optimistic when it came to the potential lineage they might share. He had to admit, he wasn't sure he should take his mother's word for it either. She'd shown him who she was over the years, and at that point in his life, he had multiple reasons not to trust her. Logan knew that his mother would always do whatever it took to get her way, yet he still couldn't quite figure out why she was pushing him to pursue a relationship with Willow. Her endgame remained to be seen, but he'd be foolish to think she didn't have one. He shrugged it off, though, intrigued to meet the only other living family member he might have.

They'd agreed to meet for coffee, just the two of them initially. Afterward, they planned to head back to the house so that Willow could introduce him to Garrett and their friends. Logan wasn't sure how long he'd stay, but he was grateful that Willow had offered to put him up in the guest suite. He pulled underneath the portico at the Little Nell and chatted with the valets, who fell hard for his vintage Bronco. Glancing at his watch, he realized he was a couple of minutes late, so he handed them the keys before reaching into the backseat to grab his wallet. He took a deep breath and headed inside to meet the woman who just might be his sister.

She would have known it was him, even if he hadn't stopped to search the room. Willow had purposely tucked herself into a corner beside the stone fireplace so she could check him out without being noticed as he arrived. She thought he looked just like his voice sounded, exactly as she'd imagined him. Willow felt tears involuntarily prick at the corners of her eyes. Embarrassed, she reached up to brush them away with her fingertips, watching him walk toward the hostess station to inquire about her. She allowed herself another moment to study him, this man who could be her brother.

He was tall and had light-brown hair, worn short, and a strong, almost chiseled jaw, a feature that she wondered if they'd both inherited from their father. He was dressed casually in jeans, and from the reaction he received after chatting with the hostess, he wasn't short on charm either. He turned back to scan the room again, leaving the poor woman blushing behind him, trying to regain her composure. After a moment, he found Willow, and their eyes met.

Willow smiled nervously, standing as he approached, unsure of whether or not to hug him. She went with her gut, leaning in for a brief embrace, and was surprised when he pulled her close, hugging her tightly for a few moments before releasing her. They stepped back, studying each other up close for the first time.

Logan stuck out his hand, smiling softly at her. "I'm Logan. And I sure hope you're Willow, because otherwise my instincts are terrible."

Willow laughed, the tension broken. "Yes, I'm Willow. It's so nice to meet you, Logan. Finally." She paused, not really sure what to say next.

He beat her to it. "Yeah, let's not let twenty-seven years go by next time."

They sat down at the small table where she'd been waiting for him and ordered two coffees when a server stopped by. Willow could feel herself staring at him as he interacted with the waitress, but she couldn't help it. She was trying to find a clue about whether or not he was family. She'd known from their phone conversations that she would like him. Garrett's warnings to guard her heart were ringing in her ears, though.

Logan turned his attention back to Willow as the waitress left. "So, as cool as it is to finally meet you, I'm not gonna lie. It's totally weird to be looking at you and wondering if we really are related. What do you know about the circumstances of all of this? Do you know who my mother was to your father?"

Logan could tell from her expression that this was the painful part of the conversation, so he decided to tread carefully.

"My mother was a secretary in your father's company for about a year back in the early nineties. That's how they came to be . . . acquaintances, I guess. My mother didn't tell me too much, just that she left her job shortly after she learned she was pregnant. We've never really been close."

Willow thanked the waitress, who'd come back to deliver their coffee. Taking a sip, she was honest with him. "That's the most surprising part of all of this. I always thought my parents had such a happy marriage. They never gave me a reason to believe otherwise. I wasn't even two when you were born. I know now that the stress of everything they went through to have me must have taken a toll on their marriage, but they never showed it. I can't imagine that my father could have cheated on my mother."

Logan shook his head in disgust, blowing out a breath. "You've never met my mother. She's a physically beautiful woman, even to this day, but believe me, it's only skin deep. She has the heart of a viper. My guess is she saw your father as a means to an end and was surprised when he didn't leave your mother for her. It would have been a new experience for her. She's gone through a few husbands, mostly for financial gain."

Logan took a sip of his coffee, humiliated by what he had to tell her.

"My mother only found out that your father had died when she stopped getting her regular checks from him. She'd been blackmailing him since she got pregnant with me, in exchange for her silence about my existence. She claims that he continued to pay her year after year so that your mother would never know, and then after your mother died, he paid to protect you from knowing."

Willow was stunned that her father had known for all of those years that he had a son and never wanted to be a part of his life. And he'd seemingly made that choice to protect her mother and her? She felt conflicted about the information, as if she were somehow at fault for Logan never having had the opportunity to have a relationship with their father.

"My God, Logan. She never told you? And my father. How could he have known about you and not wanted to have some kind of relationship?"

She knew the answer. It was what she'd loved most about her father for all these years, what she'd told Garrett about at Christmas. It was her father's devotion to Willow and her mother. In the end, it had cost them all so much. In order to avoid breaking his wife's and daughter's hearts, it had cost him his son. And it had cost Willow her brother. Until now.

Logan reached across the table to hold her hand. "I know what you must be thinking, but I don't want this to change how you felt about your father. From what you've told me about him on the phone, he was a kind man and a great dad to you. It's all he was capable of. He was protecting the family he'd fought hard to have. We need to accept that, now that he's gone. It's not going to change anything for us to hate him. And, like I said, my mother is a master manipulator, and I'm convinced she is the one to blame here. Besides, we don't even know if I'm really your brother, Willow. What if she is making this whole thing up just to continue her sick extortion? I have to warn you. There is a reason she's pushed me so hard to meet you. Honestly, though, I'm only here because I had to meet you and make my own decision as to whether or not you were someone I wanted to get to know."

Willow stared at him, amazed at his practicality in handling such a sensitive issue. It was another quality that reminded her of her father. Shaking loose the memory that was too painful for her now, she stared across the table and squeezed Logan's hand. "For now, we are going to operate like you're my brother. Because, Logan, call me crazy, but I think that you are. I feel it in my bones. So *your* mother and my father aside, we are going to spend the next couple of days making up for lost time. We will worry about the motives of others later. Let's start with you meeting some people who are really important to me. The DNA results will get here when they get here. If that's OK with you, that is?"

Logan paused for a moment, then took the napkin from his lap and set it on the table, rising from his chair with a smile. Willow did the same.

"I'd like that, Willow. I'd like that very much."

# CHAPTER
# TWENTY-SEVEN

Garrett had gotten up to look out the front window so many times that Wyatt and India were afraid he was going to wear a path in the hardwood. They were all eager to meet Logan, but Garrett was understandably anxious for Willow to return from her meeting. He'd wanted to go with her, but she insisted that she wanted to meet Logan alone for the first time. The longer she was gone, the more he second-guessed his decision to let her go by herself.

"She's tougher than she looks, you know."

India hoped that by teasing Garrett, she'd lighten the mood. The three of them had been sitting around the family room trying not to watch the clock for the past ninety minutes. They'd chatted briefly about the ranch, and about Willow's new house, but the conversation kept coming back to Logan and how likely it was that he would turn out to be Willow's brother.

Garrett wasn't ready to commit to the idea just yet. "I reserve my judgement until I meet him. I've got a pretty good radar when it comes to people, so I'd like to think I'll be able to tell if his motives are pure. I know Willow is a good judge of character too, but I can't help being worried about her, alone with some guy she's never met."

Garrett was still staring out the window while he spoke. He got quiet for a moment, then suddenly turned to walk back toward the couch and join them, grabbing a magazine as he sat down and opening it to a random page. "They're here. Let's not seem like we've been sitting around talking about them. Act casual."

Wyatt snickered. "You might start by turning the magazine you're holding right side up, dummy."

India chided her husband for picking on Garrett when he was obviously unsettled, so they were busy bantering back and forth when Willow and Logan opened the front door to come inside. Garrett casually glanced over his shoulder before tossing the magazine on the coffee table nonchalantly and standing to say hello.

Willow could feel that they'd been waiting for her to return with Logan. Smiling, she closed the front door, leading the way in to where her friends were gathered.

"Guys, I want you to meet someone. Logan, these are my good friends, India and her husband, Wyatt."

They shook hands, saying hello before Logan turned his attention to Garrett.

"You must be Garrett. Willow has told me so much about you. It's really nice to meet you, man."

*Damn it.*

Garrett didn't want to like Logan right off the bat, but he couldn't help himself.

*The guy is freaking likable.*

"Nice to meet you, Logan. I look forward to hearing a lot more about you too." Garrett could feel Willow watching him, gauging his approval. He knew it was important for her that they gave Logan a chance, so he decided to go easy on the guy for the time being. "Can I get you a beer? Glass of wine?"

Garrett watched Logan, waiting for even the smallest slip.

"Sure, I'll take a beer, but only if you and Wyatt are having one. Thanks."

*OK. So he knows bro code. Good.*

Logan made himself comfortable on the couch next to Wyatt, so Willow sat down on the other side of him. Garrett returned with five bottles of beer, passing them out to everyone before taking a seat opposite the couch on the hearth.

"So Willow tells us you're a ranger. How long have you been in that line of work?" Garrett took a long drag of his beer and sat back to listen and observe.

Logan told them his story, including his time in the Air Force and how it had led him to become an Expert Ranger. By the time he got to the part about his recent winter survival training, both Wyatt and Garrett were on the edge of their seats, firing a million questions at him left and right. They were obviously impressed by his job, and Logan had such an easy way of telling a story, he had them in his corner before long.

Wyatt knew that Logan had to be an upstanding person to have put himself through the kind of training needed for his current position. "I've always wanted to hike the Appalachian Trail. I've photographed parts of it for *National Geographic*, but I always dropped in, never really hiked point to point. And I can't imagine doing it in the winter. That would be such a cool trip to take. Where did you guys sleep?"

The men continued to talk about all things wilderness while India and Willow headed to the kitchen to fix some snacks.

India slipped her arm around her friend, rubbing her back reassuringly. "Garrett was as nervous as Jell-O while you were gone. He hasn't sat still all afternoon."

They glanced back over to see that Garrett had finally joined the other two men on the couch and was now leaning back, his leg thrown casually over his knee and his entire posture changed to reflect his now-relaxed manner.

"From the looks of things, he's finally settled himself down."

India smiled at Willow. "Logan is really nice. I don't know what I expected, but I'm glad he's found a common bond with the guys. That will make things so much easier this weekend. For all of us."

India popped the top off three more bottles of beer and took them over to the men before returning to Willow, who had started peeling some avocados to make guacamole. She handed India a knife, two limes, and a red onion, then slid a cutting board her way.

"I don't know how to explain it, India. I know we have to wait for the official test results, but I just know." She looked over at Logan again, who was now laughing at something Wyatt was saying. Willow lowered her voice. "I just know he's my brother. I can't put my finger on why, but there are little things he does that remind me of my dad. Which is crazy, because he never even knew my father. Anyway, I'm willing to give him the benefit of the doubt until we hear. Which I'm hoping will be soon."

India snapped her fingers, wiping her hands on a dish towel before walking over to the notepad that was next to the phone. "Someone called for you when you were gone. A

Robert Johnston? He said you should call him back at your earliest convenience. I totally forgot to tell you in the excitement of meeting Logan."

The color drained out of Willow's face, and she passed the bowl of half-mashed avocado to India. "That's my father's attorney. I'd better call him to see what's going on. Will you excuse me for a minute?"

Willow grabbed her cell phone and the Post-it note with his number and walked discreetly down the hallway to return the call. She was gone for a few minutes before returning to the kitchen to help India finish preparing the snacks. She didn't immediately offer any information about the phone call, so India didn't ask.

Willow thought she might burst. Carrying the tray toward the sofa, she leaned over to set it on the coffee table before standing up with her hands on her hips. Expelling a breath, she delivered the news. "Well, Logan. The DNA results are in. My father's—our father's—attorney received them today, but they're sealed, only to be opened by the two of us. He's having the envelope overnighted here, so we should have the results by this time tomorrow."

The room was quiet as everyone processed the information. Logan was about to say something, but Willow interrupted him.

"Can I speak with you for a minute privately? Maybe I could walk you to the guest apartment to show you where you'll be staying, and we could talk on the way?"

Logan followed Willow down the hallway and through the glass catwalk that connected the main house with the guest suite. Using a key she'd grabbed from a hook in the kitchen, she opened the door and led him inside. It was a charming one-room guest suite with a large, comfortable-looking bed, a small kitchenette, and a door in the corner leading to the bathroom. As she turned to face him, Willow's eyes were troubled when she spoke.

"The attorney told me something else. He said that your mother has been repeatedly calling his office, demanding to know when the results would be made available to her. He informed her that only you and I would know the results and that it would be up to one of us to share them with her if we chose to do so. I wanted to tell you that privately, since you trusted me enough to tell me about your mother earlier. It's no one else's business but yours."

Logan reached out to hug her briefly, then he stepped back to look at her. "Thank you for that. I felt like I made a little progress with the guys back there, and I'd hate to have them question me over the actions of someone I've only seen a handful of times over the past few years. My mother does not speak for me, and she never will. You don't have to worry about that, Willow."

He glanced around for the bathroom. "If it's OK with you, I'm going to use the restroom, and then I'd love to rejoin you all in the family room? Your friends are such great people. Thank you for inviting me to meet them. I can see why you love them."

Willow went back to help India while Logan tended to his business. He'd just washed up and was drying his hands when he heard his phone buzzing in his duffle bag. Reaching in, he glanced at the screen, disgusted by what he saw.

> I know you're getting those results soon. You'd better call me the minute you do. We have a right to that inheritance Logan. Don't go all soft on me boy. I'll expect to hear from you real soon.

Logan felt the same sick feeling in the pit of his stomach that he did every time he heard from his mother, which wasn't often. He usually just ignored her, and eventually she'd go away, but he had a feeling this time would be different. Tossing the phone onto the foot of the bed, he decided he'd deal with her later, if at all. Right now he had a sister to get to know, so he went back to rejoin the others and do just that.

They had a great time the rest of the evening, eventually sitting around the fire telling stories and—more often than not—cracking each other up. It was late when Willow remembered she hadn't yet stocked his guest room with towels, so she slipped away to grab some from upstairs and deliver them to the apartment. She'd just set them on the foot of the bed when she noticed his phone light up, startled by the buzzing sound it made. She couldn't help but see on the screen that it was a text from his mother.

> I'm serious boy. I'd better hear about those results tomorrow one way or another. That girl has plenty of inheritance to share and half of it is rightfully ours. I'll make sure we get it. Call me.

Willow wished she could unsee it, but she couldn't shake the words from her mind. Returning to the family room, she forced a smile when she told everyone she was exhausted and ready for bed. They all carried the dishes into the kitchen and said their good nights before drifting off to their respective rooms, but not before Logan and Willow had made a plan to meet at nine in the morning to go skiing.

Once they were in bed, Garrett knew it was time to admit that he'd been wrong.

"Logan is a great guy, Willow. I feel bad I gave you a hard time about him. I hope you know I was just trying to protect you from getting hurt. After talking with him tonight, either he's an Academy Award–winning actor or he's one of the genuinely nicest guys I've ever met. If he's not your brother, would you care if I asked him to be mine? I have to hurry and beat Wyatt to the punch."

He'd propped himself up on one elbow to study her, surprised when she only smiled at his joke. Something was wrong.

Willow decided to share with him what Logan had told her earlier about his mother and also what she'd seen on his phone. But she wasn't ready to draw the worst conclusion from it, and neither was Garrett, which surprised her.

"I think if I'd heard all that before I'd met him, I would have absolutely been ready to leap out of this bed and kick his ass out of here. But I don't know, Willow. Strangely, I trust the guy, and I think he genuinely wants to see about forging some kind of relationship with you—obviously depending on what those results tell us tomorrow."

She was tucked into the crook of his arm and Garrett was stroking her hair while he talked, trying to ignore the way she absentmindedly ran her foot up and down his calf while she listened.

"Why don't you sleep on it, have a nice day with Logan tomorrow, and when the envelope comes—open it. You can decide what you want to do from there." He paused, adding one final thought. "Oh, and if you need me to help you take your mind off of it all tonight, keep doing that with your foot. I have a few ideas of how to relieve your tension."

That was exactly what Willow wanted, having missed being alone with him all day. She scooted herself over so that she was lying on top of him, her body flush with his. He wrapped her up in his powerful embrace, and in one quick motion, he had her underneath him, his knee having parted her legs so he could reach down and show her what he'd meant. It wasn't long before his touch had her writhing under him, begging him to come closer still. He did, and as they fit together, Garrett whispered to Willow how much he loved her and always would. It was enough to send them both over the edge and into a place where their dreams that night would be only good ones.

# CHAPTER
# TWENTY-EIGHT

Willow woke to the smell of bacon and coffee and the sound of muffled voices floating up the stairs. Stretching, she rolled over to glance at the clock, realizing her alarm was set to go off in about ten minutes. With a sigh, she threw the covers off, sliding her feet into her slippers, which she'd left next to the bed. On her way to find her robe, she pulled back the drapes to peek outside, surprised to see snow falling so heavily that she could barely make out the house next door. Shivering, she headed into the bathroom, grabbing her thick white robe off the hook and slipping into it. She brushed her teeth and threw her hair into a ponytail before heading downstairs to see who was up.

As Willow stepped out into the hallway, she heard Garrett erupt into laughter from downstairs. At the same time, the door across the hall swung open, and India emerged wearing sweats, her own hair in a haphazard bun on the top of her head. Willow laughed at India's deadpan look, and they rolled their eyes at each other before heading down to see what was going on.

They found Garrett behind the counter extracting a cookie sheet lined with bacon from the oven while Wyatt sat at the counter holding out his mug toward Logan, who'd gotten up to get the coffeepot. It was a well-oiled machine.

"Well, hi, ladies!"

Wyatt was a little too cheerful for the hour, so India playfully slipped her hand over his mouth, which gave him the chance to pull her into his lap, where he buried his face in her neck.

"Mmmm. No offense, Garrett. The bacon smells great, but nothing beats the scent of my wife when she first crawls out of a warm bed in the morning."

India swatted him, laughing and trying to get away before he could embarrass her any further. Willow made her way to Garrett and slid her arm around him for a hug. She planted a kiss on his cheek before reaching past him to grab two coffee cups from the cupboard.

"These boys don't need any more caffeine, Logan. Why don't you hand me that pot so India and I can try to play catch-up?"

Logan reached over and filled their cups while India fished the cream out of the refrigerator.

"So, Willow, I know we'd planned on skiing today, but the visibility looks like it's going to be pretty bad for most of the day. I'm not sure it's a great idea to get on that mountain with a bunch of people who can't see where they're going," Logan said.

He was about to add something else when Garrett jumped in. "Logan's been telling Wyatt and me all about his winter search-and-rescue training. You wouldn't believe what he had to go through to get certified. This guy is like MacGyver!"

Wyatt swallowed his bacon, nodding his head in vigorous agreement. "Yeah, so we've been down here since sunrise—or lack of it—trying to convince him that, even though it's snowing like the devil, that doesn't mean we have to be trapped inside all day."

Wyatt stopped short, looking over at India and Willow, his hands held up in mock apology. "No offense. Not that being here with you lovely ladies all day would be bad, it's just, how often do you have a real mountain man at your disposal? Garrett and I think we should all gear up and go snowshoeing. If you girls are up for it, that is?"

Willow was watching Logan. She couldn't read him but thought that he was being awfully quiet. After a moment, he spoke. "The guys tell me that the four of you snowshoe a lot. Which is great; it's such a fast-growing sport. I've seen the number of new snowshoers triple during the time I've been in Colorado Springs. The problem is, most people don't consider the proper gear for the weather and terrain where they'll be shoeing. Around here, I think we'd ordinarily be better off with crampons, which are basically like grappling hooks for your feet. But today's weather makes that call questionable. It's been snowing most of the night, so the powder is pretty deep. In these conditions, snowshoes are better for floatation on top of the powder. Provided there isn't any kind of boiler-plate situation going on below."

Willow was impressed with how much he knew about the outdoors, and based on the dreamy looks on Wyatt and Garrett's faces, she knew they were in the throes of full-blown man crushes.

She could also tell that Logan was still working through whether or not the idea was a good one.

"What are boilerplate conditions?"

Logan finished his coffee, setting the cup down on the counter. "It's when the weather starts off warmer, creating a soft or wet base layer of snow, then a cold front moves through and causes kind of a melt-freeze crust. That's what climbers call a boilerplate. It's not an ideal condition for snowshoeing because it can make slipping and falling more likely. You're really at the mercy of your cleats in those situations. I don't think we need to worry about that, though. Garrett says you guys have had a ton of snow since you've been here, and it's pretty cold outside, so we should be OK. I just need to know that you guys all feel comfortable enough wearing the gear and that you've done it enough times to feel safe doing it in these conditions?"

They all agreed that they were willing to give it a try, so after everyone had had the chance to shower and change into their winter gear, they piled into Willow's rented SUV to head up to the nearest trailhead.

By the time they'd made it across town, the snow had subsided a little, making it easier to find the sign marking the start of the trail. They'd stopped on the way to rent gear from a shop in town, and the kid who'd helped them had told them that a few others were already out ahead of them, which didn't surprise Logan one bit.

The Rockies were home to people who liked to live on the edge, always craving a new outdoor adventure. Today's epic snowfall would draw locals to the mountains for one reason or another, like moths to a flame.

They'd each picked out their shoes, along with trekking poles for balance, and grabbed some hand warmers and bottled water for their packs before heading out.

At the trailhead, Logan checked out the map, turning toward the group while he pulled his gloves on. "Why don't I break trail first? Unfortunately, enough fresh snow has fallen to cover the tracks of anyone who went up before us, which isn't a huge deal, but I'd like to go first because the ascent happens pretty quickly on this trail. Once we reach the meadow, we can start to rotate in, which will give everyone's legs a break. Sound OK?"

They agreed, and Logan took the lead, setting out in the direction of the base of the mountain. In the beginning, they ran parallel to Hunter Creek, but true to Logan's promise, the path soon began to dramatically climb, causing them all to work harder to fill their lungs. The fact that they were at almost eight thousand feet added to their struggle.

Willow drank in the crisp wintery air, expelling it in an icy puff. She enjoyed the quiet of the woods, and before long, her heart rate moderated and the satisfying crunch of fresh snow under her shoes became meditative. The creek was gurgling over any stones in its way, providing a nice complement to the entire visceral experience.

After a little while, the trail evened out, so Logan made way for India to lead. He stood for a moment while waiting for the rest of them to pass him by, creating a natural rotation that they would continue to follow for the rest of the climb. He'd clearly done this before and knew that such a rotation was the best way to ensure that everyone got a chance to rest their legs. India lasted about as long as Logan had, so they decided they'd all better start taking turns about every fifteen minutes. They weren't able to talk much, due to exertion, but every so often, when they stopped to switch leaders, they'd pause to chat.

They'd been hiking about an hour when Logan stopped to look up at the sky in concern. "It feels like we might be in for another wave of weather soon. What do you guys say we head back and get a jump on it?"

Garrett had been looking at the small map he'd purchased earlier and spoke up before anyone else could answer. "Could we hike just a bit farther? It looks like we're really close to Benedict Bridge, and if it's not snowing yet, we might be in for a great view of downtown Aspen and Ajax. Besides, I have an idea."

"I thought I smelled smoke."

Everyone laughed at Wyatt, always quick to bust Garrett's chops. They all agreed they would forge ahead, compelled by the idea of a great potential photo op. It wasn't long before they'd made it to the bridge, and they were just in time for a glimpse of the promised view before the snow started up again.

Garrett sat down to unsnap his snowshoes, talking excitedly as he did. "So, I think we need to build a cairn together. You know, those cool rock towers we've been seeing along the way? The ones that people build on boulders in the river? How cool would it be for us to build one down there, commemorating this awesome climb?"

He pointed below, where the river was rippling out from under the bridge. There were several large boulders to choose from, so once the group had agreed on one, they clipped out of their snowshoes and headed down the side of the mountain, using a small path that was next to the farthest end of the bridge.

It was an easy climb down to the riverbed, which sat about twenty-five feet below the bridge. Once there, they began collecting small rocks from the banks, stacking them to form a base before building the tower up from there. They made short work of it, and after about twenty minutes, they'd created a structure that stood almost three feet high. There was beauty in the irregularity of it, rocks of all shapes and sizes used for the common purpose of commemorating a moment in time. Wyatt pulled out his phone and extended his arm to snap a group picture of the five of them with their creation. It was snowing harder at that point, so they agreed they should scramble back up the hill to start the trek back down the mountain.

Logan went first so that he could assist the others with their gear once they made it to the top. Willow was about to start the climb up behind India when Garrett grabbed her around her waist and spun her around. He had ice crystals clinging to his whiskered face and covering his hat, and she could see his breaths coming out in clouds as he pulled her close.

"I love you, Willow. I'm not sure I've told you that yet today, and I don't ever want to miss a chance. Thanks for indulging my rock-sculpture fetish."

Willow laughed, brushing the snow from his face with her gloved hands, leaning in to softly kiss his lips. They must have lingered a little too long, because Wyatt was hollering at them from the bridge to get a move on, so they broke apart, but not before Willow whispered in Garrett's ear, "I love you too. And I'll never forget this day. Thank you for your kindness toward Logan."

She leaned back to look him in the eye. "I know he's my brother, Garrett. I don't need a piece of paper to confirm it. And you including him the way you have means the world to me. So, thank you."

Once they were all back on the bridge, Logan unlocked his cell phone to take a look at the weather radar. "It might be pretty rough going down, guys. This snow is coming in fast, so we really need to make good time getting out of here. That path we made on the way up might be hard to see once the wind picks up, so just make sure to try to stay single file and follow in my tracks as best you can. Why don't we have India behind me, followed by Wyatt, then Willow, and Garrett can be at the back?"

They grabbed their trekking poles and set out, the snow blinding them as they went. They had to allow enough room between them for their oversized shoes, and with the visibility, at times it was difficult to make out the person in front of them. In the beginning, they could still follow the path they'd taken in, but by the time they made it about halfway down, Logan was using pure instinct to find his way.

He'd been watching earlier for landmarks to guide them back out if necessary, just as he'd been taught to do throughout his ranger training. Every so often, he'd glance back to make sure the group was all together, but he could only see India clearly, the rest of them swallowed up by the poor conditions.

Garrett was bringing up the rear, sticking as close as he could to Willow. He'd had to go to the bathroom for a while, but he didn't want to stop and risk being separated from the group. Finally, when he felt they'd slowed a bit because of a steep decline, he stepped behind a tree to relieve himself quickly so he could focus on the rest of the descent.

Willow had been turning around every few minutes too to make sure Garrett was still behind her, so when she glanced back and he wasn't there, she didn't believe her eyes at first. Stopping, she waited for a moment to see if he would materialize out of the curtain of white surrounding her, but he didn't.

Turning back around, she couldn't see Wyatt anymore either. He too had been swallowed up by the swirl of snow.

Willow felt her pulse quicken as she started back up the trail toward Garrett. After a few steps, she saw him off to her right stepping out of the woods, zipping up his snow pants. She moved toward him, and was about to call out, when suddenly her snowshoe didn't hold. She panicked as she felt herself go down hard, the wind knocked from her body as she slid.

Willow heard Garrett's muffled voice call her name, but it was too late. She tumbled a few feet down the trail, falling through a crevasse on one side that had been camouflaged by the snow. She was aware of a piercing pain in her ankle before everything started to go dark as she bounced down the side of the mountain, coming to rest facedown about thirty yards from where she'd fallen.

The last thing she would remember was being turned over and then Logan's face above hers asking her to stay with him.

She wanted to, but the excruciating pain in her side made her forget all about her ankle.

She'd close her eyes, just for a moment.

# CHAPTER
# TWENTY-NINE

Willow wanted to roll over and switch her alarm clock off, but she couldn't. The noise was driving her crazy, beeping over and over like that. She didn't feel tired, but she couldn't make herself open her eyes, no matter how hard she tried. She had to force her brain to try to figure out why before she finally realized that she wasn't at home in her own bed. She remembered falling, tumbling in a blur of snow and ice until she lay still in terrible pain. The look in Logan's eyes. The sound of Garrett's voice, desperately calling to her. It all rushed back in a whoosh, and her eyes popped open as if forced by the memories.

She blinked a few times, trying to make sense of it all, and saw that she was in a hospital room, surrounded by machines that were buzzing and blinking.

And beeping.

The alarm she'd been hearing.

With effort, she turned her head ever so slightly and saw Garrett slumped over on the couch, his head resting on his arm, fast asleep. He looked like he hadn't shaved in days, and he was wearing his old University of Washington sweatshirt and jeans. Tears pricked at her eyes, and as she moved to wipe them away with her hand, she felt a stabbing pain in her side, causing her to cry out and lie still. The noise was enough to startle him awake.

Garrett had been dreaming of this moment for the past three days. Waking up and seeing her warm brown eyes staring back at him. The reality of it was like an adrenaline rush, and he shot off the couch toward her, stopping himself from grabbing her in an embrace. Leaning over her, he placed his hand gently on her cheek, brushing the tears away and reaching to place a soft kiss on her forehead, her cheeks, her nose. She tried to speak, but he put his fingers against her lips, telling her to save her strength, which she gladly did.

Willow heard him calling for the doctor, so she closed her eyes again, grateful and relieved to know that Garrett was there. She drifted in and out of consciousness after that, vaguely aware of the commotion she had caused by waking up. It seemed like every half hour there were nurses checking her vitals and teams of doctors stopping by to review her chart with interns in tow. She slept through most of it, but at one point she thought that it seemed like an awful lot of fuss for a broken bone or two. She remembered hurting her ankle and maybe breaking a rib during the fall, but everything after that was a blur.

Through it all, though, she could feel Garrett there. Sometimes he was rubbing her hand and telling her how much he loved her. But he didn't need to tell her. She knew. She'd dreamt of him while she was unconscious. They were sitting in a swing on the porch of her farmhouse. She'd tried hard to see which house it was, but she couldn't make herself focus hard enough to figure it out. In the end, she'd decided it didn't matter. The fact that she was there with him was the headline.

After what seemed like an eternity, she finally woke up again, and this time, she felt present and truly awake. Garrett was sitting next to her, his eyes smiling back when she opened hers and saw him there.

She squeaked out a greeting. "Hi." It was barely more than a whisper, her voice in need of some exercise.

"Hi, yourself. Welcome back, my love." He brought her hand to his lips. "You have no idea how glad I am to see those beautiful brown eyes of yours."

Willow smiled at him, thinking that, even though he looked completely exhausted, he'd never been more devastatingly handsome. God, she loved this man. "How long have I been here?"

Willow knew it had been at least a night or two, since she remembered waking up and seeing him the day before.

Garrett took a deep breath, trying to determine how much she was ready to hear.

"It's been five days, Willow. Do you remember anything at all?"

His eyes searched hers, wishing he could erase the panic he saw there. He knew she couldn't have remembered anything after the fall, but he wondered if she could even recall the accident at all.

"I remember looking back for you, and my foot slipping, and then I tumbled for what seemed like a long time. From the looks of my foot, I'm pretty sure that I broke my ankle?"

She wiggled the toes of her left foot, which were protruding from a cast that went up to the bottom of her knee.

"You broke your tibia and fibula, actually. Both bones in your lower leg. Lucky for you, they were clean breaks, and low enough that your cast didn't have to go all the way up to your hip." Garrett paused, struggling with the rest. "Willow, it's my fault. I thought we had slowed down enough for me to duck behind a tree to use the restroom. It didn't occur to me that you'd turn around to come looking for me. If I hadn't stopped, you wouldn't have lost your bearings in the storm and slipped into that canyon. You never would have needed . . ."

Garrett stopped himself, his face turning white as he reached up to remove his baseball hat and run his fingers though his hair.

"I wouldn't have needed what, Garrett? What's wrong with me?" Willow was suddenly very aware of the acute pain in her abdomen, and she started to feel panicked at the worried look on his face.

"Nothing now, Willow. You're fine. You're going to be fine. But . . ."

"But what? Tell me!"

Garrett took a breath, blew it out, and then turned to look into her eyes, his voice tortured as he spoke. "You injured your liver, Willow. Badly. You've been here for five days because you're recovering from an emergency liver transplant."

Logan had been a complete and total mess since they'd reached Aspen Valley Hospital. He'd done all he could by getting Willow to the bottom of the trailhead as swiftly as possible with Garrett's help, where they'd been met by an ambulance that India had called. But Logan couldn't help reliving the accident over and over in his head.

He should have known better than to keep going with the heavy snow returning. He just hadn't wanted to ruin the good time they were having, and Garrett's idea had sounded like such a bonding opportunity, so he'd ignored his gut, which he'd never done before with any success. By the time he'd realized something was wrong, thanks to India's screams for help, Garrett had already scrambled down into the canyon to where Willow lay facedown, unmoving in the snow. Logan had practically leapt down to meet him, cautioning Garrett against moving her before he was able to determine that she hadn't suffered a neck injury. After a brief evaluation, it had seemed unlikely that she had, but her leg was likely broken. Other than that, she'd seemed uninjured, at least from her outward appearance.

Logan's extensive training had prepared him for the worst, though. He'd known that, with a fall like that, she could have sustained internal injuries, which had made it imperative for them to get her to the hospital as soon as possible. He'd lifted her as tenderly as he could, and, with help from both Garrett and Wyatt, had gotten her up to the trail that led back to where they'd parked. He'd had to convince Garrett to let him split time carrying her down the mountain, so neither of them accidentally overexerted themselves and made the situation even worse.

He now understood how people experienced superhuman strength when faced with a seemingly insurmountable task. Looking back, he had no idea how they'd managed to get her all the way down the mountain by themselves. But they had, and now they were just waiting for her to wake up from the whole ordeal.

He stood gingerly, wincing at the pain he still felt in his own side but ignoring it and pushing through it so he could walk to see Willow.

He stepped out into the hallway, checking both ways before heading back toward Willow's room. He'd gone only a few feet when he heard India and Wyatt behind him.

"Where do you think you're going, Logan? Do the nurses know you're out here?"

India rushed toward him, turning to stand between him and the doorway of Willow's room.

"They do, mother hen, but thanks for asking. They encouraged it, actually. So why don't we all go in and see how she's doing?"

India grabbed Logan's hand on one side, while Wyatt stood on the other side of him, ready to offer physical support if needed. Together that way, the three of them walked toward Willow's room and froze when they saw that Willow was finally awake. They stood quietly as they heard her asking Garrett a question.

"How could I have gotten a liver transplant that quickly? Aren't there thousands of people on the waiting list? Why would I get to jump the line like that?"

Garrett glanced over to where his friends stood with Logan in the doorway. "Why don't you ask Logan? He can tell you more. After all, he did give you half of his own liver. I think it's his story to tell."

Willow turned to follow Garrett's gaze, locking eyes with Logan and staring at him in disbelief. Before she knew what was happening, she felt a wracking sob escaping her throat and was unable to stop the flood of emotions she felt as she lay there staring at this man who'd saved her life.

Logan's own eyes filled with tears as he watched Willow realize the depths of what had happened.

When they'd arrived at the hospital and had heard that she was in acute liver failure due to the blunt force trauma of the fall, each of them had immediately begun the process of testing to see if they were a match. Only Logan and India had the same blood type, which was a prerequisite for a living donor match. But Logan knew he might share something more than blood type with Willow, and there was only one way to find out.

He'd left the hospital briefly on that second day, rushing back to the house where he'd known he'd find the UPS letter they'd been expecting to receive on the afternoon of the accident. He started to open it right there on the porch but decided to wait and do it in front of India, Wyatt, and Garrett, so they could all make the decision together about what was best for Willow.

They'd opened it in her room, where she still lay sedated and unresponsive, her body primed and ready for the one thing that could save her life: a new liver. It was decided after much discussion that, regardless of the results, his blood type and the fact that he wasn't a new mother meant Logan would be the one to donate half of his liver to Willow. After a battery of rushed tests, the doctors had explained the risks to him, and he was in surgery less than twelve hours later.

Now, just two days later, he was up and walking at the advice of and with permission from his doctors, but only around the surgical floor. He'd been transferred there to be near Willow after they'd both spent the first twenty-four hours in intensive care. The surgery had gone perfectly, and if everything went as expected, Logan would be in the hospital for just a few more days. He'd be able to resume normal activities, and even return to work, in just three to six weeks. His own liver would completely regenerate itself over the next two months, allowing him to go back to a completely normal life. The portion that he'd donated to Willow would grow inside of her to become whole again within that same time frame, and she would be completely healed inside of a year. In his mind, it had been a no-brainer. Saving lives was what he was trained to do.

And this life was more important to him than any other.

This life was his sister's.

Now, as he approached Willow's bedside, he was overcome with the emotion of it all. He had a sister, and she was a good one. A kind one. Having a family member who cared about him would be a new experience for him. Maybe her love would be enough to soften his heart, which had hardened from all the years of neglect at the hands of his mother. He'd been honored to be the best match for Willow. And according to the letter he showed her now, they had confirmation that they did indeed share DNA.

He watched Willow take in the words she was reading, her eyes filling once again with tears when she looked back up at him. Logan bent down to hug his sister but winced again when the stabbing pain in his side reminded him to move gingerly. Instead, he sat beside her in the chair that Garrett had vacated for him, but not before Garrett gave Logan a quick embrace.

That was the best part.

Willow was a package deal.

From the moment they'd first read the results with him in Willow's hospital room, India, Wyatt, and Garrett had welcomed him as one of their own. India and Wyatt were there with him when he woke up from his own surgery, making sure that Garrett was kept in the loop while he sat vigil at Willow's bedside. They were his family now too. He would do whatever he had to do to protect this. To protect them.

To that end, he'd made sure he'd answered his mother's dozens of texts asking about the DNA results before he went into surgery. He'd lied and told her that he and Willow weren't related, after all, and that the results had been conclusive. His mother hadn't even bothered to answer him after that, and he suspected it would be a long time before he heard from her again. He hoped so anyway. He didn't want her anywhere near this new family he'd begun to create for himself.

Willow had stopped crying and was sitting quietly, surrounded by Garrett, Wyatt, and India. Squeezing Logan's hand, she swallowed the lump in her throat, unsure of how to thank him for what he'd done. "Thank you, my brother. For the liver."

Logan smiled, squeezing her hand. "My sister. That's so crazy to say. It was the greatest pleasure of my life to do this for you, Willow. It wasn't even a question for me. I think I knew the moment I saw you. My soul recognized yours. I can't help but think that our father would be pleased to know that we have each other. I don't blame him, Willow. You have to know that. He was just protecting you, and now that I know you, I can see why. What he couldn't give me during his lifetime, he's made up for by raising you the way he did. I'm grateful to have the time we'll have from today going forward." Logan paused, his brow furrowed. "Just one thing?"

Willow's smile faded, her face growing serious as she waited to hear what he needed from her. "Anything, Logan. I owe you my life, for heaven's sake!"

Logan tried to keep his face serious, but he lost the battle, breaking into a handsome grin as he looked around the room for their friends to back him up. "Next time there's a blizzard? Let's just stay in and play Scrabble."

# EPILOGUE

After what seemed like an endless winter, hibernating meadows finally started to reemerge from under the heavy white blankets of snow in the Rockies. The buds on the aspen trees in Willow's front yard were fuzzy and pregnant by May, ready to explode into summertime, when they'd wave proudly in the mountain breezes until turning a glorious yellow just a few short months later. The months of May and June in the Roaring Fork Valley were known as mud season, but this spring, there hadn't been a lot of additional rain or snow, so the melt-off was the only source of water, creating less muddy, more favorable conditions for outdoor enthusiasts.

Willow wouldn't say she'd been much of an outdoor enthusiast herself since moving to Aspen, thanks to her new liver. She hadn't been allowed to start driving again until late March and had found it nearly impossible to let the others do everything for her in the meantime. Logan had to lay daily guilt trips on her about not ruining his perfectly nice gift by taking unnecessary chances before he'd finally convinced her to relent and focus on her recovery.

Susan and Finn had flown out to Aspen to meet with Willow shortly after she and Logan were released from the hospital. Willow and Logan had spent seven days in the observation wing and had been home for about a week. Susan insisted that the two of them stay and recover in her and Finn's home in the West End, since it was already furnished with all of the comforts that they would need. Susan and Finn enjoyed getting to know Logan during their week-long visit, encouraging him to remain in the guest suite for as long as he needed it.

"Honestly, if I didn't know you, Logan, it would only take one look at you to know you're related to this pretty gal. And you both have the same tenacity, that's for darn sure." Finn had fallen hard for Logan, just like the other guys, impressed with his training and work ethic. Logan had taken a medical leave for his own two-month recovery period, intending to return to Colorado Springs in March, but Susan had a better idea, which she'd shared with Finn on the second-to-last night of their visit.

"India told me that Willow is struggling with where she wants her life to go from here. It's understandable, of course. When you go through a medical crisis, your priorities certainly crystallize."

Finn raised his eyebrows in agreement. "I know that. Those few moments I spent on the floor during my heart attack brought everything into focus for me, for sure."

Susan smiled, reaching to place her hand in his. "I have an idea, Finn. What if we gave her the reason she's looking for to stay here in Aspen? She has her house, so that box is checked. What she's missing is some roots. We know that Garrett would move here to be with her, that's a given. Have you seen the way they look at each other? It's so beautiful to see. But what if we could convince Logan to relocate too? The three of them would be the perfect team to get Walland House up and running, and they'd have accountability to each other and a real reason to stay here long-term, which is just the kind of commitment we're looking for."

Finn raised Susan's hand to his lips for a kiss, chuckling at the twinkle in her eyes. "Now who's busy coming up with grand ideas? Susie . . . that's why I married you. Someone has to be the brains behind all this beauty."

They couldn't wait to share their idea, and with just a few phone calls, the rest of the details fell right into place.

When the former GM of the resort back in Tennessee had heard about Willow's accident, he'd offered to step back out of retirement until they could find a more permanent replacement. Susan knew that she had another Finn on her hands. These dynamic men thought they should retire in their sixties and seventies, but they still had so much to give. Michael Cummins was more than happy to extend his tenure with the farm, indefinitely if needed. Susan wasn't surprised in the least.

With the flagship resort in good hands, Susan and Finn officially asked Willow to stay on and become the general manager of Walland House in Aspen while convincing Garrett to move West as well in order to establish heirloom farming practices on the newly acquired ranch. Willow and Garrett couldn't believe their good fortune. *The mountains are calling, and we must go.* It was right out of a John Muir essay. But that wasn't the best part. Susan gathered them all in the family room of the house in the West End to make the pitch to Logan.

"We've decided that there is just one thing missing from this plan of action that we've been concocting. It's my and Finn's opinion that Logan would be the perfect complement to complete the Walland House team."

Logan was stunned, but it didn't take much convincing for him to agree to stay on to head up and help run the extreme outdoor activities they planned to offer on property. It would be a new chapter for him in a place that had the landscape he loved, and more importantly, he would have the luxury of time and space to get to know his sister and Garrett better.

India and Wyatt had gone home to Tennessee shortly after Willow and Logan had been discharged from the hospital, needing to get back to their babies. After hearing about the new plans, they were understandably sad to be losing their friends to Colorado but were looking forward to being together soon enough for the Food and Wine Classic, which was coming up in late June. This year they'd just be observing, soaking in the atmosphere of the festival and getting ideas, since the resort wouldn't be fully operational until the fall. They'd take what they learned this year and be ready for the following summer.

While he had been a little reluctant to lose Garrett, both professionally and as a friend, Finn felt good about the abilities of his remaining garden staff to pick up the slack back in Tennessee, and he admitted to Garrett that he'd already hatched a plan to try to move forward without him.

"We need more land managers like you, Garrett, not less. It's up to me to take one or two of those young guys we've got back at the resort and try to grow them in your mold. They'll have big shoes to fill, but I'm not going anywhere anytime soon, so I'm willing to devote the time and resources. We've got enough good people to cover the resort and the new orchard. You worry about getting the gardens at Walland House operational. Heck, I might even see if one of those young bucks would accept a transfer out here to work with you."

Logan and Willow had stayed back in Aspen together while Garrett traveled to Knoxville to facilitate the move. After multiple promises to Garrett that they would follow the rules, Willow and Logan finally convinced him to leave them alone for the week. They figured that, between the two of them, they had a whole liver; what could go wrong?

Once in Knoxville, Garrett had given notice to his landlord, arranging with a moving company to pack and ship his stuff out to Aspen as soon as possible. There had been even less to do at Willow's place. Most of her stuff was still in boxes from when she'd moved in, so after taking inventory with Willow over the phone, Garrett signed off with the crew on what stayed and what got shipped.

Walland House had gone from idea to reality, just like that. Everyone was excited to expand the cherished brand out West, with the best possible team in place to do it.

Initially, Garrett had missed Tennessee, but he'd grown to love Aspen in the five months since he'd been there. He and Logan had grown close, and, most days, he felt like he'd been blessed with a brother at the same time as Willow. Spring had eventually made the turn to summer, the season that locals loved best because the days were long and mostly spent outside. Aspen was a casual town with no dress code, an educated population, and great legs everywhere you looked, thanks to the active lifestyle.

But there was one powerful reason that Garrett knew he'd never leave.

She was fast asleep next to him.

It was the twentieth of June, the morning of the opening day of the Food and Wine Classic. It was also the five-month anniversary of Willow's accident and a day that Garrett had been thinking about for weeks.

He lay still, watching as Willow stirred and started to wake up. Her eyes fluttered open as if she could sense him watching her, and when she noticed that he was, she turned to rest her cheek against her hand on the pillow.

"Hi."

"Hi, yourself. How'd you sleep?"

She smiled, scooting closer to him, tucking her feet in between his legs to snuggle. "I slept great. How about you, birthday boy?" She stretched enough to kiss him softly on the lips before pulling back to study him once more. "You don't look like a man who's thirty."

Garrett slapped her gently on the bottom, causing her to try to squirm away, but he wouldn't let her go before he'd gotten another birthday kiss. Finally, when she managed to reluctantly break away from him, she scampered out of bed and slipped into her robe, peeking through the blinds out the window. Looking back at him, she had a smile on her face.

"Wanna see your birthday present? It's right outside."

Garrett yawned and stretched his arms over his head. After a moment, he threw back the covers and strode over to where she stood while Willow watched him, admiring the view. He took her breath away, and she giggled when she realized his birthday outfit was perfect.

"Something funny?"

Garrett untied the belt of Willow's robe, reaching up to push it off her shoulders, letting it fall to the floor at her feet. She blushed, still a little self-conscious about her postsurgical body. She covered her scar with one hand, still smiling shyly at him.

"Now it's a party. I was just thinking that you're literally in your birthday suit, but now I guess I'm following the dress code too."

Willow got serious in a hurry when Garrett slid his hands down her arms, lightening his touch as he brushed her hand away, and lay his own hands on her belly above her scar.

"I love this part of you."

He dropped down to his knees, gently trailing his fingers along the tender pink flesh where they'd had to cut her. Willow shivered, closing her eyes. He reached forward to place kisses all around the scar before standing again to pull her into his arms. "Every time I see that, I'm reminded to cherish each and every day we have together. I love you so much, Willow."

Garrett was about to show her just how much when they were both startled by the persistent honking of a horn coming from the yard. Willow grinned at him, reaching down to grab her robe.

"Unfortunately, this will have to wait until later. Hurry up and throw some clothes on. Your gifts await you, and it sounds like they're getting impatient."

They rushed around, quickly dressing and brushing their teeth before heading downstairs to the front door. Willow opened it, walking out first and stepping aside to watch Garrett's expression.

He couldn't believe his eyes. There in the yard was a classic green John Deere tractor with a big red bow on the front. What made Garrett laugh, though, was that Finn was behind the wheel while the rest of their friends stood around hooting and hollering birthday greetings. India and Wyatt were there with Susan, who had the babies in a double stroller, and Violet was holding Evan while Rex chased Sadie around the yard, trying to keep her from climbing up to sit with Finn.

"Happy birthday, Garrett," Finn yelled out over the noise. "Susan and I figured that if you're going to try to get the ranch in any kind of shape over the next year, you'll need some proper equipment. We already used her to cut a path through the aspen groves between this place and Walland House. Makes your commute a lot easier."

Garrett was grinning from ear to ear as he circled the tractor, giving it a closer look. He hugged each of their friends, happy to be seeing them for the first time since they'd officially moved to Aspen. Logan was the only one missing, and Garrett was looking around for him when he heard the sound of tires crunching on the gravel drive behind him. Willow sidled up next to Garrett, slipping her arm around his waist as he turned to look up the drive, a sly smile on her face.

"There's just one more thing. You can't take that tractor into town, and I know the lease on your Jeep is up soon. Rumor has it you told my brother that you've always had your eye on one particular kind of car. So we went out and found one for you."

Logan was just pulling in, smiling wildly behind the wheel of what Garrett immediately recognized as a 2009 Land Rover Defender Ice edition. Garrett's jaw dropped, and he stood there wide-eyed while he watched Logan throw the car into park. Garrett was speechless.

"Not only is that a birthday gift, it's a thank-you from Logan and me. Garrett, you've taken such good care of us these last five months. Neither one of us could have done it without you."

Logan was walking toward them, the keys to the truck dangling from his fingers. "She's all yours, man. And I left that thing you asked me to grab for you in the glove box."

The men exchanged a look, embracing briefly before Garrett turned to shake his head in awe at Willow.

Wyatt kicked at some imaginary rocks at his feet, mumbling under his breath. "Damn, I never got no truck from my girl. What's a guy gotta do?" India shoved him playfully, reaching over to give him a kiss instead.

"Let's get out of here and let these two have their morning back," India told Wyatt. She turned to Willow and Garrett. "We'll meet up with you guys tonight in town for the opening of the festival. Happy birthday, Garrett. Sorry we got you out of bed so early. You guys enjoy your day together." She paused, smiling and winking at Willow. "If you don't mind, we're taking Logan with us. There's someone I want him to meet."

Logan raised his eyebrows in surprise but readily agreed to go with them. Willow couldn't wait to get the scoop from India later that night.

Once everyone had gone, Garrett and Willow climbed into the Defender and took it for a spin, ending up a few miles away in the parking lot of Maroon Bells. Willow smiled, happy that Garrett had decided to bring her here on such a gorgeous morning. It was early enough that the sun was bathing the top of the mountains from the most perfect angle, and the air was still, so the reflection of the twin peaks was pristine in the calm lake.

They could hear the clicks and whirs of camera equipment as they made their way past the dozens of photographers who had arrived earlier that morning, well before sunrise, to capture the awesome image. Some of them would remain in place all day long to capture the same shot over and over as the light changed throughout the day. It was arguably one of the best times of the year to visit, as the level of Maroon Lake was still high from the runoff, and the surrounding fields were bursting with wildflowers.

Garrett took it slow, even though Willow had been gradually increasing the amount of exercise she'd been doing. They walked hand in hand, choosing to take the path that encircled the lake rather than a trail that started to climb into the adjacent woods. Arriving at a spot where a large flat rock jutted out into the water, they sat down, taking their shoes and socks off, rolling their pants up, and dipping their feet into the icy lake.

They sat that way for a while, discussing the weekend ahead, talking about Garrett's new truck and tractor, and marveling over the serendipity that had brought them together and ultimately out to Aspen. Even with the warm sun on their backs, the water cooled their body temperatures down quickly, and after a while they stood to go. Willow was gingerly making her way to the edge of the rock when Garrett stopped her.

"Actually, Willow, I forgot something."

She turned, and there he was: down on one knee, watching her and waiting for the moment to register.

"I forgot to tell you what I really want for my birthday."

Willow's face registered shock, and her hand instinctively flew up over her heart, her eyes filling with tears. Garrett knew he wouldn't forget how she looked in that moment as long as he lived.

"I want you. I want your kind heart and your incredible sense of humor. I want to open my eyes each and every morning for the rest of my life and have those chocolate-brown beauties of yours staring back at me. I'm a simple man, Willow. A farmer. I plant things, and they grow. I planted the seeds with you almost a year ago now. The seeds of intention. I intend to be with you forever, Willow. The only way I want to grow is to grow together. With you. If you'll have me."

Garrett reached into his pocket, pulling out a small black box.

"Logan gave me his blessing when I asked him for it yesterday. He even picked up the ring for me. That's what he had stashed in the glove compartment. I sure hope we didn't knock the diamond loose on the ride up."

They watched together as Garrett opened the box. Willow could see it through her tears: the most beautiful antique-looking diamond ring, set in rose gold. She clamped her hand over her mouth, nodding her head yes, then dropped to her knees to meet him. She reached up and took Garrett's face in her hands, wiping away the tears that had rolled down his own cheeks.

"Will you marry me, Willow?"

After she'd answered him, but before she kissed him, Willow had one last question: "How did you know I'd say yes?"

Garrett threw his head back and laughed with her, in the shadow of the mountains where they'd grow their life together.

"I don't know. I guess I just had a feeling."

# ACKNOWLEDGMENTS

If you've made it this far into the book, I can't help but think that, in some way, we've made a connection. That is what life is about for me. I feel most alive when I've connected with others. Sometimes it's small: a smile exchanged on the way into a store. Other times, it goes a little deeper. It's the single reason I feel so filled up by finding ways to give back.

In November of 2016, terrible wildfires ravaged the beautiful area in and around Walland and our beloved Smoky Mountains. Thousands of acres burned, and many people lost their homes. The connection I feel to that place is powerful, and so we couldn't help but try to assist in some small way. After a call to action on social media, many friends, family, and even strangers sent in donations. The generosity blew me away. As I write this, we are preparing to travel to East Tennessee to distribute the money raised, along with comfort quilts to those who were affected by the fires. Thanks to all of you who felt the connection and gave so willingly. And thank you to Kathleen Price and Mission of Love for the work you do to make our world better.

I wasn't sure there was going to be a sequel to *Walland*. When I finished writing it, I began drafting a different story, but after a few chapters, I realized that I wasn't fully present in that new world because a part of me was still consumed by thoughts of my "friends" in Tennessee. I opened up a new document, just to see if anything would flow, and boy did it ever! Garrett and Willow weren't going to let their story go untold. I got plenty of encouragement from my friends to explore this continuation of what we'd dubbed the Hesse Creek series, and now I'm working on a third book that continues the story, which I plan to publish in 2018. I've got to go where the pen (or keyboard) takes me!

Speaking of my friends, I'm really blessed to have some great ones. I'm slow to trust, but at forty-five years old, I feel like I've finally found my tribe. Two of my oldest and dearest friends have played particularly instrumental roles in my life and now my writing career.

Lisa Hauptman Salyers was my college roommate and is the keeper of all *my* secrets, so she can spot them a mile away when I sprinkle them into my stories. Thank you, Lisa, for insisting on that one last hike in Aspen last December in search of just the right photograph for the cover of *Seeds of Intention*. I think we picked a winner, and I'll never forget that beautiful but slippery walk in the woods with you. Thank you for being my person and always having my back.

Few people can get me belly laughing like Terri Overbeck Carrick. She's been to Walland with me for two photography workshops and again with our families, so she understands my fondness for the place. She even took the author photo for *Walland*. Terri, I feel safe with you and know you have my best interest at heart always. Thank you for being a perfect and patient traveling companion, even after I kept you awake with the clacking of the keyboard at three in the morning. I love you, my sister. And I love your family like my own.

Dawn, Erin, Kara, Lekshmi, Paula, and Shannon. The friends that would drop everything and read those late-night pages sent to you by your reclusive author friend, always ready with an encouraging word for me when I needed it most. I love having each of you in my life, and I'm made so much better by spending time with you. I've known some of you for ten or twenty years and some much less than that, but I'm certain that this is just the beginning in so many ways. I adore each one of you. The broader community we are a part of is filled with even more awesome, diverse women—too many to name here, but you've each touched my life in some way. Living in a place like this, surrounded by so many cool chicks. Life is good.

To my friends who are faraway, yet so close: Kerry, Sean, and Scott. There aren't many days that go by when you're not in my thoughts and your're always in my heart. My family in Michigan and West Virginia, and my in-laws in Peoria—I'm the luckiest girl alive to have people that love me and support me unconditionally. Gina—you're the sister I never had. Thank you for always being willing to carry a heavy box for me. I hope to return the favor someday. I love you. Julie— you're a rock for our family and have been so supportive of my books. We love you dearly.

Patrick Henry—your light went out too soon. I know that this is not goodbye. Carry on, my friend.

To each person who took the time to read *Walland* and provide your feedback, whether verbal or in a lovely review on Amazon or Goodreads: please know each comment meant so much to me. It's a vulnerability like no other to share something you've created with the world, and to have it be well received seems like more than I could have ever hoped for.

It turns out that once you ramble on for eighty thousand words or so, you need to have some really excellent people on your side to make lemonade out of the thing. I'm beyond grateful to have discovered the awesome team at Girl Friday Productions to set me in the right direction, first with *Walland* and again with *Seeds of Intention*. Meghan Harvey, Courtney Calon, Rachel Christenson, Christina Henry de Tessan, Stefanie Hargreaves, Michelle Hope Anderson, Erin Cusick, Devon Fredericksen, and Kristin Sheppard (from Giant Squid Media by way of GFP), thank you for your guidance and never-ending patience with this weird girl who reached out to you to help her publish her first novel and then gave you about thirty minutes to do so! I promise to be more organized moving forward. I not only have smart, funny, and interesting women on my team, but feel like I have you all as friends now too. Thank you!

The people behind the scenes are some of the most important. Our family has been so fortunate to have had the same friends and advisers for over twenty years. Sally Gries, Ed Bell, and Brent Ballard. Thank you for being the glue that holds us all together, and for all of your sage advice over the past two decades. We couldn't do it without you, and we cherish your friendship. Pam Ziegan, you must know by now how we would fall apart without you. Much love! Marcia Wexberg—thank you for everything. Wishing you the best next chapter in life. And Dan McMullen, we've only just begun, but I'm thankful to have your years of experience behind me as I navigate the legal waters of the publishing world.

The Chicago White Sox have been so generous with our family for so long. I can't imagine someone exists who is more thoughtful and connected with his employees and their families than Jerry Reinsdorf. To Christine O'Reilly and Sheena Quinn: thank you for making sure I have had every opportunity you could think of to advance *Walland* on this interesting journey. From the *RedEye* article to the amazing launch party at the ballpark; I owe you more than one!

Amazing photographers inspire me, and I know two really incredible women who practice the craft beautifully. Heather Anne Thomas, if it weren't for the inspiration as a result of your amazing workshop, who knows if *Walland* would have made it to the page? Thank you for teaching me so much about the special way you look at things through the lens, but also for your support and friendship. Sonia Mani-Joseph, you're one of the kindest and funniest people I know. You have more talent in your little finger than most have in their family tree. Thank you for putting me at ease and helping me to enjoy the process of being photographed. I'm grateful for your keen eye and also for your friendship.

Thank you to all of the local bookstores that have supported me along my journey! Phil from Fireside Bookshop in Chagrin Falls, Ohio; Anderson's Bookshop and Barbara's Bookstore in the Chicago area; and Bonnie at Barnes and Noble in Peoria, Illinois, and at Vanderbilt in Nashville. I loved every minute I spent tucked within your stacks, meeting people, and signing books. To Jill Berry, my favorite librarian. Thank you for your nomination letter for *Walland*! To *Windy City Live*, Kenny McReynolds, Carole Chandler, and Today in Nashville; thank you for having me on your shows, helping me to get the word out about the book and how it connected to our different philanthropic endeavors. To WOIO and WJW in Cleveland, and my dear friend Mark Nolan on both WOIO and WMJI (because why not?!). Thank you for making this Cleveland girl's day and having me back to the old stomping grounds. *Hinsdale Living* magazine, *The Doings*, *The Hinsdalean*, and Kirk Wessler from the Peoria *Journal Star*, along with Cleveland.com, *Cleveland Scene* magazine, and the *Chicago Tribune*. This fledgling author is so grateful for all of the publicity! Stephanie Krol of SKPR, thank you for all of your help in getting the word out about *Walland* to all of the above! And Marissa DeCuir, Angelle Barbazon, Ellen Whitfield, and Sydney Mathieu of JKS Communications; I look so forward to our new partnership as we embark on the press tour to prepare for all-things *Seeds of Intention*.

My family is my everything. My brother, Nick, lives in Colorado, and I miss him so. I can't help but think that maybe I needed to include the Rockies in this series so I could feel a little closer to him. I love you, little brother. And to my Aunt Merilynn, my mom's baby sister. When I talk with you, I can feel my mom a little closer. Thank you for your unwavering love and support and thoughtful comments along the way. You mean the world to me.

Finally, to my dad, Jerry; my husband, Jim; and our kids, Lila and Landon. You are my nucleus. Every decision I make is with you in mind. I will always put you first. I love you all so much, and I'm eternally grateful for your support and encouragement. I can't wait to see where this next year takes us.

Go out and plant your seeds, people! Do it with pure intention. What the world needs now is love, sweet love.

(Plant a few extra seeds of that variety, if you're so inclined.)

XO,

Andrea

# ABOUT THE AUTHOR

*© Sonia Mani-Joseph Photography*

Andrea Thome is a former broadcast journalist, having covered both sports and news during her career. Her love for travel permeates her Hesse Creek series, from the foothills of the Smoky Mountains to the Colorado Rockies. Andrea currently lives in Chicago with her husband (a retired professional baseball player) and their two children. She spends her spare time traveling, volunteering, pursuing her passions for photography and writing. Her debut novel, *Walland*, is the first in the Hesse Creek series. See a gallery of her photography and connect with Andrea at www.andreathome.com.

Made in the USA
Lexington, KY
28 September 2018